BLOOD
SUGAR

BLOOD SUGAR

A NOVEL

JIM DeFILIPPI

HarperCollins*Publishers*

HarperCollins books may be purchased for educational, business, or sales promotional use. For information, please call or write: Special Markets Department, HarperCollins Publishers, Inc., 10 East 53rd Street, New York, NY 10022. Telephone: (212) 207-7528; Fax: (212) 207-7222.

FIRST EDITION

Designed by Claudyne Bianco

LIBRARY OF CONGRESS CATALOGING-IN-PUBLICATION DATA

DeFilippi, Jim, 1943–
    Blood sugar : a novel / by Jim DeFelippi. — 1st ed.
        p. cm.
    ISBN 0-06-016879-X
    I. TITLE.
PS3554.E365B5   1992   92-52598
813 .54—dc20

92 93 94 95 96 ❖/HC 10 9 8 7 6 5 4 3 2 1

This old song to my family and friends

I

THE BIND

It was just too bad Pearley was home on loony leave, using turpentine on his daughter, instead of here showing ElRay the ropes one more time.

Well, at least the dead man's eyes weren't following ElRay around the room; that was good.

A while back, two weeks, there had been that stiff down in the projects, sitting on a lettuce crisper, refrigerator door open, both his bare feet flat on the kitchen floor, hands cupped on his knees like for a coffee break, his throat opened up wide by a Garden-Weasel his wife had borrowed from the neighbors. Guy was fast bloating up with all his fluids, stretching out his stained sleeveless undershirt.

That stiff's eyes had followed ElRay all over the place, driving him crazy, making him want to violate the sanctity of the crime scene by putting a bag over the damned red-and-purple-and-green-skinned head.

But all in all, by comparison, this stiff here this time looked pretty good. Sure the guy was pretty old and cold and blue-green and ugly, but plenty of *living* folks were a lot of those things too. And at least these eyes were steady, not cruising.

Yeah, the man in the bed looked all right, other than the being dead of it. Not swelled up yet, sort of healthy-looking. A white man turned blue-green by circumstance, but not all that much whiter or bluer than most whites, ElRay figured. And pretty good muscle tone, probably had worked out some, good pecs for an old-timer, the muscles relaxed there just above where the rose-colored quilt ended. And despite the smell of the newly dead, a smell ElRay could recognize now, it didn't seem like the stiff had shit himself. Of course, that could still come.

Two flies landed on the dead left eyebrow. ElRay went over and waved them away, like a traffic cop, and he felt himself swallow something that had almost made its way up and out of him.

ElRay had been taught that all deaths are homicides until proven different, so this was in truth a potential crime scene, and his first one to work, sort of. He steeled himself to do a good job, make a perfect debut. Well, not actually a debut—he had done the stiff in the lettuce crisper and a couple vehic-homicides and a kid's suicide in Willingham Park, but Pearley had really handled all the judgment calls on those.

In truth, ElRay had just sort of helped out on them, tried to look busy and stay out of the way until the detectives and the morgue arrived.

He helped out, he stayed out of the way, he strung yellow tape, and he got coffee. These were the things that a patrolman just five and a half months out of the academy did, especially a young, black, educated, ambitious patrolman—a self-proclaimed mover who was going to make gold badge in under five, although he didn't self-proclaim that part of it to anybody, not even to Julia or to his own mother.

And especially not to Pearley, who would have laughed and whistled a three-second-long, sarcastic "Shit" at him and then shook his head and grabbed his belt buckle. But Pearley, who had shown him a lot in five months, wasn't here now. And Bates, the kid ElRay was teamed with until Pearley got back, was even more of a rainbow than *he* was. Bates still wore his academy-issue socks, and he was probably downstairs by the fireplace now, trying to look busy and stay out of the way until the detectives got here, letting senior Patrolman ElRay J. O'Keefe nail down the securing of this here crime scene.

ElRay stayed busy, making choices. The cut-and-dried stuff was done. His log showed that at 1:35 A.M., he and his partner had been sent to 135 Willard, Munsey Hill, to answer a call involving a body.

On the scene, they were led by the decedent's wife up to the bed-room, where the decedent was propped up in bed. The wife, ID'ing herself as Mrs. Audrey McKenna Wright, said that she had returned home about 1:00 A.M. and found her husband dead in bed. Cold. No ambulance necessary. Her call.

ElRay first determined that no first aid needed to be rendered, Wright being dead and Mrs. Wright looking upset but not in danger of going into shock. ElRay led her out of the room; she chose to go sit in the kitchen, refused to call any friends or family for support. He got the name and number of her family physician, but she said she didn't need one, thanks. She just sat—hurting, controlled, beautiful enough to lace your eyes out.

ElRay had again ascertained by pulse and heartbeat search that the man, Mr. Milton Wright, was indeed dead. ElRay had his partner use the black-and-white's radio to call it in to the desk, as ElRay had begun stringing the bright-yellow barrier tape. The desk would notify the Detective Room, the Crime Lab, and the ME.

Get in, help out, call it in, close it up, don't let anybody else in.

And don't touch anything you don't have to. Hell, this was a house that told him don't touch anything anyway, dead man in the bed or not. This house just about screamed it out at him. Money Hill Tudor, stone outside, Oriental inside, furniture meant for metal polish and investment, not for sitting. A Money Hill money house.

A money bedroom in a money house. The only thing out of place was the dead man and the ugly electric metal thing lying on the nap of the tan rug there in the corner. ElRay had seen a tool like that before, couldn't place it. In a book. Maybe it was just some machine all money people used. For who knows what—get rid of wrinkles? Who the hell knew. Didn't matter; just don't touch it, that's all.

ElRay looked around again, looked at the body, and decided that he had made all the right calls so far, all the major steps were taken. But beyond that, there were plenty of little choices still to be made. Should he ask the widow again if there was anyone they could call for her?

The widow was definitely a stone fox, even at her age, and you could tell she'd been doing everything just right for herself, to look the way she did.

Should he ask her about that ugly damned pointed electric thing with tentacles on the rug? Should he call North Shore, even though from now on this man's only relationship to a hospital would be for research and body parts?

On each of these judgment calls, ElRay figured he could go any of three ways. First, he could do things like the academy had taught him to—but of course they didn't cover a lot of this stuff there, like electric machines with hoses lying in the corner of a bedroom. Or he could do it like on television—but he had to be careful of taking too many cues from cop shows; too phony. Or he could do things like Pearley would have—even though Pearley had a style all his own and Pearley wasn't here now.

Pearley was on leave because he had gone apeshit for a while. Actually, it was Pearley's daughter gone apeshit, but Pearley himself was running a close second.

Pearley's daughter just kept trying to paint herself fluorescent colors and then climb up a tree. It had gotten so bad that Pearley said every time he had to pluck her semigloss and glowing body off a limb, he felt like he was some wonking migrant from Jamaica, picking fruit piecework.

Pearley's wife had chained herself to an ice chest and walked off the Staten Island ferry twelve years ago. Ever since then, Pearley had been raising the three kids by himself and, in his own proud words as well as everybody else's, had been doing a pretty much screwed-up job of the whole thing.

So now Pearley was home on loony leave, pruning off all the low branches from the trees in his backyard and using turpentine on his daughter and preparing to slap silly any shit punk who came by for her, punk sporting shaved temples and a Metallica shirt and a red and runny nose.

Which of course left ElRay here basically all alone with the rainbow kid and the wife and the healthy-looking dead man in the bed.

ElRay again checked the stiff's eyes, open and scared of something bigger than him. And both the guy's ears were discolored; not much—ElRay wondered if it was bruises or just something that happened with the blood draining after death. Should he point it out to the detectives, if they ever got here? How about to the ME? Probably not. He'd look rainbow if it turned out to be something that happened to every stiff's ears whose head was propped up.

"What the hell, kid," they'd say or they'd think. "You never saw a body before? They didn't teach you in school that Whitey's ears go blue, bluer than the rest of him, when he's dead?"

ElRay forced himself to move a little closer to check out the ears. The flies hadn't returned. Don't touch anything. First he turned, held still, and listened to make sure that the wife was still downstairs. Wouldn't want the widow coming in, yelling at him to stay away from her husband's beautiful blue, blue ears.

They had scrapes on them, and little flecks of blood and raw skin. Like something had rubbed him there on the sides of the head.

ElRay heard the front door open downstairs, looked out the front window, and saw an unmarked detective vehicle parked crooked in front of the house. OK, get down there now, let them know you've been in charge, let them know that you know what you're doing. Let them go out of here tonight thinking: That kid'll be gold badge in five years.

Halfway down the stairs, ElRay noticed that the two detectives talking to Bates were Homicide, cops he knew. Good.

This tec team was Mutt and Jeff. One was Sergeant Joe LaLuna, a bit of a star in Homicide—a lot of years, some good publicity cases, always a pro, liked by the uniforms, brass too. Sheeney's boy. Good Italian looks to him, the kind of guy who walked like he didn't have to let you know anything—quiet muscles. Somebody had said LaLuna could clear cases quicker than anyone else in North Homestead. Lieutenant material, smart money believed, slated for head of Major Crimes after Lieutenant Sheeney went over there and then retired. Yes, LaLuna would come up a winner, it was said, if the politics of the thing worked out for him.

He was standing there, his thumbs hooked in his pockets, nodding at Bates. Bates was trying to keep looking at him, log the names into the entry log on his clipboard, same time.

LaLuna's partner was a little runt everybody called Winky Dink. He was about a foot shorter than LaLuna and about three quarts slimier. ElRay didn't think he had ever heard the greaseball's real name. ElRay couldn't figure if LaLuna kept him around because the guy was good or just to score points by comparison.

"Decedent's upstairs in bed, sir," ElRay told LaLuna. "ME, Lab, on the way. The wife's in the kitchen there, she seems to be handling it OK."

ElRay figured he was handling it OK too. Ignoring Winky Dink, talking just to LaLuna, was right. Probably everybody did it that way to the little greaseball, who probably was used to it by now.

ElRay felt like, Go ahead, Sergeant, ask me anything, I'm ready for any question you got.

LaLuna looked at him and said, "Is she happen to be wearing this big-ass onyx blue ring at all?"

Any question except that one. "Who, sir—the wife? Rings I'm afraid I didn't notice. She *is* married to the decedent, though. I know that much."

Damn. There's one wonking smart observation. The husband and wife, they're married, sir. Good, ElRay, perceptive as shit. But why's he asking about rings for? What was that—a trick question maybe?

"It's all right, O'Keefe, it's just something crazy popped into my head. It has no bearing. Hey, where is she—she's in the kitchen there, right?"

"Right, sir." A half-turn and point that way. Using the "sir" was overkill. Hey, but he did know my name, huh?

ElRay followed the two detectives toward the kitchen. Another call now. Should he introduce the tecs to the widow, or just shut up? But he couldn't introduce them; he only had one name. Ma'am, this is Detective Sergeant LaLuna and his partner, we all call him Winky Dink.

Or maybe just: Mrs. Wright, the detectives here would like to ask you a few questions. No, too television.

Both detectives stopped short at the kitchen doorway. ElRay thought they might be waiting for him, so he walked past them, stood inside the door, and reached out one hand toward the widow, sitting there at the table, smoking. ElRay held his hand a bit below belt level, and both detectives grinned a little at him as they walked past. Not bad grins, just ones that seemed to say, You're doing all right, kid, ain't this a great job we got here?

ElRay kept standing there by the door as the detectives pulled out chairs and sat on each side of the woman. Perfect. Beautiful. Just like a script.

But the script changed when LaLuna, instead of saying something that ended in the word "ma'am," said, "Hi, Audie, how's it been going?"

And the widow looked up from her cigarette smoke and blinked and answered him, "Hello, Joe. You mean other than that?" And she hiked her thumb in the direction of upstairs, up to where her dead husband was lying in bed.

These little Chinamen, each an inch tall, were walking across the top of the walls where normal people would have just had wood molding. Wallpaper trim on walls with no wallpaper.

LaLuna hated this place. Fat-cat, overstuffed, a house built to laugh at other houses. The leather there would be laughing at any hint of Naugahyde—like the big, soft, slow-exploding recliner that LaLuna had back at *his* house, in front of his TV.

And those one-inch Chinamen were lined up and marching pharaoh style along the ceiling line—what, friezes?—smirking at any plywood or pressboard as they went. And the plaster walls would be chanting, "Hey, the real stuff, real stuff here," at any mention of Sheetrock, right?

Even the Money Hill neighbors would probably rag on this place, call it maybe the Oriental Princess or something. And would they be talking snide and dirty over their bridge bidding about the lady of the house—what, the Occidental Slut maybe?

She was sitting in the living room now, curled up on the couch, smoking, twisted over to one side.

This was no place to find Audie McKenna. A woman born rich— she used to call it "well off"—but not born for a place like this.

The two-hour widow had her bare feet tucked up under her ass on the underupholstered leather couch. The sleeves of her bulky sweater were pushed halfway up her forearms, and her skirt was black-and-green plaid. Her eyes were reddened, but only around the outsides, not in the white, not the blue of them. That part of them looked untouched by the dead, by the years.

What did that mean, then—a lie? A lack of common concern? Did that show a facade, LaLuna kept wondering while he stared at her, the absence of any true-felt grief? Or did it just mean that there were some layers of beauty that even a tragedy can't penetrate, just too damned thick?

She had told him her night out in a monotone, like a TV reporter, standing back, not involved.

Still, LaLuna knew she couldn't ever be at ease here in her dead husband's house, sitting on his expensive little sawhorse of a couch. And LaLuna remembered that it had always been that way for this woman, she had always been somehow not in mesh with her surroundings. Even thirty years ago, his sex dreams of her had always been of the nude descending the wrong staircase.

And the warmth of her had always been wrong against the cold black tabletops of Hoover's bio lab, her skin seemed to suck the splinters from the plywood flooring of the bed of the LaLuna-Lawns Chevy pickup truck.

Back then he had sworn to anyone who would listen that Audie McKenna could stand up and wave to her friends at an assembly better than any girl he had ever seen.

She told him now how she had been out of the house for the evening, at a rock concert; she was saying it again for him, still calm. When she got back, she said, her husband was dead, up in bed there. No, no history of heart or stroke. No, no medication.

LaLuna had pulled a shiny-silk chair over to where she was. Winky walked by and looked at both of them, and Wink held the look a minute, reminding his partner that the stuff they had talked about before, it would have to come up again later.

Before, during the Crime Lab–ID search, Wink had quietly cornered him in the upstairs hall and whispered that he thought Audrey might be having her sex life catered these days by the American Farm Equipment Corporation.

LaLuna had whispered back, had told him to go stick his head in the master-bedroom toilet bowl.

Wink told him he already had. "See," Wink said, "I beat you to it, Joey, I found it too."

SOP said they didn't search until Crime Lab had it sealed, gave the scene over to the detectives, but they both liked finding stuff first. Crime Lab, like most people paid to do only one thing, usually did a shitty job of it, no pride invested. Just rubber gloves and blue Luminall spray to raise blood spots, toil, trouble, and bored-all-to-hell looks.

"What d'you think?" LaLuna asked Wink about what they both had found.

"Geez, I don't know, Joe, let me think here. The residue of a white powdery substance flushed down the toilet as the cops are coming. Sure beats me. I have no clue. Sugar? Saccharin maybe? Guy had sugar diabetes?"

"Yeah, OK, fine, we know. Crime Lab'll collect it?"

"Nah, they're gonna let Slabb the Drab pick it up. She got those nice clean little Good Humor sticks, those cute little Baggies, plasticky things. Crime Lab says ME gets all the good stuff, so they let them do the job."

"How do we know it'll be Slabb tonight?"

"They checked the on-call roster. There was Sunshine's name, right there on top of the dance card for the evening."

"I hope she'll be OK for this."

"Oh, yeah," Wink had assured him. "If not, she can fake it all right."

Audie finished telling him again how she had gone out for a while, seen a Chuck Berry show with someone, eaten, come back a widow. She shifted nicely on the couch.

He looked again, third time, for the big blue ring, and he didn't see it. So instead, he told her, "You still wear your hair pretty long, I see."

It was just one more stupid thing he had said to her. He used to collect them, write them all down—The Stupid Things I Have Said to Audie. He kept at it, that list could have gotten like the Vietnam Wall by now, a mile-long black tribute to life's little tragedies and mistakes.

She said yeah, she did still wear it long.

"I have to ask you those places you went," he told her, "if you can document it."

"Yes, Joe, I can document it. I probably could even get you the damned ticket stubs and register receipts, you want. Do I have to do that now?"

"No, you don't. But some names now maybe. A name. The guy."

"The name is Chet," she said finally. "Chester Zumrad. Small businessman. Stub saver."

He wrote it down as she spelled it.

"Different kind of name."

"It's just German, I think," she said.

He told her it could be.

An hour later, just before the ME got there, Audie was really talking to him, telling him almost too much, telling him about being married and still running around, and her life and how things had been with her and her now-dead husband.

Mostly she had just seemed tired out by all of it. "Shall I count the ways?" she said. "But that was the deal of it. Get him happy, and I go out for the evening. All right, but it got harder and harder—yeah, well, you know, not harder and harder. So."

"The drugs, dope, don't help. What he think, they did?"

She hesitated. "What drugs?"

"You have to flush better. Up around the rim. People think they flush something down the toilet, throw it in the garbage, down the disposal, it's gone. No."

"Well, I didn't realize that you and Winky were such good house-keepers. How in the hell are you two still together anyway?"

"It's a long story. I'd like to tell you sometime."

"Well, so," she said, "the two of you, you guys are better than the crew I bring in Thursdays. Ty-D-Bol. Joe, do you think I need a lawyer for some reason here?"

"I don't think so yet," he told her. "We're just concerned with the death, but maybe it wouldn't be such a bad idea. Talk to one at least."

She shrugged, like she was considering.

"How about the bruises, Audie?" he asked. "Did you do those?"

She asked him what bruises.

"On his ears there, side of his head. It looks like somebody got something strong, someone with muscles, around his head and squeezed it. I'm sorry, I have to ask this stuff. Did you do that to him?"

"No, not last night."

"Ever?"

"Who is *that* question for, Chief?"

"Yeah. Yeah, all right. I'm sorry."

"OK." She waited a beat, then said, "Sure, I guess, sometimes, bruises. I told you, Joe, I did a little bit of everything to my husband at one time or another. You know, every available body part in and out of every imaginable orifice."

"So, you're not in Pep Club anymore?"

"But not last night I didn't. Just a textbook copulation, over and out. Those bruises aren't mine."

"Did he have other women?"

"Everybody has other women. Nobody special. Just whores and things. No one with a name."

"Last night?"

"Not after me, no."

Joe asked her, "What kind of drugs he do?"

She told him, "Just coke. Tooting. Some blow, years ago, of course."

"Nothing more?"

"What—crack, you mean? Heroin?"

"Yeah, I guess so."

"No. Never."

Wink came into the room and said, "Sunshine's here."

LaLuna looked at Audie and said, "That's Dr. Slabb, the medical examiner. All right? Just quick now, Audie, last thing—what about that milking machine?"

Wink hung around to hear this. The widow had to laugh a little bit. She looked at both of them, and she told them, "Well, you know, the Pulitzers had their trumpet, didn't they? It was mostly just a joke. I picked it up at a farm auction up in New Hampshire, last summer, gave it to Milton for his birthday. I had it all cleaned and polished up. Mostly for him it was just the sight of all that chrome and metal and tubes and rubber. Yummy?"

"Audie, Wink and I are simple men. What?"

"My Christ," she said, looking away but still smiling, "you would be amazed at the different ways two people—maybe more, I don't know, I would believe …? There must be a lot of glowing farmers up in New Hampshire."

Winky said he didn't think so. Dr. Sharon Slabb came in.

"Audie, this is the medical examiner," LaLuna said. "Sharon, Mrs. Audrey Wright. Her husband's body is in the bed, upstairs left."

The two women looked at each other. Slabb gently took the woman's hand, looked down at the rug, told her how sorry she was. Slabb told her that she would try to make things as placid as possible for her and for all concerned.

Then Slabb walked up the stairs, eyes focused straight ahead, as if she were concentrating on something that wasn't there. LaLuna knew that once Slabb was in the bedroom, she would reach into her brown, real-leather bag, pull out a syringe about a foot long, like something you would use on cows, and she would drive the thing fully into the dead man's heart, right up to its glass cylinder.

Later on, Slabb came down to the kitchen, where they were now. She stood by the door, gave LaLuna a look. He went over to her by the doorway, Audie still sitting at the table, smoking, cup of tea in front of her. Slabb started to talk to LaLuna, but she kept missing his eyes, glancing over his shoulder, back in at Audie. When it started to annoy LaLuna, he turned to look. Audie was just sitting there, hanging around in her own smoke, mostly just looking back at them.

LaLuna took Slabb's arm, and they left the kitchen for a minute. He made Slabb tell everything to him a second time. After they had walked around the living room, Slabb still explaining things, LaLuna came back into the kitchen, over to Audie, sat down, and he said, "Audie, listen, she says the body's been moved."

An apparently genuine "What?" from the widow.

"Dr. Slabb, she tells me somebody moved the body."

"How would they know things like that?"

"How the blood settled and congealed, I guess. It was all in the front of the body, apparently. Your husband dying, flopped on his face and spent some time lying there. Sorry. The doc thinks maybe the hallway, downstairs. They're spraying for blood there. Audie, did you haul him, prop him up in bed there like he was?"

"How could I do that? He weighed a hundred eighty pounds, Joe, for Christ sake."

"Audrey, did you move his body?"

"No, Joe," and she took a drink of tea. He had seen her add some booze to it.

She stayed very calm for a while after that. Everybody quiet, Slabb working the body, Crime Lab floating around, Wink and LaLuna reminiscing about high school.

Wink said he wondered if Audie could be one of those ladies who would seem pretty much in control one minute, quite fine, thank you, until something went wingo with them inside, and then they would go nuts on horseback, frothing and blowing off steam. LaLuna and Wink didn't really remember that about her; they didn't think so.

Tonight, with a lot going on, she'd come close to that when Slabb was all done with the body, had wired some white tags through the bare toes, then the coroner crew had started zipping it into the thick black body bag.

Audie was up there watching, standing by the gurney that would take it out to the truck.

Then maybe Audie was hit with the fact that her husband wasn't coming back to this place, she was here all alone, because what she did, she made a noise and said something about his "comfort and pain," and she went and got a blue terry-cloth robe from the main bathroom.

She had somehow quietly gotten the body bag half unzipped and one dead arm into a sleeve of the bathrobe before the boys in white could get her away from the stiff and Slabb was on the phone for the personal physician.

LaLuna brought Audie back downstairs, to the first-floor commode, where she stayed for ten minutes, bad noises coming out at him through the door. She came back out and started talking, spitting out the words.

Nonstop, she told him about how Milton was really her second husband but that her first one, Derek—did Joe know him? had they met once?—he really didn't count anyway because she just had married him to help him beat the draft. It had been early Vietnam, and Derek had flunked out of C. W. Post and was worried and had told

Audie that if she would marry him, then she would save him and that they wouldn't even have to ever screw, that it was just for the paperwork of it.

So Audie, young and dumb, had done it—had driven her mother crazy by it—and then, when she found out that Derek had really meant what he said about not screwing, she divorced him in a week and then turned him in to the draft board. And he had been one of the first guys in the navy to die. Lots of them in the marines and army were already dead, but he was an early one for the navy.

The papers had printed his picture and death notice, and after that she got terrible phone calls, perverted peaceniks telling her about her sailor boy's body. In the mail, she even got a picture someone had taken of them together, didn't know what it meant.

But Milton had been different from all that; it had been a real marriage. Real love, real marriage, ten years, tin anniversary. Milton was smart, and he had gotten rich in the offensive-radar-armament business. All the government contracts for the radar used for defense were pretty well sewed up, but Milton's company was pioneering semiconductors or circuitry or something that hooked onto a Vulcan machine gun for the decks of ships, and the radar aimed the gun. Milton and his partner, a scientist-businessman named Felix Marmasette, were using lasers now to do the same thing, and Milton was so smart and getting richer all the time. On offensive radar.

And flea repellent, crazy as it was. Somehow, his R&D department had secured the patent for a formula used in flea collars for dogs and cats. They were too small to hang on to it, to protect the patent, it had been raided, but they still were getting contracted-out work from some big national pet company—not Hartz Mountain but one like it, she forgot the name. So it was radar and flea collars.

She had loved him, she said, really.

Audie told LaLuna, "You'd probably never know it, Joe, but this tonight has probably been the most difficult thing I have ever lived through. I mean it. All things aside. This night could be the watershed of my life, I know that already. Sorry I went nuts there. Anyway, I have some phone calls that have to be made. His mother and family, mostly. They'll all be a pain in the ass. The sooner the better, I guess, or I'll never be able to do it without losing it. So, Detective, do you have any other questions for me now?"

Just one, LaLuna was figuring, just one. The question would have been: Christ, Audie, is it possible that I am still crazy in love with you?

He didn't ask it though.

THREE

Joe and Audie had been in the bed of Joe's father's red Chevy pickup with LaLuna-Lawns on the side of it and "Perfidia" by the Ventures on the radio, running on battery because the engine was off. Joe was kicking for leg room and release.

Song almost to the bridge, Joe almost to the bra clip, they both heard hands clapping loud and "Stop that! Stop that!"

It had been a long time coming. They had both gone to Hoover for four years, fed in from different junior highs, and had seen each other around the halls, but that was about it for a couple of years.

There had been no shared classes, just passing in the hallway. Audie was college prep and Joe was of the giant middle track, a program supposedly designed to produce kids who could do anything but really gorged with kids who would go on, for the most part, to do absolutely nothing. Joe got C's in courses somewhere between *Beowulf* and building birdhouses.

Midtrack Joe liked to think that he was really part of no group at all at Hoover. If he had to classify himself, though, he would have called himself a rock. Yeah, he usually would wear jeans turned up two inches at the cuff and the standard white tee-shirt up top. His hair always looked wet, and it was curly and had stubby sideburns. He would have worn a leather jacket if he could have afforded one, but he had corduroy instead, dark green with a leather collar.

So, as far as he could tell, he was a rock.

He was not a greaser. He only became really aware of that word years later, and he always associated it with Hollywood and John Travolta and things that were not of the real world.

And he knew he wasn't a hood. He would have denied that, and he *did* deny it sometimes when *Compare* Martino, his godfather, flipped the term at him. Hood stood short for hoodlum. They were the guys who jumped cars for profit, never for fun, and talked about scams and quick money and tried to listen to opera instead of rock and roll. All of them aspired to become affiliated with career criminals. Hoods wanted to wear shiny, sleek suits with yardstick-thin lapels, maybe even with shades, dark shirts, and white ties. Sheldon Leonard style.

The rocks, like Joey, held tight without aspirations to their own little power base at Hoover, controlling a certain well-defined turf of certain classrooms, the lunch hall, the street, and the grudging admiration of peers. There were certain places they felt they could go and comfortably belong, and one of these places would have been the now rocking bed of the step-side pickup truck, but it wasn't the place if you were there busy rocking along with Audrey McKenna, of the Heights, and an angry adult voice, full of authority and shock and shame, was choking out, "Now stop that! You two!"

The strict rock code of behavior and uncompromising rock view of what was right and what was wrong led a few of them to become cops, and at least one to become a homicide detective.

There had not been that one blistering moment that convinced Joey that he had to build himself into something, had to get to a point in his life when he wore suits and brought home pretty good money each week. Instead, it had been a series of images stuck on him throughout his school years. His mom, pushing the family pickup—LaLuna-Lawns—the same pickup his foot was denting from the inside. His dad, sitting on the soft edge of the big double bed in their room, in his underwear, his big fingers cranking the stupid little tin arm of the machine the old man used to resharpen his Gillette Blue Blades.

Joe's mom had been so damn visible pushing that truck. Her two hundred forty pounds leaning into the truck's doorframe because the starter had gone from working to hesitating to clicking to nothing in a week. Her low-cut Keds were twisting into the pavement of Northern Boulevard with strain and torque, and a bunch of guys—they had been out in the schoolyard playing punchball till the fifth-period bell—had gone, yelling and joking, over to the stubborn truck and by simple force of numbers and youth and joy had whisked it off somewhere, Joe couldn't remember where. Guys he didn't even know, some of them not even rocks, helping to shove, and his mom so damn visible through it all.

And his dad had been so *in*visible so much of the time, there sharpening his Blue Blades, face full of sad determination and concentration, the gray undershirt worn see-through at the front and back, holes in both sides.

These images gave Joe a picture of himself with a suit and pretty good money—not too visible, not too invisible. Once, Winky had told him that it was Mrs. McKenna, Audrey's mother, who had driven Joe from Hoover into the Air Force when everybody agreed college was out of the question, and had driven him to make staff sergeant under four, and had driven him to the police force after that, air police experience in tow, and had driven him to the gold badge of the detectives, and finally driven him to a name in Homicide, a pretty good name, with a job and suits and OK money.

But no, Winky, it hadn't all started with, or been fueled by, Mrs. McKenna on that afternoon in the bed of the truck with Audie. "Audrey! Audrey, right now!"

It hadn't been that at all.

Audie and he had started out with coy looks in a common lunch period and a couple of common friends making contact for them, and then a couple of uneasy dates alone. Audie was a queen, top five of the school, easy, so the date was mostly her sitting quiet and Joey trying to act nice, which he was, but he'd never felt like he had to act it before.

Date, date, date, that's all. He hadn't loved her until the Sunday he took her to the football Giants.

Pro football was just shedding its second-class status as a national sport back then, and you could still get bleacher tickets on a first-come, first-serve basis the morning of the game, if you made it up to the Stadium before eight.

So that's what the guys did—the Long Island and the IRT to the right-centerfield booth, every Sunday morning, fall to middle winter, when the Giants were at home. It had always been a guys' affair— Wink, Joe, some other rocks—and there had been a few looks when he showed up with Audie that one time, but he held a little too much status to hear any remarks. Besides, she was so beautiful with her black beret, pulled straight down, not angled like a fag or a Frenchman would do it, and the four inches of her blond hair curled out around the bottom of the hat. And she smiled at the guys, and who the hell in their right mind could resist anyway? They all just had to love her.

By 8:00 A.M. they were part of the line curling around the Stadium, by nine the booth opened, by ten they were in their seats, right above a ramp opening so no one could stand up, block your view.

The guys sat there smiling and anxious and reverent, still four hours to go before kickoff, and Joe kept checking out Audie without getting caught at it. She seemed to be enjoying even this part of it. The fifty-five thousand other seats in the Stadium were empty and echoing, reserved, and the fans in the bleachers were packed together, jealously guarding their seats, rationing out their caches of wine and coffee and sandwiches, ducking behind collars to slip the wind, pounding their sides to drive out cold. He offered her his scarf, and she smiled and didn't take it. He had no cash for a pennant or team picture or anything. Anyway, no vendors worked the bleachers.

The bleacher crowd usually had two crosses to bear on these Sabbaths—the cold and the boredom—and the boredom would have been the worst of it, except that she was there this time, and there were miracles happening all the time in that place.

Here was one. A small red plastic football appeared in the gray-brown Bronx sky right above their heads. All their voices chanted as one, adjusting pitch and volume to the flight of the ball. "Whoaaa-aaaaaaa-ooooooooooo!" The ball fell to earth and was immediately rocketed again toward heaven, then again and again, with the voices still chanting in sync with its flight. Even though only a few hands ever touched that red plastic ball, ten thousand people were in the game. Finally, bad toss, the ball sailed over the mesh onto the playing field. The crowd all groaned together—the city cops made retrieving the ball impossible.

But suddenly—yeah, right there, there it is, there, see?—a second ball was gliding above them—Joe couldn't remember if this one
was red too—and everybody's boredom and cold were gone again for
a few magnificent moments. And he looked at Audie, and Audie was
laughing. Then, again, the ball sailed onto the field and was gone.

Everybody sat there in stillness for a time, waiting: maybe thirty
seconds, it seemed like more. What were the chances that a third
plastic football would be in a group of ten thousand people? What
were the odds of that?

And then, then the sky had filled with food. Cupcakes and
bananas, fruit bars and pickles and peaches, rained down upon them
from the heavens. The juices sprayed their skin and the aromas filled
their noses. Their brown bags were empty, but their hearts were
filled, filled with magic and well-being and awe, as the food was recy-
cled again and again, up into the air. People that Joe figured to be
stockbrokers or ministers were flinging the food along with the
bussies and the stooges and the rocks and the hoods.

Maybe his memory was overworking, maybe his sense of that
moment was exaggerated, but Joe would swear to whoever would listen that the very sun and sky were blacked out that day by the flying
food.

And the one sight he *did* remember perfectly, the one that he
knew really *was,* really had been, was Audie McKenna there beside
him, her face skyward, laughing, and her palms held upward, as if to
receive the gifts of the world. Lipstick and mustard and grapefruit
juice, and she couldn't stop laughing, and he couldn't stop loving her.

Later, during the game, she would even share the binoculars and
fulfill the binoc holder's duty of shouting out the yardage gained or
lost by counting the steps Phil King or Mel Triplett had taken before
being hauled down. The seats were that far away, who cared? It was
her and the binocs and her hair and her beret, now speckled a little
by the rain of food. How were you ever going to stop loving that?

And so, from that Sabbath on, they had become Joe and Audie at
Hoover. They were Joe and Audie in the middle of a mixture of confusion and admiration and envy and joy, from both the students and
the teachers. And the two of them loved all of it.

For her birthday, Joe had shopped longer than he had for anything in his life. He had finally found a big, blue-stoned ring that looked like an Indian had made it. Onyx, that what it's called? She kissed it and wore it all the time.

But there were forces at work back then, forces Joe did not understand and could not trace. He only knew that first she had backed out of a few dates because she had to baby-sit her brother Ronnie. Then Joe had been made tight-fist furious at Audie because of a date she made with some guy, a date Joe never knew really happened or didn't, and never asked her about. Instead of asking, he let himself get strung into a double date, blind date, with someone from another town, somebody's cousin named Anna Marie Popstooka. It had gone so bad, he had gotten home from that date nauseous, and he blew lunch into his family's toilet at exactly 12:35 A.M.

And his friend, the matchmaker, the cousin, had told him it was kismet or something, because his girlfriend told him that Popstooka had blown her cookies too, at the exact same time. Star-crossed barfers, Joey wasn't impressed.

Audie confronted him with tears, publicly, about the Popstooka affair, and what the hell are you supposed to do with all your friends watching anyway? So he did what he was supposed to, told her to fuck off. And then he saw her without the ring, hanging around with Dennis "Smokey" McQueen, of her status and station in life.

Joe and a couple of rocks had crashed a party where McQueen had passed out drunk on the rug. Joe's buddy Winky had offered to drag McQueen home, told everybody later he had given the jerk a Sea Monkey enema, using the hose and the bag and a solution full of those microscopic sea creatures you always saw advertised on the back page of comic books. Wink's stunt had gotten famous; he'd even passed around pictures he'd taken of it. McQueen's friends tried to beat Wink up for it but could never catch the little bastard.

Joe just smiled about it and took Popstooka to the prom and saw Audie there in red satin with McQueen. Joe stared at Audie until he thought he had her staring back at him, but she was really looking past him at Popstooka, because Popstooka was dropping her gum down into her water glass to keep it fresh during the meal. Joe got mad and threw the water on the floor and told Popstooka he could afford to buy her a new stick of gum after dinner, for Christ sake.

And he looked around and saw Audie smiling at that, smiling but not smiling mean, smiling maybe like you would smile up at food falling into your face in the bleachers of Yankee Stadium.

And so later that night they had managed to talk on the beach at Covehaven, where everybody went prom night. He was barefoot, with rental tux, she was barefoot, with red gown, and they walked a bit and talked, it didn't matter about what.

And the moon and the water made little rippling lines on her beautiful face as he told her he'd call. He did, and pretty soon after that they were back there at the beach, late, and they'd talked again and he'd undressed her a tiny bit, like a gentleman, and she'd stopped him, like a lady, and they'd planned a wedding and a life, sort of starting off in theory, pretending, but it was getting more and more real. Planned a wedding and a life, and the wedding took more planning than the life did, and with Joe, for once, everything was all set and in place.

It was probably the last time he'd ever feel so set about everything. Things stayed like that for a while, with the glory of perfection folded up in the back pocket of Joe's jeans along with his homework.

They both knew that their days of Popstooka and Dennis "Smokey" McQueen and confusion were over, and it wasn't too deep into that summer that they had found themselves with each other in the bed of the pickup, Joe sweating and kicking for leg room and release and them both suddenly hearing "Cut it out, cut it out" and the hard slapping of hands.

Audie's mother's face was there above them, and they rolled over and tried to stand up. Kneeling was the best they could do, but it put them at eye level with Mrs. McKenna, the swollen face of Zeus. Joe felt his blood drain.

In the silence, they heard a snap, and he and Mrs. McKenna looked over to see Audie resnapping her jeans. Joe hadn't realized he had gotten that far, and despite it all, this started him getting hard again. But his thing had gotten folded back onto itself somehow and, reinflating, hurt like hell. He tried to think of how bad things were right now.

They were even worse than he thought. Because from the moment Mrs. McKenna's face appeared over the tin wall of the truckbed, things were over for them. It took him a long time to realize it, and nobody ever actually said so, ever told him, certainly not Audie, but that was it.

In the fall she'd be off to Wellesley or Skidmore or somewhere, he'd be off to the marines or the Air Force or jail.

When she left that fall, he tried to forget her. As he was looking for Popstooka's number in the book, he told himself again that it had all been Audie's mother's call. Bad deal. But he knew that was lying.

It hadn't been her mother's call, or Joe's call. It had been Audie's call all along.

And now it was thirty years later, maybe half a lifetime, and Mrs. McKenna had died a long time ago—the papers said cancer, but people said booze—and he thought maybe he loved the widow Ms. Audrey McKenna Wright as much as ever, as much as he had in the Yankee Stadium bleachers with Andy Robustelli, number 81, running onto the field shaking hands with a kid quarterback who never made it, Lee Grosscup, number 11.

Maybe he still loved her as much as he had in the bed of his father's step-side Chevy pickup truck, LaLuna-Lawns.

Whenever Winky Dink Hraska had a lot to drink, he'd start telling everybody his father invented Maypo. It wasn't anything he ever really decided on or planned, just something that happened. That's what he was doing now.

"Your father didn't invent any fucking Maypo," Joe was answering him.

"I'm just telling you my father invented fucking Maypo, that's all. You don't have to wonking believe it or not. Like my cat said about his breakfast—now I'm sorry I fucking brought it up. That's all. You don't gotta believe it at all, I don't care."

They were sitting in Hraska's black Chevy Celebrity, out in front of Hraska's place. They had started off the night at Zack's Blue, had a couple V.O.'s there, then gone to the Splotch, then to Donelli's, then to a bunch of places Hraska couldn't remember. They all blended.

It was at the Splotch, Hraska thought, that they had tried to talk about the Audrey McKenna case and the forensics of it.

Joe said he had been looking at Audrey's picture in the old Hoover yearbook. It was right across from Smokey McQueen, the guy she had gone out with back then. A jerk-off.

So Joe and Hraska had decided to think up everybody in the world named Smokey. Just to see how many of them were jerk-offs, what percentage it would come out to be. They had to quit, though, because the only other Smokeys they could come up with were

Smoky Burgess, the old ballplayer, Smokey Robinson, the singer, Smokey the Bear, and Smokey Rizzo, a child-molester and part-time arsonist they both knew.

So they decided to name an all-fruit ball team instead. Right field was easy. Darryl Strawberry. Milt Plum, except he was football. Hraska had said that he thought Plum might have pitched in college, though. Ty Cobb was the Georgia Peach, but nicknames didn't count. The whole thing degenerated when Hraska brought up Luke Appling.

"Luke Appling?"

"Yeah, you know, like apples."

Later, two guys they knew from Bunco came over and tried to get Hraska to draw on the bar's TV screen with the Magic Markers they got from behind the bar.

Drunk cops were always doing that to him. It was because of his name.

There had been a cartoon show on TV when they were kids, *Winky Dink and You*, starring Winky and Jack Barry, the guy who would later go on to host some tacky quiz show. At eight years old and older, Winky loved *Winky Dink*, couldn't live without it. That's how Theodore John Hraska had received his name for life.

The gimmick of the show was, you sent in for this kit that had some crayons and a piece of cheesecloth to stick on the TV. Then you drew stuff on the screen that would help Winky in his adventures. Jack Barry would say, "Quick, kids, draw the footbridge so that Winky can get away from the Gila monsters. Here, follow my finger with your red Winky Dink crayon." Or else he'd say, "Hey, kids, Winky's Italian grandmother has lost her mustache. Let's help her out and draw it back on with your big black crayon. Press hard now."

So the *You* in the title *Winky Dink and You*, it really meant something.

But hell, Hraska was just a little kid; he had gotten out of hand a few times and drawn stuff right on the screen without any cheesecloth, because his folks were too damn cheap to let him send away for the kit. A lot of Windex and ass whacks in those days. A lot.

And goddamn Joe LaLuna, his much loved partner and friend, never minded breaking a silence to tell everybody in the department, or in the Room, where the detectives worked, about these youthful indiscretions of Wink's.

But anyway, it was good that Joe and his partner got to share a few drinking nights like this now and again. Hraska punched in his Celebrity's cigarette lighter. Lately, with Lou Duva getting sicker and sicker and meaner and meaner, Joe couldn't get away from her at all, not even for the PBA's official and semiofficial blasts, much less for a night of just hitting spots, throwing beer back up into the pitcher from whence it came.

Joe's wife, Madeline, looked like Lou Duva, the fight manager you saw on the tube every single fight, so that's what Hraska called her, especially when he had been drinking. And he didn't care who heard it. Joe didn't mind. The lady looked exactly like Lou Duva, that's all, and every year went by, she got to look even more and more like Lou Duva. It was simply a fact.

She had just about every sickness there was, in her ears and legs and skin and everywhere. The latest thing, other than the rashes, the doctors suspected she was pissing away her own protein, a little bit at a time.

She always came up with diseases and with conditions, like this pissing away protein thing, that weren't completely covered by medical, so they cost Joe a fortune. Plus the woman gave big money to every shyster with a collar they used to have on TV. She had lifetime, luxury-suite reservations at about fifteen different religious resorts, none of which still existed, some of which never did, and it'd gotten poor Joe into debt way over his stupid wop head.

It was such a shame, Hraska figured. Here's Joe LaLuna, his life buddy—more than that, his superior in just about everything—married till death to something like that, somebody spending money like water and getting flushed away a little at a time every time she sat down on the thunder box.

And Joe, still a good-looking guy in his upper forties, paisan dark, with all his hair still, black with a little gray, quiet, soft-spoken, distinguished, the guy who could clear homicides faster than anybody else in the history of the department. Six in an afternoon once, Hraska swore to it.

Many times, questioning an iced guy's squeeze, she would start coming on to Joe right there across the bloodstains and dark fluids and yellow crime-scene tape. Like to say, "As soon as these guys haul the dead meat out of here, want to go buy me a drink someplace?" With that guy, leg was always on call.

And Joe making out like he didn't catch the scent, didn't feel aware of anything, shrugging it off and going home at the end of the shift to Lou Duva, who was always in a bathrobe, even on hot days. It was almost so sad.

Joe said, "Get out. I'll keep the car, pick you up in the morning."

You could see he was thinking already about what Lou Duva would say to him when he got home. Joe held the booze a lot better than Hraska, so on drinking nights, rare that they were, Joe would usually wind up driving him home and then picking him up in the morning, his own car. Was one of the Corporal Works of Mercy, right after Visit the Sick—Drive Home the Drunk.

Joe was like the brother Hraska never had, even though he had six of them. They didn't count, none of them, not like Joe did.

Hraska didn't want to get out. "So," he said, "what do you think about the Audrey thing?"

Joe wasting his life away with Lou, that's what made this Audrey McKenna thing so great, so exciting, to Hraska. Could be something still there. There *was* something; Hraska saw it when they were talking, saw it right after Slabb the Drab had hauled off the meat.

Joe didn't answer him. He did a lot of that. Hraska repeated, "So what about Audrey, huh?" He repeated stuff to Joe a lot. Joe still didn't answer.

"Yeah, it's just kind of like old home week with me and you and her, ain't it, Joe?" he asked him.

Joe said, "Yeah, well, with me and her it is, at least."

Hraska had been at Hoover when Joe and Audrey were there. Wasn't that an amazing thing?

Joe was holding the wheel, looking out the windshield, waiting for Hraska to get out. When he didn't go, Joe said, "Yeah, well, the cocaine killed him."

"Yeah, that's what the wonking autopsy said."

"What did it say?" Joe asked. "How much, a two and a half?"

"'Topsy said two and a half micrograms per milliliter of blood," Hraska quoted for him. "Potentially life-threatening amount. We can drop the 'potentially' for that guy."

"Plus it could have been a lot more than two and a half, Wink, you know that," Joe said. "The dope continues to break down, whether the guy with it in him is dead or alive. Even in a test tube it does that, Slabb said. So it could have been a lot more than that. It's not like booze, where you can get an exact reading in the blood."

"That's right, yeah. Course, there was the booze too," Hraska said. "What, I think she said three ninety milligrams per hundred milliliters, something like that. That'd borderline kill you too."

"Audie said he was drinking vodka, she didn't know how much. That and the coke would kill you, sure."

"Yeah," Hraska said.

Hraska sat there.

"What do you think about the foot?" Joe asked, finally.

"I don't know," Winky said. "To me it's just a foot."

A kid, Dumpster-diving down by the Locusts, had found a human left foot, severed pretty clean, wrapped up in some butcher paper. Joe and Wink had been given the case, called a few hospitals and morgues, checked a few files, lost interest. Lieutenant Sheeney would ask them about it every couple of days. Winky kept trying to explain to Sheeney it was just a foot. Sheeney would forget it eventually. As long as the papers didn't pick it up, they'd be safe.

"I hope this all doesn't ruin her," Joe said after a while.

"Ah, what do you care. It hits the papers, the *Post* sells some copies, that's all."

"You think it will?"

"It might. Shit, they were both rich, the 'topsy it said they were screwing, they apparently used various farm implements for agricultural gratification—that's news, ain't it?"

"The papers don't find that out," Joe said, and he looked over at Hraska.

Hraska said, "No, of course not, not at all. But shit, Joey, what do you care anyway? Audrey, hell, from what I can recall of her, she was always such a pansy ass anyway. Wait, can a female be a pansy ass? I don't know."

Joe looked back out the window. After a long time, he said quietly, "I don't think of her as a candy ass."

Hraska said, "Hey, I didn't call her a candy ass. I called her a pansy ass. I think. So, do we think about charging her?"

"What, the drugs? No, come on. Hey, I don't know what we recommend," Joe told him. "You think we just turn everything over to Philbrick, let them bind her over, or not? Not our call?"

"Yeah, and Philbrick makes the call on PC, smiles if it turns out right, calls a press conference if the GJ indicts, leaks that it was Strickland's call if it turns to shit with dismissal, huh?"

"That's how it'll work," Joe said.

"Yeah, but how long can Strickland not figure out the guy's after his job, after his balls, you know?"

"Maybe he already got his balls."

"Yeah, well," Hraska said. "You know, with Philbrick on this Audrey thing, that cocksucker might just get into something. Slabb says somebody moved the body for sure, you know? What's that mean? All crapola. Who knows for sure? You know Philbrick—could do anything with it, go any which way. Still, I think about it, Joe, you say you don't feel something about it is right, I don't know. I just don't know—who cares?"

"Tell you, Wink, this one turns to something, I won't feel like letting go of it."

"You don't feel it's right?"

"I don't know. What?"

"I don't know," Hraska said. "To me it's nothing to lose sleep over, not worth any Bobby Lewis nights, that's for sure. What, something, you think, it ain't right?"

"Well," Joe said, "I got to think some more about it."

"Yeah, all right, paisan," Hraska told him, opening the Celebrity's door, getting out. "So you g'head, you go think some more about it."

FIVE

That afternoon, the deputy chief medical examiner of the town of North Homestead, county of Nassau, had argued with her mother about *Beetlejuice* or *The Whales of August*. Both only a dollar, not new releases.

"Look at that ugly face," her mother said, pointing to Michael Keaton in makeup on the box. "How come you never want a show with a handsome man in it?"

"Mom, *Whales of August* has no men at all," she answered, taking the box from her mother's hand. "Look, it's Bette Davis and somebody else."

"At least it's drama," her mother said. "It will have a story, I guarantee. Now, how about this one with Goldie Hawn and this handsome fellow?"

"Mom, please."

"I'm sorry, I'm sorry, Sharon."

They kept looking. Her mother pointed at Tom Hanks and said, "This one looks just like Bernie, down at work. It's true. It used to be movie stars couldn't look like regular people. Clark Gable. Now they all look like people at work. It's pretty awful, really. If I wanted to see people who looked like the people I work with, I'd go to work. I could, too. Terry is always asking me for overtime. I just don't have the time, with all I have to get done at home. But isn't it true,

Sharon? Don't the people at work look just like the people in the movies nowadays?"

"Mom, all the people I meet at work are dead. And I'm busy cutting them up into pieces."

"Not now, please, dear. I'm trying to pick."

Mom was in her Guttersnipe mode. She had five modes in her life. In descending order of irritation, they were Loretta Young, Fog, Chucklehead, Guttersnipe, and Blitzkrieg.

In Guttersnipe, she would never actually call Sharon a useless and crushing disappointment as an offspring; she would, instead, just butter those ideas thinly between her words and then deliver them with a sigh and a smile.

Mom's modes had been degenerating all day. First, she was annoyed that Sharon had slept late because she hadn't arrived home until four-thirty in the morning from the Wright necropsy.

This one hadn't been easy, and these things were always a pain. The doctor was expected to work quickly, precisely, efficiently, meticulously, no matter what. Once the body was out of the cooler, it would lose its bloom in a matter of minutes, the texture and color draining like water. Bad if you were trying to take pictures. And just moving the dead weight around on the table, even with a deiner helping, was tough. And even with exsanguination, there'd be blood everywhere to sop up, or, worse, enough peritoneal fluid to float a battleship. There was only so much you could sop up with your lint-free paper towels by Scott. Hard to use a chalkboard for notes, with your hands wet. Smear. Plus their best striker saw had started shorting out. And even with the double-action shears, ribs would splinter or crack instead of cutting neatly, slices of tissue would turn out serrated, no matter how much you tried for a clean, one-cut motion.

And Bobby Dekar would notice, let you know about it later. Doesn't matter, Bobby. And he always ranted on about the no-touch technique that he preferred. Reduced contamination, but it was like trying to eat peanuts in the shell using a knife and fork. Bobby, just let us pick the damned things up.

Necropsies were tough, even for people in the sharpest frame of mind.

So Sharon had gotten home exhausted, and when she had come

downstairs that morning, Mogie Hattes was already there in the kitchen, jiggling his keys in his pocket and pretending to smile at her while he talked to Mom about her shopping list.

Then, on the way to the Grand Union, Mom had complained about a head and neck ache and told them again that she would have to do something about her eye prescription, that Dr. Andress made it just too strong the last time. Mom took off her glasses and studied them, as if she could figure out the curvature of the lenses and do something about it right then and there.

After, the kid at the checkout had challenged Mom on four coupons and turned back three of them, two on expired-date raps and one because it was only good on the fifty-pound bag of Captain Pussy Kitty Litter, an amount Mom said would be enough for an army.

Of course, with Mogie driving them in their own Cadillac over to Smash Video—even though Sharon hated to be driven anywhere by anyone, but mostly by Hattes with Mom in their own car—Mom had been ostensibly in "Loretta Young." It was only when they had left Mogie outside and come into the video place that Mom had downshifted three gears in one yank, right into Guttersnipe.

Her mother cut across to another aisle, the one named "New Releases," and she started talking to Sharon through the pegboard holding the videos. Sharon hated when she did that. Sharon couldn't see the person she was talking to, and everyone else in both aisles heard everything. She thought maybe that was one reason her mother always did it that way.

"I didn't hear you get back last night," her mother's voice said through the little holes in the board. Sharon was looking at concert videos, not recognizing many of the titles or even the names of the groups.

"I got back late," Sharon said. "I had to do the work right then. You know those are the new rules. At least for now they are. It can't go on. It's a silly, sensationalistic way of running the procedures."

She had tried complaining to her boss about his new policy. He'd just quote the scripture, Pulvertaft, 1950, for her: "'Necropsies should be neither hurried nor perfunctory, and should take place as soon as possible after death.'" Dekar was just looking for ways to enhance his résumé, that's all.

"But, honey, you're the boss," Mom said, "one of them anyway. You're the head doctor; let somebody else take those night calls and on weekends."

Her mother hit the "boss" and the "head doctor" extra hard. Probably to impress the high school sophomore working the counter, so that he would come over and ask Sharon to be his bride.

One of these times, Sharon would shout back through the peg-board partition, "Oh, I don't mind, Mother. The feel of the cold flesh through my rubber gloves, the cutting into the stomach for the undi-gested-food survey—it breaks up the evening for me. Just the sort of thing a bachelor girl such as myself enjoys."

But this time she said, "I'm only on call a few times a month, Mom. I take my share—actually, a little less than my share."

"It's just that it cuts in, to your time, I mean, and what with your jujitsu and all, I figured ..."

"It's not jujitsu, Mom, it's Laotian. We'd better decide. Mogie will get tired of waiting out there."

"Don't worry about Mogie, he'll be fine. He's an angel. Was there any trouble? Last night?"

Sharon didn't answer. She walked around and stood by her moth-er in front of "New Releases." Then she said softly, "What do you mean, any trouble?" She heard herself sounding mad and didn't try to change it.

"You know, dear, any problems with the—procedures, you call it."

"No, Mom, of course there wasn't any problem," she said. She looked around. She was still holding *Beetlejuice*.

"Who was running the investigation?" her mother asked.

"Joe LaLuna was. Why?"

"Oh, is he the nice, quiet Italian one with the horrible little part-ner, we met them once at Carvel?"

"Yes, Mom. Joe is nice. Joe is quiet. Joe is Italian. Joe is married."

"I didn't ask you that, did I? Did I ask if Joe was married at all?"

"How come you didn't ask if his awful little partner was married? Wouldn't he be a cute little pocket-sized son-in-law for you?"

"I didn't ask if *anyone* was married, did I? You're imagining things, dear. Let's just get a show, that's what we came here to do, isn't it? I was just chatting about your job. I'm very, very sorry that I chatted."

"Right, Mom, let's just get a video."

"Of course we should," her mother said. "We've made poor Mogie wait long enough. He didn't even want to come in. He's happy with anything we choose, although I believe what he likes is a good musical."

"Mogie's a saint, Mom. I'm sure he knows all the musicals."

"Please, Sharon, no sarcasm right now, if you don't mind. I have my fill. Let's just get ourselves a show. Mogie will be happy with whatever, I'm sure. By the way, did he say to you that you should call him that?"

"What—Mogie? No, he didn't. I just did."

"Well, I think that's good, dear. You two. The two of you."

"If he only had a son. A younger brother."

"Sarcasm, dear, remember? Please?"

And Sharon knew already that she would not be able to sleep that night. They would go to Buy-Lo before they went home, and they would all three walk out with a package.

And then after the filet of sole that they had bought on sale, and after the video, Sharon would go upstairs and leave her mother and Mogie Hattes be. But Sharon would stay awake. She had gotten to bed too late this morning after the necropsy, thinking too much about coolers and cavities and fluids spilling over Formica and tired fingers and trims. So she had slept too much and wrong and woken up too late.

She would be awake and sweating this evening, replaying things. The external on Milton Wright, patterns, marks, lesions. The double-incision Y-cut, from each shoulder, meeting at the chest: keep cuts hidden for the open-casket service. The join, then the single cut down to the pubic hair. Cut the rib cage, lift the chest plate, all the organ systems, stuff the shell with cotton, sew it back up. The cranium—cross-cut, peel the scalp, open cranium with an O-cut, lift, and remove. She'd put it all back, she'd comb the hair. Sharon would see all that again tonight. Comb the hair again.

And she would listen to different voices asking questions that she didn't always understand, questions asked by voices that didn't go with the faces that she would see, like voices coming through an intercom in the necropsy room, through a pegboard partition in a video store.

She wouldn't recognize the faces, but the voices would belong to Joe LaLuna and to her mother and Mogie Hattes and the checker at the Grand Union and Beetlejuice and Mel Gibson and even to Milton L. Wright, deceased, whose body she had cut into with her scalpel just this morning.

And all the voices would be asking questions.

And finally she would roll over onto her stomach and try to make herself calm, and she would almost make it, almost be off.

But afterward, some of the voices would still be there, still asking questions quietly, asking, "What killed me? What's killing me?"

And one of the voices would be her own, and she would be wide awake again.

"All right, Mom," Sharon said to her mother. "Let's just get *Whales of August*."

Two swans were twisting and squawking, pecking hard at each other's necks, fighting over a crust of Pepperidge Farm cinnamon raisin toast. As their necks feinted and drove in and came back out, beaks holding feathers, a duck snuck in and stole the toast.

Audrey looked up, to see a man approaching her bench. She threw her cigarette down, snuffed it out with her toe, licked her lips.

The man coming over was short; his hands were in the pockets of his opened black trench coat. Under it he wore a black turtle neck and dark-blue Dockers. He had on white high-top Reeboks. His straight black hair was pulled back into a ponytail, revealing on his left ear a diamond stud that dangled a golden circle.

He looked like someone who would be managing a marginally successful art gallery, maybe running a Social Security check cashing racket at night. Actually, he turned about a third of a million dollars each year by convincing executives to switch jobs with other executives in different industrial fields and corporations. No matter what the economy was doing, he never seemed to run out of fields or jobs or companies or executives willing to try a switch. Lately, he had been talking a lot about taking the business and affiliating it nationally.

He came over to Audrey there on the bench, bent over, took her face in both his hands, and kissed it.

"How's it been, love?" he asked her.

He sat down on the bench next to her and put his left arm over the back of it.

"Lousy. I can only stay awhile," she told him. "I've got a lot to do. Thanks for coming. I have everybody starting to come over this afternoon. Milton's henchmen are already here."

"The family? When's the services?"

"I don't know yet. They have to release the body to me. The police do. Then we have to get it upstate."

"Why? Why do they, the police, have it?"

He grabbed onto the black lapel of his coat with his right hand, took hold of his elbow with the other hand.

"I don't know. It's just until they find out what he died of. They should let me know soon, they told me. I know the cop running the show. I dated him. In high school. Isn't that crazy?"

"Don't let them shmooze you around, a woman alone. Don't take shit. Does anybody think there's going to be a problem? I mean, about anything?"

"Joe, the cop, he seemed fine. Even his partner was in high school at Hoover. They're both fine. The people I'm battling now are Milton's. His mother and his sister. Wouldn't you think they'd give me a few days, a honeymoon until the funeral's over, before they started intimating how I killed him?"

"What are they doing? Those cunts. I swear. They say you killed him? What?"

"Oh, you know, nothing to put your finger on, just the little things. His mother moaning about life on the North Shore, you know, as opposed to life upstate. Life-style killed him, *my* life-style. Nobody's ever died upstate, did you know that? Couple million people born up there in history, nobody's ever died. Those that want to die come to the Island, or to the city. They marry bitches, go to parties, and then they die young. It's the only way the herd gets thinned out. Or else everybody would be standing on everybody else's feet, from New Rochelle on up north. Listen, Chet, I can't sit here, sorry, I've got to go back, thanks. You should've been sooner."

"Wait. You called me down here, remember? C'mon. What'd you want?"

"Nothing. Just to see you, I guess. You should've been sooner. You won't be able to come to the services or anything. Don't call. They're both staying in the house. She's setting up a command headquarters or something. She has herself a damned checklist, made it out on the plane. My God—things to do to get my son in the ground. After every entry I think she's written, 'Skewer Audrey, savage her until she's curled up fetally in the back of the hearse on the way to Rolling Knolls,' or wherever. She's good. I don't think you've ever met her."

"No. When would I?"

"I don't know. I've got to go. Marmasette keeps calling me up too, driving me crazy."

"What's that guy want? Barracuda."

"I don't know. He keeps asking if there's anything he can do. Mommy Dearest and the funeral parlor guys have decided on no wake, I think, which is fine with me, but Marmasette keeps wanting to talk to me, help me out, I guess—I don't know—in my time of need."

"Yeah, relieve you of the burden of your stock and options probably. Remember, no matter what the stipulations are in the Vor-Tech makeup, you can hang on. You can put it in the courts until doomsday, you want to. Remember. I hate to talk business, but it's your company as much as anyone's now. Don't do anything now. Call me, you have to. Audrey, you be careful of that guy."

"Thanks, hon. Everything's all right. I'll call when I can. Don't call. They'll be around, Sis and Mom."

He leaned over and took her face in his cupped hands again and held on until she stopped talking, stopped shaking. Then he started singing quietly and slowly to her, "Maybelline," asking, "Why can't you be true?"

He had taken her to a Chuck Berry concert at the Memorial Auditorium the night Milton died. Chuck had been great. A bright-red jumpsuit, still chicken-walking frontwards and backwards, getting almost as low as he used to on *American Bandstand*—what, thirty-five years ago?

Hit song after hit after hit, no lead guitar in the group, just old Chuck, playing it behind his ear, two strings at a time. Chet had explained it to her. Instead of a phony bid for an encore, Chuck told everybody to come up on stage and dance. Masses did, and of Chuck you could see only his red guitar, held straight above his head, still keeping the beat, hitting the notes. They had stood on their chairs and clapped above their heads for a while, then they had gone up on stage too. Danced.

Later, at Burger King, Chet had told her, "Rock 'n' roll has killed so many of its children, it's good to see that it's taking such good care of its father."

It was a practiced line, coming out like that, but it was still rough-polished and interesting, just like Chet himself. Just like his having them sit there with Whoppers dripping, drinking fifty-year-old wine from a bottle he had snuck in. Just like him.

Chuck Berry to Whoppers to fine wine.

No, there was a break in there. She hadn't told Joe LaLuna, but Chet had gotten a beeper signal to call one of his snitches as they left the Memorial Aud that night. Chet was always getting those—fuzzy calls at crazy hours to meet people at bad bars. He always went, to find out about the latest executive about ready to jump ship, or about some new position opening up somewhere. What kind of person made money selling information to corporate headhunters? Did these snitches dress in Italian silk or in spotted army fatigues?

She didn't know. But Chet had gotten a beep from one of them right after Chuck Berry, right before Whoppers and wine, and they had separated for a half hour and then met again at Burger King.

They had talked and eaten and drunk for a while. He was her steel-belted radical, that's what she called him. Sometimes he could spend hours explaining to her why the FBI had to be disbanded and how to price baseball cards.

The manager of the place, maybe twenty-five, with a blond mustache—Chet called him "der Burger Meister"—had spotted the wine and thrown them out. They had loved it.

After that, they had made it, standing up. It was in the park by her house, and they were the same height. There was a tree there, a low-crotched apple tree, and they were both in his coat for a while, not caring if anyone saw them there in the dark. The panties she had sweated through during Chuck Berry were gone, curled into a roll and peeled off her, and she had made her way to Chet's little bit of chest hair, for kissing and licking, and then she was just floating up heavy, her feet way off the ground, her twitching body supported by him and a tree trunk and a little bit of ecstasy, sliced thin.

After, he had wiped the little pieces of bark off her ass with the flat of his palm. He called it "doing a little gardening back here." And she had headed home to a dead husband.

She had called 911 and then, while she was waiting, called him.

"He's dead."

"Sure?"

"Stiff."

"Better hang up."

"OK."

"I can't come over."

"I know."

"I can't come over now."

"I know that."

Now Chet was there in the park with her, telling her that her in-laws were cunts, holding her face in his hands, singing the chorus to "Maybelline," about starting back doing the things you used to do. She wanted to go back to the tree, get him back there to the tree with her.

She wanted to use her own blood, use it to wash the thoughts out of her head and then down, down through her body, down to her legs, where the thoughts could mutate and at least do some good. She wanted something about herself to do some good.

There on the bench, she felt a bit of Chet's lip between the edges of her front teeth, and she let herself moan a bit, a little of it forced, but the hearing of it made her want everything more.

She rolled her body toward him and they kissed. She was holding the kiss when she sensed a movement over Chet's shoulder, and she looked up.

Joe LaLuna was maybe five yards away and saying to them, "Excuse me, hey, could I ask you some questions maybe?"

From the first, LaLuna had figured Chester Zumrad for a little, pompous, condescending piece of fag bait who probably had Audie all faked out and spreading for him because of her confusion and guilt.

"He seems to be a good friend," he told her when they were back at her house.

"Yes, he is," she said.

Yeah.

"You two involved?" he asked her.

"You mean lovers? Yes. But he only comes around sometimes. He's very busy. With a lot of things. In some ways, he's bigger than life, Joe. A genius, you know?"

"Great, you seem to know lots of that kind. Congratulations."

Zumrad hadn't wanted to leave them, back there in the park, had just hung around, hunching his puny shoulders, being a pain in the ass, giving LaLuna the "What you can say to her, you can say to me" kind of crap. When Audie had told him it's OK, he had looked at her quick and she shut up.

LaLuna found himself wondering about bruises on her. Would she stand for that garbage? LaLuna wouldn't. No.

"Look, Mr. Zumrad, I'll be talking to you about this case soon. Please, c'mon now," LaLuna had told him.

Chester hadn't liked that. "What case? This is a case now, is it, Officer?"

LaLuna studied him, little guy trying for a sort of pissed-off, nothing-to-hide attitude. Not quite making it, though. Yeah, Chester, this is a case now, maybe. LaLuna told himself that first impressions, hunches, they break your balls, the long run. Forget this guy. Nothing. Still, though, LaLuna figured, still.

LaLuna had finally scared him off with a notepad, some questions about his business and background, and a promise to meet with him real soon. Chester kissed Audrey, holding on to her shoulders too rough, too long, LaLuna figured, almost decided to smack the little bastard. Then Chester let go of her, stepped back, smiled at them both. She seemed frozen; LaLuna tried to look calm; Chester strolled off, singing "Maybelline" by Chuck Berry.

LaLuna had taken Audrey back to her house to talk. The door had been opened for them by a white-haired witch with pearls and white skin and expensive false teeth. She acted like it was her place, not Audie's. Audie introduced her as Milton's mother. LaLuna nodded, didn't say he was sorry. Then a colorized version of the same gal came in, Milton's sister.

The daughter's demeanor told them: If old whitey here dies, I take over. Make yourself at home.

LaLuna used his badge, his notebook, to get rid of them both, but everybody concerned knew that they'd be hovering around. Big house, thin walls, big ears; Audie didn't seem to care. Surprise, though: Mom and Sis headed on out of the house, said they had to get some things done.

Audie told him they were probably going shopping for funeral wear, would love it. She sat LaLuna down like an old friend. Which he was, right?

He told her the autopsy, the bones of it, and neither of them had much to say about that. She just blinked a couple of times, like maybe trying to force tears back, or cough them up, when he had to say, "Cocaine tox."

He had started her talking and had somehow mentioned his wife, not by name, just by "my wife." In passing, like a vaguely familiar hitchhiker you felt guilty about not stopping for.

"You have kids, Joe?"

"No," he told her. "We haven't had much luck there."

They had lost two. Little, imperfect Jeffrey, the reason for the groundbreaking of the marriage—the poor kid had never made it home from the hospital. And Daniel had been eleven when he was run over by a Cambodian who said he hadn't been drinking.

For three months LaLuna had wanted to kill the little bastard, had planned it, but the Cambodian had beat him to the punch, dousing himself with Good Gulf one-step charcoal lighter, waiting ten minutes for it to saturate, then flaming up.

At his funeral, a tiny Cambodian woman with black warts on her face, wailing like Phyllis Diller laughs, started yelling at LaLuna in Cambodian until he left.

"You?" he asked Audie.

"No," she said. "No kids. We wouldn't know what to do with them. Wouldn't have. So, Joe, how come you hate Chet so much? I'm not complaining about him, you know."

"I don't know. I didn't cover that up too good, huh? I don't know, maybe he reminds me of guys I used to hate in high school or something."

"Like who?"

"I don't know. Guys who weren't like me, you know?"

"Oh, you mean Ricky Phalen and the crowd, and Bob—what was his name—the Corvette? And guys like that?"

"Sort of, I guess, yeah."

"And Smokey?" she asked, smiling.

Joe shook his head. "He was such a flea."

"What do you mean? So your friend little Winky had the right to enema him up?" Still smiling.

"Come on, Audie, that was a medical procedure." He was smiling too now, enjoying. "You had such an eye for quiffs, for fleas, back then, I swear."

"Hey, I dated *you*, didn't I?"

"See? That's what I mean."

"And what do you hear from your old friend? The one with the gum? Still chewing on her cud?"

"Oh, Christ, you mean her?"

"Yeah."

"Popstooka. That was her name. Popstooka. I think lusty thoughts of her whenever my dog gets sick."

"Oh, I bet."

"God, I don't know. She used to make me throw up, you know. Only girl I ever knew could make me vomit at will, with just a look of her eye, a touch of her smile."

"Sounds like Cole Porter lyrics. That's chemistry. Somebody told me you had married her, though."

"What? Popstooka? You crazy?"

"Yeah, somebody said."

"Nah, I never married Popstooka. I been married over twenty-something years. Christ, Aud, I'd be dehydrated by now. You nuts? Nobody can vomit twenty-five straight years and live. I never saw her again."

"Oh, well, I don't know, somebody said. I figured at least you'd still be buying her gum for her, on the side."

"Yeah, well, they must know, all right. I guess I must have married her, they said so. No, Aud, I married a girl you don't even know. Not from town. You don't know her."

"Twenty-five years, Joe. God."

"Yeah, well, something like twenty-five. I could figure it out, I had to."

"That's a lot of love, Joe."

"Yeah, well, it's a lot of years, I guess. A lot."

"Too many?" she asked him.

LaLuna looked up, said, "I got a comfortable spot, Audie. That's not bad. I can lie in bed, when I'm not working, and I know every sound in that house. A Cape, out on Houser Street, for years now. I can lie in bed there, Saturday mornings, listen to the things I know, you know, the flies banging their heads against the glass. Sump pump in the cellar, it clicks on. Drips from the faucet in the little bathroom. Washerless, they said that wasn't supposed to happen. Ghost in our toilet tank, churns up the water for couple seconds, then it's quiet. You own a house, there's always a lot to do, you know. A million things, every day off. You know how it is with a house. Hey, it's not bad."

"Joe the home owner. I never heard you talk so much."

"Yeah. I don't know, I've just been thinking about all that stuff."

"Sounds like you love the place."

"Love it? Nah. I'm comfortable there, that's all. You know, I can get up in the middle of the night, pitch black, go downstairs for something, got a full dormer, get something to eat, and in the dark I'll know where to step on the landing so I don't step on the dog sleeping there, dumb mutt. I know the place that well."

"We never lived in this house like that, Milton and I didn't. Not like you guys live in yours. I don't know, we were, just here, that's all. Instead of being someplace else. It didn't matter to us."

"Madeline, my wife, she's sick, she calls me up to bring home stuff from work. Bread and stuff. Just like television, you know. Ozzie Nelson."

"Milton and I, I'd pick him up his cocaine for him. He'd get low, ask me to pick some up. That was our groceries, Joe. That was our *Father Knows Best*. I'm Donna 'The Mule' Reed. What's your wife got?"

"Just sick. How come you for the coke, Audie? He couldn't get his own stuff? Didn't care about getting you in trouble?"

"It's because I know the guys. Should I be telling you any of this?"

"Hey, I'm not Narco, I don't even give a shit about that. I'm Homicide, that's all."

"Well, I know the people. Guys in certain condos that you cops all know about anyway. One guy at a ski outfit store. Big-time. And a hairdresser in the Franklin Mall. Hey, you cops know all these places, I'm not telling you anything. But I used to use before Milton did. So I introduced him."

"You still use that stuff?"

"No, Joe, I gave it up. It was in, I used it. It was out, I stopped. No big thing. I'm just waiting around to see what the next self-destructive fad will be. Remember glue in high school? Goddamn airplane models for the eighth-grade boys? God. Kids. Noses. Kids of all ages."

"Yeah. But your husband kept using when you quit?"

"Well, I guess maybe so, sure he did. Not a big thing. And anyway, he needed something. He worked hard at the business all day. I had the time, he gave me the money. I would go out and score for him. No big."

"Audie, it's what killed him."

"Well. Joe, he's used more than that and lived, that's all I know. He's used more, he's drunk more, and he's gotten up to go to work in the morning, you see? Joe, am I in trouble here? Is anybody? I should know, I should be told."

"I don't know, Audie. I told you the autopsy. It's more of a mess than big trouble, I think. It could go a hundred different ways right now. You know, Kenny Doyle—remember him?—died of drugs."

"No. The wrestler, with the neckties? He was a senior, we were juniors? I think I dated him. He died of drugs?"

"Yeah, he did. A couple years out of high school."

"He didn't seem like it, did he? OD. Well, he shouldn't have."

"Yeah, but he did," Joe said.

Audie asked, "Do you remember that guy's zits? God, they were like—a couple more, they used to tell him, he'd have to wrestle as a heavyweight. Remember that?"

"Yeah," Joe said. "The poor guy. You had to feel sorry for him, huh? Zits like that."

"Ah," Audie told him. "He shouldn't have picked them, that's all."

Joe laughed. "Shouldn't've used, shouldn't've picked his pimples. God, Audie, you've gotten cynical," he said. "Unyielding as hell."

"Hey, Joe, your knees still hairy?"

"What hair? What?"

"You know," she said, "your big, clumpy, black Italian knees. You still got them?"

"No, I don't," he said. "My knees aren't hairy. What kind of stuff are you on here?"

"God, you mean you shave them now?"

"No. They just are not hairy, that's all. You probably got me confused, sweetheart."

"Oh, you got electrolysis then, huh? I've got a girlfriend did that to her sideburns. I bet you two know each other, probably bumped into each other each week down at the electrolysis parlor."

"Yeah, right, we did. Hey, girl, my knees are fine."

"Pull your pants up."

"What?"

"Go ahead," she told him, "pull your pants leg up. I want to see the rain forest. You have dandruff trouble, or you use Selsun Blue on the kneecaps? They say first impressions are very important, you know. Knees like that get dandruff, you'll need snowshoes to walk with."

"Yeah, well, I hate to be crude here, girl, but you've forced my hand. So I'll tell you; I think most human beings, given a choice between being stuck with either hairy knees or cross-eyed boobs, they would choose the former."

"What the hell are you talking about, you freak, you?"

"Oh, come on, McKenna, I hate to say it—everybody at Hoover used to discuss it endlessly. When you wore one of those sweaters of yours. It looked like Mortimer Snerd got in there somehow and was staring back out."

"You freak." She made a face, threw a pillow at him. He ducked. "It seemed to me there were not that many complaints from the boys of Hoover High about me and my goddamn nipple placement."

She looked down at herself.

"Shall I pull up my pants leg now? We'll trade off?"

"You pig. You freak. Do you remember Winky's gross sign at the Miss Hoover assembly?"

"Yeah," Joe said. "Got him suspended, right? What, twenty or so of Hoover's loveliest, including yourself, the eventual winner, parading across the stage in bathing suits, and that moron thought he could hold up a sign that said—"

"'Show Us Your Tits.'"

"Yeah, 'Show Us ...,' and no teacher or principal was going to see it, right? And at the same time snapping pictures like a goddamn madman. What a moron. Got him three days in jug, I think it was. What a guy."

"Joe, why do you still hang around with a guy like that? Is it for the dress-for-success hints you can pick up from him? I guess I had heard he was still your partner, but I am still bowled over by that fact. Why do you?"

Straight-faced, LaLuna told her, "I try to see Christ in him."

"Yeah," she answered. "We all do."

"No, really, I guess he just is so goddamned joyful about everything, he's a good remedy for me, a good antidote."

Audie asked him, "How come people can't stay happy like that, huh, Joe? How come *we* can't? How come we didn't?"

He asked, "Who didn't?"

"Come on, Joe," she said. "You were never Smilin' Jack, you're worse now. You know. Neither of us did. Almost nobody does. Nobody goes through life like Winky does. Nobody gets out of here alive, that doesn't matter, but nobody gets out of here happy, that's the shame of it. That's what makes all of it such a tragedy, don't you think?"

"Too heavy for me," Joe said, "and, well, if it's philosophy we're talking now, then Winky is a cosmic freak. When Armageddon gets here, he'll be flipping channels, seeing what's on. He'll find something to watch. He's got his own hard code, nobody like him, you're absolutely right."

"Joe," she asked, "am I in trouble? About the cocaine?"

"I don't know, Audie. I told you I don't know. We'll see."

"Joe. No shit."

"Audie, I'll find out. I'll do something."

"Would you, Joe? Please?"

Then she told him she had been lying, nobody had told her he had married Popstooka. Then she told him Chester had left her, for about a half hour, that night.

The air-conditioning had turned the Naugahyde into black ice. LaLuna wished he had worn a sports coat or his Mets jacket over his short-sleeved blue madras shirt. Every spot where his arms hit the booth froze for a few minutes before his body heat managed to warm it up some.

Zack's Blue was a cop bar for most hours of the day. Smoke and noise. Peanuts too soft to eat, mixed drinks too hard to get. Different shades of country and old rock on the jukebox—and LaLuna knew them all. All the fistfights here were sloppy, one-punch affairs, and it was a place you could go where the call "Officer down, officer down," just meant that someone else had passed out drunk.

Dr. Sharon Slabb, across the booth in a dark-blue summer dress Whistler's Mother would have worn to a wake, had added a sweater, but she didn't seem to notice temperature. She never did. Joe checked it out, figured she had washed her hair.

"You look a little uncomfortable, Sharon. You OK?" he asked her, just to make her a little uncomfortable. It would grease things to come. They were both doing a lot of waiting as they sat there. Waiting for their drinks, waiting for the smoke to clear, waiting for an opening.

"No, I'm fine," she told him, trying to smile. "It's just the place, I guess maybe."

Dwight Yoakam on the box. Old stuff. Cowboys and lovers, guitars and Cadillacs, enough bass and beat to please the crowd.

"It's a cop place. We're cops. It's natural habitat. And I've seen you here before," he was telling her.

"Well, I know. I guess it's you too."

Christ, this was the absolute easiest female in the world to make uncomfortable. Now LaLuna wasn't sure if he should be raising or lowering the lady's level of concern. So he told her, "We're a couple of cops having a drink. That's all right to do."

He hit the word "drink" a bit too hard, though. She was nursing a wine, he had a beer. The favorite in Zack's was something called a Marked Man, basically a self-assembled, ale-assisted boilermaker with a few twists. But now wasn't the time.

"I know it's not a date, you cowboy," she was saying, looking down and getting redder. LaLuna figured this lady to be as self-conscious and hypersensitive as anyone who cut up stiffs for a living could possibly be. "It's just something I'm not used to. I *am* with my mother, you know."

"Yeah, I know." The opening. "How she doing?"

Dwight Yoakam ended. ZZ Top now. Punched in by a new blue, someone not yet studying the retirement regs. Somebody's cigar started to make LaLuna's eyes burn. Somebody else said, "Jungle music."

"Well," Sharon said, "fine. Fine. She's seeing a guy."

"Yeah, I heard."

"You heard?" He didn't give her a reaction. She went on, "I thought she'd date Buck Rodgers, the crew chief from 911? But she turned quickly away from that. I don't know. She's dating someone else."

"Serious? So, I bet maybe that whole thing might end up with you putting in more time in dives like this, huh? That would be all right too, right?"

No reaction. Just a sip of wine. No Patsy Cline.

"How is it?"

"Good. Fine. Not my drink of choice, as I'm sure everybody knows by now."

Good. Here we go. Could just that little bit of wine be lubricating? Hard to believe. "Yeah, well, there is the office rumor that you like your Scotch," he told her, bringing his thumbs up from his belt and sipping from his beer, just to take the edge off the comment.

And then this frail, pale, string-haired schoolmarm of a coroner looked up from her wine to tell him, "That's right. Some nights I could drink a cesspool full of Scotch. And I do. But you've already heard that already."

"Yeah, well, I have. I drink too. Everybody drinks."

"I don't drink on duty time. I hope you've heard that too, haven't you? Have the office fat-mouths given me that much, at least?"

"I guess they have, sure," LaLuna told her, "but mostly, I'm sorry, but they concentrate on your look. Mornings, you know?"

"Oh, I do suffer for my sins. They're right on that."

"But, uh, if it makes you feel any better, the word is in that from noon until quitting time, you're the best ME we have, maybe the best in the East, as they say."

"Who says that?"

"Hey, everybody, everybody says that. I guess Winky does, he was the last one I heard it from, I guess. And I believe it, we all do. The best there is."

She just stared at him. No expression. He knew drunks can't get drunk on one wine. Maybe they get drunk on atmosphere. Or self-secreted body chemicals. Probably taught to do that in coroner school. Good trick.

No, wait a minute. The lady had been drunk when she came in. Drunk but good at it. LaLuna the cop hadn't seen it at first.

After a while she said, "I'm sure that's not the only thing Sergeant Hraska says about me and mine. I'm sure he has a million comments about me and my mother and my drinking. And all the other things they talk about."

"No. Not really. Winky's OK. You got to know him."

"What's there to know?"

"Well, I told somebody else just before that he's just a cosmic freak, that's all. So you got to know him. We were friends in high school, did you know that? Lot of years together."

"I heard that," Sharon told him. "That's no excuse. I went to high school with David Berkowitz, it doesn't mean I need to have the Son of Sam as my partner."

"I don't know what you have against the Wink, though, really. I don't even know why we're talking about the guy. He's not even here now."

"I guess I have against him that he's so crude, so below you, Joe. He cheapens you just being around the ground you walk on. If I were you, I would get a partner worthy of yourself, or none at all. I've heard so many disgusting things he does. At parties ..."

"Oh, you mean the Sea Monkey enema thing? Hey, that's his signature. That goes way back, to high school. It's just a gag."

"That makes people very sick."

"No, there was a rumor some drunk-up cop from the South Shore got rushed to emergency, didn't even happen. It's just a gag, makes a mess."

"Let's please talk about something else, please. Plus I know he doesn't like me. Probably because I'm a woman who cuts up deads for a living. That's probably a job meant for real men, in his mind."

"No, he doesn't dislike you, I think. I never got that from him. He told me once he just doesn't like MEs, that's all."

"Why? We're too ghoulish for him?"

"No. Believe it or not, it's because of Quincy," LaLuna said.

"What?"

"You remember 'Quincy,' the television show? The guy from 'The Odd Couple' played an ME? Well, Winky, for all his loud-mouthing, really hates shouters. Comes from a quiet upbringing, believe it or not. You probably haven't seen it, but a loud voice around Winky is like Arab fingernails on a Jew's blackboard. He just hates it, knocks out his bridges. And that Quincy guy, well, I guess he was a yeller, sore throat kind of a guy."

"So for that Hraska hates all MEs?"

"Well, his mind. You know. *You* figure."

"I bet he and the boys do a lot with my name too, huh? Dr. Slabb—stiffs on a slab?"

"No, not too much. That stuff gets pretty old early on. That's a one-trick pony, all right. Goes by real quick."

Sharon leaned forward now, hunching her shoulders a bit. LaLuna thought of his dog doing that, thought she might be getting sick. Then he saw she was just taking him into her confidence. "He says things about you too, Joe, you know, when you're not around. Things like … about your wife."

LaLuna smiled. "Lou Duva, right?"

"Yes. And you let him? That doesn't bother you?"

"No, hell. He says that stuff around me too. That's his mind. Sharon, you got to learn to differentiate, girl. Besides, I told you, he respects you. Noon to quitting time, all of us, we all think you're the best there is. I told you that."

"I never drink if I know I'll be on duty."

"Right. You're not on duty now—you want another wine? Something else?"

She shook her head.

"How often you on call?" LaLuna asked her.

"Twice a month maybe. Almost never."

Willie Nelson singing now.

LaLuna put his beer down and started speaking slowly, looking right at her. "But it can be a problem once in a while, Sharon, am I right?"

"No. Just about never."

"But sometimes," LaLuna insisted, trying to sound like he wasn't insisting. "Sometimes, though. Right? Bobby Dekar's stupid-ass same-day service, right?"

"Right. 'Necropsies should be performed, et cetera, et cetera.' Joe, listen, with Wright, if that is what we're talking about, and I bet it is, I had the kid Kerry Stamfield right there as my deiner, and John Dreeve came in too as it was going on. They watched everything I did."

"Sharon, that true what they say about Dreeve? He likes stiffs? I mean, *really* likes them?"

"Never mind that. There's gossip everywhere. It's stupid."

"True. We all got secrets, but I heard people have enough on Dreeve make him do anything."

"Oh, I'm glad you're into blackmail too, Joe, it's very complimentary to you. Did you ask me about the necropsy?"

"The autopsy, I did, yeah."

"And I said I handled it fine. That's why you asked me here, am I right? We're not here as friends, or fellow cops. We're not here so you can be cheating on your Lou the fight manager. A man looks like you could do a lot better than me. I'm smart enough to know that, Joe. Please grant me a little something, please. Maybe something just this side of wisdom for once."

"First off, Sharon, I don't cheat on Lou Duva, OK? Second off, I could do a lot worse than cheating with someone like you. You're a lot more than you think you are, you just don't know it yet. You will someday. And third off, third off—and this is the tough one—yeah, I am here with you about the Wright thing. I'm sorry. It's true."

"Joe, I did everything procedure on that. Check with the boy, Dreeve, if you want. You've already checked the report. There's no way in the world you or anybody can contest that postmortem. All my work is letter-perfect acceptable, so all right?"

"Sharon, I understand. There's no way in the world I would cause you any pain or trouble. Please know that, for me. I know that the work you did was acceptable. I know everything you do is acceptable, more than acceptable. I would never cause you any trouble. Do you know that?"

"I know that. Now. I guess."

LaLuna wished that he could order another round, fast. He looked around. Plankley, the bartender, was way down the other end, looking at a hard-boiled egg. LaLuna said, "Tell me about this guy your mother's seeing."

"What do you mean?"

"This guy. You said your mother was dating." He smiled. "They still call it dating at their age, or what? Spooning? Sparking? I'm kidding you."

Then Sharon came as close to raising her voice as he'd ever heard her, or ever thought that she could. "Oh, for Christ sake, Joe, you mean you know about that too? What's wrong with you guys? Don't you ever say anything that just means what it says? Don't you ever do anything just to do that thing? What are you doing to me? Leave me alone, for goddamned sake, please, Joe. Jesus."

LaLuna held his palms up at her. "Sharon, all right, all right. Please, let's just help each other, that's all I'm saying here."

"What? What the hell *are* you saying?"

"We can help each other. You were drunk when you 'topsied

Wright, right? They got that stupid-ass same-day service, and you had to do it, right?"

"I don't need any help. I got called in from home, it was eleven at night, midnight, and I did a perfect job. That's all there is. You can't blackmail me, you fucker, you."

"Sharon, there's nobody trying to blackmail you. Just listen, please. This guy your mother's with, he's a shit punk, right?"

Sharon just looked off, then down into her wine. She said she should go.

"Come on, Sharon, everybody knows it. You got a funny name for a coroner, you drink a lot, you love your mother, and you hate the shit punk she's been running around with—is that right?"

"You're not interrogating one of your perps now, or whatever the hell you crudes are calling your crooks this year, Mister Dick. I am no perp, damn you. I went to Columbia University for many, many years. I am registered."

Joe said, "Shh!" and he held up his hand a few inches from her face, began to reach to her face, and then grabbed his own temples with both hands. He said, "Sharon, you're right. I've spent too many years sweating assholes, pardon, and now it seems that's the only way I know how to talk to people."

She was crying now.

He went on. "I swear to God, I'm here, I brought you here, to help out both of us. I swear I won't, don't want to hurt you. I really do like you. I get depressed as hell whenever I just pass you in a hallway, everybody does, but I really do like you."

She told him she liked him too.

"Good," he said. "That's good. So here's the deal. Let me get rid of this piece of shit your mom's been carrying around on her shoe with her. Let me get rid of him for you both, her and you. You know I can. I can do that for you."

"How much do you know about him?"

"Not too much. I'll find enough to know. I'll get him out of the whole wonking state of New York for you. You and your mom will never see him again."

Still crying, she told him, "My mom and I are best friends, Joe. He's a sneak, Joe, he'll end up hurting her."

He told her he knew that. He said he wouldn't hurt the lady. Mom'd never even see him, or know much about it. LaLuna'd just force the piece of shit's hand. Guy'd leave. "You know I can do that. And I'll be glad to. For you."

"For me," she answered, "and what do I do?"

"Well," he said, "I don't know how else to say it. You redo the Milton Wright stiff for me." She turned her face away. "Sharon, Sharon, there's something there, something you and I and everybody just missed. I know there is. Just coke and booze? Please."

"Coke and booze is plenty. Joe, what the hell is going on? If I am noon to quitting time the best cutter east of the Mississippi, then you're the best at clearing cases. They all say you can clear cases like Kleenex, Joe, like—"

"Yeah, Winky says I clear homicides like Jerry Lee Lewis clears wives."

"That's right. So the Wright case is cleared, Joe. You should be heading on to other things, shouldn't you be? How about the foot from the Dumpster?"

"You know about the foot?"

"Of course, Joe. I have the foot in my cooler."

"God, that's too bad. I'm sorry."

"For what? What do you think we keep where I work, lamb chops? We have all sorts of parts, in and out, all the time. Feet and hands and organs and even heads. Cold-storage bins. All the time. What do you think anyway?"

"Enough to build a human, huh?"

"Well, a dead one anyway."

LaLuna laughed. She laughed, cleaned her nose.

"Yeah, well, sure, a dead one, I would think," he said. "Yeah, Sheeney keeps telling me I should clear that foot thing. I just don't have the time."

"Maybe you don't have the time because you stay on this Wright thing. It's cocaine tox, Joe. Very simple. Move on, my friend. It's done and it's finished and it's a dope death."

"Sharon. Mrs. Wright purchased the coke. She brought it home for her husband. She served it up."

"Oh, come on, Joe, this isn't some lady backup singer shooting

John Belushi with a speedball. So she's the one bought the cocaine, that doesn't matter. There's no manslaughter case here. You know that."

"No, I don't know that. With Philbrick grooming for full DA someday, looking to leapfrog over stupid-ass Strickland, who don't know shit about what's happening anytime, and the lady's rich, and there's that thing they were doing with that wonking-ass milking machine, whatever the hell that was. It's all of it good press for their office, Sharon. It scares me. Grinding her up will make such good juice for the flesh eaters, you know? I worry. Sharon, I just don't know what's going to happen to this lady."

Still Willie on. Angels flying close to the ground.

Then Sharon asked him, "How long have you loved her, Joe?" Sharon asked him that. Pretty good, must read Ann Landers a lot.

"I don't know. Off and on. A long time. Not now anymore, I don't think. But a long time ago. I still care, though."

"Joe, admitting to staff that I have to redo the stiff will kill my career. You know it will. You think Philbrick is ambitious. I work for Bobby Dekar, Joe, remember that? He makes Philbrick look like Mother Teresa."

"No," Joe told her, "that's just it. You don't do anything wrong. I can be the prick here. I get confused on a couple of points on the toxicology, I screw up the 'manner, cause, and means' crap, I messed my paperwork, I ask for a redo, and you be the good guy and give me one without even checking with Dekar first. 'Just to shut the prick up, Chief,' you tell Dekar. He appreciates. You look good. You do a couple hours OT, and your mother's free to go food shopping with you on Saturdays again. Everybody wins. Everybody except the turd, who's gone forever, compliments of me. Come on, Sharon, what do you say here? Huh? Physically you can do it, right? I mean, it can be done, huh? I know they've redone 'topsies in the past."

"Sure," she said. "We just go to the trim room, collect the fixed tissues, and process for microscopics and everything. We replaced everything nice and neat."

"Well, no need to tell me the hows of it. But *if* you could do it, Sharon, if you *could*, I mean."

"Joe, I'm not going to find anything."

"Hey, you're the best there is, we've already established that much. You don't find anything, then you don't find anything, that's all, that's fine with me. It's just that, the guy's done a lot more than that night, he never died from it before. So I ask, why that time?"

"Worse yet, I could find something that will put your homecoming queen away. I don't think so, but who knows, Joe, maybe I will."

"Well, that's fine too, then. That happens, at least I know who to blame for what. And what to cry about."

Reba singing with some guy, then a Beach Boys.

Sharon looked sadder than usual as she left him there in the ice-cold black Naugahyde booth, upholstered like a coffin. He was still freezing to death. He sat alone, was about to yell for a beer, then he yelled to her instead. She came back. He whispered that if things turned out, there might also be a fifth of Dewar's in the deal for her.

When she went out of the bar, she was smiling at that but still looking very sad. The Beach Boys sang about, fun, fun, fun, until they took away her T-bird.

NINE

Why'd you say Sharon had to work, sweetheart?" Mogie Hattes was soaping himself.

"I don't know, exactly. She just said something extra came up."

"Well, lookie down there—something extra has come up here too."

"Oh, Mogie, you're just plain awful." Ellen Slabb slapped his shoulder.

She was fifty-eight years old, and she'd never showered with someone else before. Before this. She was taller than Mogie, so she could keep her eyes on the bald top of his head, where the water was spraying off the tanned skin. The tiles were gray-white with discolored grout that she should have scrubbed. She told him he was a nut.

"Yes, Officer, yes I am," Mogie said. "But I am a young nut, and there is the difference. Well, a young-acting nut anyway. A fifty-year-old nut, acting like a twenty-year-old nut, and getting you, my sweethead, acting and looking like an eighteen-year-old nut. You're beautiful, you know. Care to soap me up?"

He was sixty, at least; Ellen knew that. Who cared. She soaped him and tried to think about the chipped tile right around where the shower curtain rod went into the wall, but that didn't help much.

So she thought about Sharon. Imagine if she came home just now? What would she think of her mother? Ellen thought about that night a month ago when she had come home and passed Sharon on the walk, tears in her eyes, drunk, going somewhere fast, to the store, she had said. In the Caddy and gone.

Mogie had been waiting for her inside.

"Ellen, my dear, my sweetheart," he had said, looking sad, and he always looked so happy it broke her heart. "Sweetheart, you have a good daughter. Don't ever forget that. She's good. She's troubled, but she's a very, very good person through it all."

"Mogie, what?"

"I only wish she wouldn't drink so much, that's all. If I had to count the number of good people's lives I've seen ruined by that bottle in my years. As they say, better a frontal lobotomy than a bottle in front of me."

"Mogie, what happened?"

"Oh, nothing happened, nothing at all is what happened. What? But in her mind, maybe it did. Maybe in the drunk haze there, there's guilt. Guilt for nothing. Can't a drunk thirty-odd-year-old spinster give her mama's man a hug? Can't she let the loneliness and sadness of her life overtake her for a weak minute, for half a minute, without going to pieces over it? Was she that wrong, Ellen? Does she have to punish herself for that?"

Ellen hadn't said anything.

"Could we talk to her about AA, you think, about the problem?" Mogie asked quietly, later. She hadn't heard Sharon come home that night. In the morning, she was fine. Nobody had ever mentioned it. Everybody was fine.

Mogie was unscrewing the shampoo and saying, "Sweetheart, your man's got some problems."

"What?"

"Here, baby, cup your hands, I'll pour. You remember Rennis, my son-in-law I told you about, with my cleaners up in Anchorage?"

Mogie had told her many times about how he had retired from the Air Force up in Alaska, right before the pipeline went through. He had taken his mustering-out pay, all the back leave money they owed him, borrowed a bit from the bank, and started a dry cleaners. The pipeline came in, there were new buildings and money and people, all with dirty clothes they didn't have time for, and before he knew it, Mogie had a chain of places right across Anchorage and up into Fairbanks.

He promised to take her up there sometime, told her how beautiful it was. They could take the ferry from Seattle, see Mount McKinley.

"Well, the boy's gone and made some moves, and now, I'm afraid, the whole big schmear is in trouble."

When Mogie's daughter married, Mogie had given his holdings over to them and left for the East Coast, where he had grown up. His son-in-law was apparently slowly running all that Mogie had built into the ground, although Mogie never criticized the boy for it.

"From what my little girl says, the boy fancies himself some sort of a moviemaker instead of a dry cleaner. Otto Preminger or something, I guess, the kids. He's been putting all the profits into these TV commercials they've been producing for the places. He's been writing them and directing them and doing whatever else. But get this." Mogie was reaching up to massage the shampoo into her scalp. "They're all in Italian, if you believe it or not."

"Italian?" she asked. "What, the commercials are? Are there Italian people up there?"

"No, of course not," Mogie explained. "The boy says it's a gimmick. He makes these commercials look like old Italian art films, and then in the subtitles he talks about Hattes Cleaners. But I think I know the people of Alaska well enough to say that they don't take their cleaning to a place because some Guinea movie, excuse me my French, on television tells them to. Isn't that crazy? But anyway, the kid's young, he's having fun with his creativity juices, apparently, but these things are not cheap, from what my little girl tells me, and that's where the profits have been all mostly going for a year or two now. Can you believe it?"

"Oh, Mogie, that's just awful. Watch my eyes, honey."

"This is baby, it don't burn, sweetheart. So anyway, he's also extending at the same time, overextending, getting new pressers and things for the shops, that he don't need, and those things, let me tell you, are thousands and thousands of dollars, especially when you have to ship them up there from the lower forty-eight, thousands of pounds for thousands of miles, that all adds up, of course."

"Maybe you should stop him, dear. I know he's your son-in-law, and you love them both, but maybe you should head right up there and put a stop to things. After all, I'd hate to see everything you built just get frittered away like that. It just isn't fair."

"Too late for that, sweet, too late for me to take charge again. I put it all in their name, of course, when I left. Their game now."

"Mogie, you're too good to people sometimes."

"I have been told that for my entire life, adult life and before. But I don't learn. I just figure, what the heck, they're young kids, anxious to get started, they need a place to start, to get going, heck, give them the business, damn the torpedoes, full speed ahead. Right?"

"Well, can they pull out of it, on their own, do you think?"

"Sweetheart, I just don't know. Hunting season. It's hunting season up there in the Great Land now, you see? And hunting season, you'd have to see it to believe it—the place just literally closes down. Same thing in trout season. Maybe it's trout season now, yes. It's a very metropolitan area now, believe me, not at all like when I started out twenty years ago, but some things die hard. Come hunting-fishing season, it's little old Alaska again, and everybody closes up and packs up the camper and goes. Which of course means that nobody, nobody, nobody gets what done? Can you tell me?"

"What?"

"During hunting season in Alaska, nobody gets what done? Nobody takes their what to get what?"

"What?"

"Nobody takes their clothes out to be ...?"

"Dry-cleaned?"

"Exactly." Mogie dropped a soap bar. He bent over to pick it up, and she looked away. Saw a stain on the tile. "Nobody goes to the cleaners. Which means, if I may play upon my words here, my daughter and her husband are being taken to the cleaners, so to speak. Because, while everybody else in the state goes hunting for deer and bear and caribou, there's one group who stays right at home and hunts debtors. And that, my dear, is the same group who stays home and hunts debtors in every state in the Union and every province of Canada and beyond—the bankers. The bankers. And that is who is hunting my little girl right now, I'm afraid. Bankers with papers. And they've got my little girl right in the cross hairs of their sights. So to speak."

"You mean, they'll lose the place? All of them? Couldn't they cut back, sell a few shops, pay off for the others?"

"Oh, my sweet babe, you don't know business, do you? I only wish it was all that simple. But with them, it's all or nothing at all. Let's just take down the sign I hand-painted twenty years ago and rechristen the place the First National Bank of Alaska Dry Cleaners, Inc."

"Isn't there something we can do?"

Mogie stared at her through the mist, drips on his nose. He said, "Baby, I've loved you before, many, many times. All the time, in many, many different situations, but I think I loved you the most when you said the word 'we' just now. I thank you deeply for that. But this problem is not a 'we' problem, my sweet dear, it's a 'me' problem, and I refuse to implicate you in it. Don't you worry that beautiful little freshly shampooed head about it. Things have a way of working themselves out. For now, we'd better just rinse and get out. I think we're beginning to lose the hot."

H raska was talking about the foot someone had found in a Dumpster, telling them about how Sheeney had been pushing Joe and him to get on it, clear the damned thing.

Hraska told them, "I mean, what can you do here—round up the usual suspects? 'Hey, anybody with a foot missing, please report to Crime Stoppers, call this number, no questions asked. Hey, you, buddy—yeah, you—come over here. You got feet? Oh, yeah? Well, let's see them, then. You got two of them or just one?'"

The four of them were in an end booth. Joe had got them all there together, funny mix.

"See what I mean?" Hraska asked them all. "So I told Sheeney, I said, 'You know, boss, it's not like a head or something. It's just a foot. Now, a head—I mean, yes, a head would be quite different, I'm sure, Lieutenant. But this, of course, is not that.'"

Hraska was just doing what he did. His mouth moving, moving, moving, while his eyes did the work, the real action, checking out stuff—the place, the mood, the people; mostly the people.

The place was easy—Libby's Diner. Twelve revolving stools at the counter, six booths, lots of chrome around, lots of glass, neon, a linoleum room in the back, added on, for parties and some low-level gambling. SOS—same old shit.

But the mood was harder to read: confused, confusing. And the people, the four of them there, that Joe had brought together, they were a fascinating mix indeed.

Hraska's eyes kept checking them out, quick, as his mouth kept moving.

First, directly across the cracked and brown-stained Formica from him—Slabb the Drab, she who wore glasses on a string back when glasses on a string wasn't cool. She was looking, as always, like Sister Mary Rosalie after they announced over the convent PA that God had just died. A slow and painful death, agonizing. Apparently left everything He owned to a bleached-blond showgirl He had met in Vegas. That's how Slabb looked. Like always.

Slabb hated Winky Hraska, which was par for the course, and she loved Joe LaLuna, also par, and she was squirming around here in the booth now, incredibly uncomfortable and just plain depressing to look at. Par. No reading on her to Audrey, Audrey to her, yet.

Sitting next to the Drab One, Joe, his partner—my man, Joe the wop—changing every day now, sitting here mooning at Audrey McKenna like he was back in the smoking area, thirty years ago, leaning on a Schwinn, puffing, eyes glazed over because Audrey McKenna was strutting by, pilly little sweater on, books clamped to tits, heading off to fifth and English. Joe baby, get a hold. Take stock, for Christ sake. Please, son.

Since those Hoover days, the Joe he knew didn't lose his hold. Hraska had seen Joe go through a lot, stuff that took years—losing his kids—also stuff that took just a second, stuff they didn't talk about, and Joe always held the center, every single wonking time. What's happening now? Suddenly, a high school babe and anarchy? Joe babe, the good husband, the man who had access to the widening legs of beautiful women everywhere and never took advantage. So what's happening now?

And finally, right next to Hraska there in the booth, the hardest one of all to figure, Audrey herself, Audrey Wright—Wright's dead—née McKenna, drinking her coffee, smoking, there beside him, grazing elbows. Hard to figure, because he couldn't check her out like he could Joe and Slabb, across from him, hard to figure because Audrey's always been hard to figure, impossible even on a good day.

Hraska's mouth kept moving for them, his eyes kept checking for stuff. Joe, Slabb, Audrey. What a wonking mix.

"It is in my heritage to perform, I believe," Hraska was telling them. "In my blood. My grandfather was what we'd today call a stand-up comic, back in Poland, in the thirties. But of course, come 1938, and the Blitzkrieg, well, the act's comic appeal naturally suffered some. Hard years for a funny man, '38, '39, right through the war and '46, '47, '48. What's to laugh at, there and then? What's to joke about? The crowd, they didn't want to hear it anymore. So he gave all of that life up, came over here to America, late 1940s, I think, and spent the rest of his years working menial, mending bowling shoes in various alleys around the area, never complaining, never begrudging, never talking about his previous life as an entertainer, just sewing and pounding those red-and-white bowling shoes back together, people are tough on shoes when they belong to somebody else, the old guy making ends meet, feeding his family, busy, busy, all the time, working all hours to get the job done."

Finally, Joe said something, said, "I'm surprised he found the time to invent Maypo."

Hraska told him, "That wasn't him, Joe. You know damn well that was my *father* invented Maypo. Maybe the ladies didn't know that. Who I'm talking about here, ladies, is my maternal grandfather, a comic turned hard times."

"No relation to Maypo," Joe explained to them.

"Only by marriage," Wink told them, winked. "A lot of people don't believe me on that, don't believe *anyone* invented Maypo, because it seems so much a part of the natural universe. But this is not so."

Hraska's eyes caught Slabb the Drab, Ol' Sunshine, looking across at Audrey. He twisted a bit to see Audrey's reaction. Something more than the usual forced, common contempt for a chatty cop going on here? Something more than the bewilderment of it all? Something else? Who the hell knows?

Joe, being even more quiet than usual all day, not answering even more than he usually didn't answer. Joe had been the one brought them all together here, so what the hell was it going on?

All of a sudden, Joe said he wanted to thank everybody for com-

ing, kicking things off like a good party host, classy, like an MC working a lounge act.

Slabb said, "Joe, this isn't the right venue."

Hraska wondered when it was people started saying "venue."

The waitress refilled the coffees, dropped off a Danish for Hraska. Hraska mentioned to her that she should lance that fever blister
or else get it done professionally. So she told him his nose looked like
a moonscape. So he told her that was his one flaw, which made his
perfect beauty even more attractive to others. He told her also, don't
expect a big tip.

She left, and Hraska turned to the other three and asked, "Did
you see that thing? That could be cancerous, couldn't it? Bad thing to
be exhibiting here on the job, might even violate OSHA directives, I
don't know."

Slabb said, "Joe?"

Joe said, "OK. I wanted Audrey to be here. I know it's irregular, I
apologize, but nothing here is regular anymore. Audrey and I, you
know, are, you know, we know each other. I wanted her to hear what
you have to say."

Audrey finally getting a little jumpy. Shifting in the corner of the
curved seat, asking Joe what was going on, then looking over at Slabb.
Hraska decided to shut up awhile, let it play.

Joe said, "Audrey, Sharon here, Dr. Slabb, has been kind enough
to redo the autopsy on your husband."

Joe had been acting off kilter, not exactly edgy, just like he was
expecting something, waiting, like for a repair guy to get there for
your water heater. Watch the clock, smoke, walk around, don't say
much.

"What? What for?" Audrey asked him.

"I asked her to."

"What for?"

"Oh, a lot of little things. It was messy. The coke. The amounts.
Your implication in it. I wanted to smooth things for you, everybody."

Audrey looked over at Slabb and asked, "What did you find out,
Doctor? The same findings again?"

Slabb looked down. "Not entirely," she said.

"Some things were … inconclusive the first time, on the preliminary report. By my findings. I called Joe up and told him I'd like to tell him what changes we'd come upon this time. Irregularities. I haven't even finished writing the postmortem report up yet. This is so irregular." She looked up at Audrey. "I don't think you should be here. Just for your own sake. And procedures. And ethics."

Joe said, "Look, we're all here now, right or wrong. Come on, Sharon."

"Well, we redid the toxicology, remained basically the same, most areas," she told them. "Alcohol to blood three ninety mg's to a hundred ml's, two and one-half micrograms of cocaine complex per ml of blood."

Hraska looked around the diner. He asked himself if there was anything more depressing in the world than an ugly broad talking about a dead guy and what the guy had in his system.

A half hour later, he wasn't so sure.

Tito, who worked behind the counter at Libby's, had come over and told them there was a call for them. Hraska took it, since Joe was so enthralled by the stuff Slabb was telling them.

It was Sheeney on the line, telling them to get over to a house on Oak Bluff; an Eagle Scout had slit his father's throat while the guy was asleep. Kid used a camping knife. They got over there, apparently the father had been a gambler, had been stealing the kid's old comic books to sell for vig cash. Some of those old ones, cherry *Shazams*, *Batmans*, ones like that, they were worth a grand or more, so the kid slit him for lifting them.

Hraska himself had hung on to some *Scrooge McDucks* in his day, but his mother had thrown them all out, naturally. Might as well throw out the old IBM stock certificates while you're at it, Ma; clean house, why don't you?

They had asked Slabb to drop Audrey off as they left the diner. When they finished with the bloody Boy Scout and were heading back in, Joe was telling Hraska how much he hated needles, his whole life, even as a kid.

"Yeah, and in the eye, huh?" he told Joe. "I mean, I don't mind taking a needle in the arm, or on the ass, somewhere like that. Remember, we were kids, the big thing was, get bit by a dog, you hadda get rabies shots, in the stomach, remember? They'd say, a painful series, right in the stomach. And hell, first day of basic, I must've took ten of them wonking injections, pop, pop, pop, in the arm there. You too, I'm sure. Of course, at Dix, they used those guns, remember them, the lasers? Except first guy through always moved his arm a little bit, and rip, here he comes out with blood all down his arm. I think the first guy through, they pick someone they know he's gonna jump, or else they give him a little nudge, don't you think? So that everybody else in the squad can see him bleeding and say, 'Uh-oh, here comes me next,' don't you think? But anyway, in the eye like that, huh? How'd the Slabb ever miss it first time through, though, you think?"

"Hey, it's a hard thing. Give her credit. She used the glass, the magnifier, but who would have thought. And they usually don't examine the back of the eye. Till she saw some lesions, she said, tracked the hemorrhagic track. Whoa. Even reopened the skull, checked it out, back of the eye. Give the gal credit, Wink, she did the job. A needle in the eye. God, I hate all needles. I never even give blood because."

"Yeah, well, but speaking of eyes, the Slabb missed it first time, I think, because she was cockeyed drunk. Pie-eyed."

"Nah, give her credit, Wink. Our man uses a surgical needle on Wright, the holes heal in a couple hours, they're gone. Plus into the middle of the eyeball? Who's gonna see? Even a top FP like Slabb, you're not gonna find that."

"The guy's dead, they don't heal, my friend. Only a living corpse heals puncture wounds. And it was our *man*, you said there, huh, Joe, not our girl?"

"Come on, hey. I prefer to think."

"Yeah, well, we can figure out now what the wonking bruises on his ear were from. Hell, someone would have to hold my head down with their wonking legs too if they wanted to stick a wonking needle in *my* eye. Hell, they'd have to use a wonking vise hold my head still. No way about it."

"That says man too, of course. Wright was a fairly big mother, solid."

"Yeah, but smoked on coke, steamed on booze. Anybody could've. Course, there's the other way too, isn't there? Joey, let's say it, the sexual angle. There ain't no man alive wouldn't mind Audrey wrapping her thighs around his head for a little while. Even a husband, for Christ sake. He's lickin' the chicken, having a good time before he lets her go out on the town with her beau, he opens his eyes, cheats a little to see how things are going, get an extra thrill by looking, opens his eyes, bang! She's waiting there on top of him with the hypo. Stick!"

"Come on, Slabb said looks like the guy died in the downstairs hallway. Was dragged up to bed."

"Oh, I forgot, this was Arthur and Kathryn Murray here: they only did in their own bed. Missionary style. Come on, Joey, I know you loved this girl in high school. Hell, everybody did. Hell, I did. She's a big girl now, though. She's come a long way, baby, doesn't have a long way to go, to get to the far end. The girl was using a fucking automated milking machine on the guy, don't forget, for Christ sake. So what, she couldn't know that he'd like to muff dive, let him go there while she's kneeling on top, squirting a little bit of the insulin out the hypo, getting ready for the injection? Stick it in me, baby. Now. Please. Pow. It's in. He's dead. She's on the town. She's hanging on to her faggy beau's arm, asking him, 'What tunes you think Chuck Berry'll do tonight?' Hubby's back home dead, holding on to one eye like a hot stick just went in, doing a Basil St. John imitation. 'Oh, sweetie,' Audrey's out telling the fag, 'don't you hope it's "Johnny B. Goode"? I love that one.'"

"Winky, don't hold back. You got some suspicions about the lady, I'd like to hear them."

"Yeah."

Back at the desk, Joe made a call.

Hraska heard him say, "Sharon? Joe.... You got her home OK?...Did she seem OK?... Did she seem she was taking it OK?... Good.... Thanks.... Thank you.... Yeah.... Sharon, tell me about the insulin again.... Yeah.... Yeah.... OK, I see.... Yeah.... Uh-huh.... How much?... Yeah, OK. Thanks, Sharon. Oh, hey, Sharon? Really, thanks, I mean it. For it all, right? You can rest assured, you know what I mean?... Good. That's good.... Yeah, so long."

Hraska asked him, "Audrey OK?"

Joe said, "Yeah, I think so. Slabb thinks so."

"What'd you want to hear, you asked her?"

Joe said, "About the insulin again. Did you know that?"

"No, I'd heard something once. What, maybe a guy out in California? And von Bülow—didn't they try nabbing old Claus on that? For Sunny-girl? I don't know. I guess the only thing I really know about insulin is diabetes."

"Yeah, sugar diabetes, the old greenhorns called it. As if there's different kinds. The stuff they give diabetics, it's made from a cow or a pig's pancreas, or sometimes even a grow-your-own that's human. Gets in the blood, it's all the same. But Slabb's a pro, I tell you. She notices a low sugar content in the spinal fluid. Gets it analyzed, it's a ten-milligram count. Normal's eighty to a hundred, somewhere in there. So she does a radioimmune test, assay test, something like that—lady knows her shit."

"I used to like essay tests," Hraska said. "Could bullshit my way."

"Assay. Listen, this test, it has something to do with putting pig insulin into a rabbit, the rabbit develops antibodies, they're tagged with radioactive isotopes or something like that."

"Yeah, I remember Slabb telling us that. So the rabbit died, so Wright was pregnant when he was offed, right?"

"Listen, then you pump this stuff into the decedent—that's the 'stiff' to you—and the stuff reacts, and you can count how much insulin is in the system, in the blood and the tissue. Wright had eight hundred units."

"And you don't home-grow that much, am I right?"

"Yeah, you don't grow near that amount."

"And Wright, he wasn't diabetic."

"Nope."

"So then," Hraska said, "it came in through the eyeball."

"Yeah, in through the eyeball."

"When they were balling."

"No. Maybe."

"So then, who we looking for, Joe?"

"I don't know. Someone works in a hospital maybe? A diabetic? Someone knows his clinical and anatomic pathology, huh?"

"Oh, well, clinical and tonic pathology expert. Could be anybody, then. What's that faggy boyfriend you told me about do—he's not a doctor, huh?"

"No, nothing like that. I wish he was."

"Well, Joe, my friend, I'm going home, but it has been a good day, has it not?"

"Yeah, I guess so. We got a lot."

"We got just one thing makes me happy, pal, just one solid fact to sleep upon tonight."

"What's that?"

"That fucker was murdered."

LaLuna's morning had been a complete blow-off, no work on Audie's case at all.

He had to bend his duty day around two court times, ten o'clock for a prelim on a DWI, with death, eleven-thirty for a bail hearing on a guy who had used an industrial meat-pounder on the woman he had been living with for seventeen years, on and off.

Plus they were trying to get a search warrant for a public landfill where they thought a hood had dumped his dentist's body. Invited the doc somewhere, discussed an accounts-due problem, had him taken out with the trash.

So LaLuna had done some time in the Room, with a bunch of other shirtsleeved detectives on typewriters and computers, had fit in some paperwork—first some new reports, 507's, and follow-ups on the Boy Scout who killed his father on the comic books, then some older stuff, odds and ends, fifty-five ways to get yourself killed.

LaLuna worked fast, efficiently, hands moving to different stacks of paper, keeping his mind on only those facts that were at the end of his hands and fingers, letting Winky bullshit away for background music.

After the court prelim, he had driven over to get a prescription for Madeline's ears, $129.95, would last about a week, then came back to the Room, his desk, the noise and confusion.

Tiny Tim Mallarny, a homicide cop with three weeks to go for twenty and out, had died the month before, and the squad had officially decided that LaLuna would take over what had been Tiny Tim's most important duty assignment—running the annual World Series Pool. So somebody had dumped Tiny's manila folder marked "W. Serious. Pool" on LaLuna's desk when he was gone.

LaLuna looked through, tried to sort it out. It was a good pool, evolved slowly over the past ten years or so. Twenty guys in the squad, each put in ten bucks. You got one secret pick, could take anybody from either team. Then there was a draft round. You drew your draft spot out of a hat. Every player on the rosters' name on the blackboard, players chosen, their names erased by Winky, who ran the draft portion of the pool, then a third player, drafted in reverse order.

So everybody got at least one star, maybe two. You got four points for a dinger, three for a triple, so on, one for a ribbie, run scored, stolen base. Dailies and overalls.

"How about a walk?" somebody would always ask.

"Nope. Not in the box score."

"How about a sacrifice?"

"Not in the box score, is it?"

"So? We could keep track, we watch the game?"

"Yeah? Who you gonna trust?"

That was the problem—who you gonna trust?

Pitchers were trouble too. Every year they changed the scoring on them. What, maybe a point an inning pitched? Half a point? Half a point an inning pitched, minus one for every earned run?

"Nah, who's gonna take a pitcher, then?"

So who you gonna trust?

They could work it out. It wasn't fall yet. The pool itself had good bones to it. Sheeney called on the interoffice, asked LaLuna about the foot again.

"Lieutenant, we called ER's, we're on the wire, we're on the chalkboard, we're at guard mount, nothing yet."

"Clear it, Joe, all right?"

"We're trying, Lieu, we are."

"Big Bob wants it cleared, Joe."

"Lieutenant, I got a question. Tiny Tim's World Series Pool, I got it now. You remember if an error, you lose a point? I can't find it here in the paperwork."

"I think so. I'll get back. Remember the foot, huh, Joe? And clear the Boy Scout quick. Big Bob wants that to Philbrick a little bit faster than you could do it, so OK?"

"OK, Lieutenant. I'm pretty sure an error's minus one."

"I think so too, Joe. You got the pitchers straight this year?"

"We'll have to meet, a rules committee or something."

"Joe, how come Slabb redid the 'topsy on that cocaine guy in bed?"

"I sort of asked her to. Loose ends."

"Joe, what the hell?"

"Call here on another line, Lieutenant, you want to hold?"

"Nah, get lost."

"OK. Try to remember about the errors, huh?"

"Yeah, OK. I'll get back. Joe, what about stolen bases?"

"Not in the box score, Lieutenant."

"Yeah, not in the box score, not in the box score, that's what we always say. I had wonking Rickey Henderson that year he stole everything wasn't tied down. Wait a minute. They are too. Stolen bases are in the box score. I remember they are, definitely."

"Gotta go, Lieutenant."

"I think I must've got jewed that year—you know that?—now I think about it."

The call on the other line was a reporter doing a story on a landscaper who had raped and then killed a society lass; the kill had happened about seven years ago. The papers liked it, a Lady Chatterley thing—he had been mowing her lawn and wonking her for a good while before—and now he was up for parole. LaLuna had cleared the case, and so he gave the reporter a couple of innocuous quotes before heading to court again for the bail hearing.

He was back to the Room before twelve, hauling Big Macs, and he and Winky ate. Winky asked him if McD's carried onion rings. They couldn't remember. Years ago, Wink had known a starving actor who had got a break doing a McD's onion ring commercial, then they decided not to go onion rings. Ads never ran. Poor shit.

"Now, though, I think they got them," Wink said.

"You know what I did for an hour last night?" LaLuna said, trying to twist open a catsup pack. "I looked at the old *Aristocrat* again, the year we got out. It's getting like a mania for me. You still got yours?"

"Use your teeth. The *Aristo*crap, right? Sure I got mine."

"That's right, the *Aristo*crap. I'd forgotten that. You ever look at yours?"

"Sure I do, Joe, everybody does. Whose picture you look at the most? Let me guess. Mr. Metzger in his lab coat, so fat they used him for movies, they couldn't find a screen? Watermelon Peavey and her buckteeth? Me in my wrestling digs? Come on, who? Page forty-eight we talking?"

"Yeah, yeah, you got me, Wink. You're right. Just sitting there, staring at her, making sure Madeline doesn't come in. Long time. Page forty-eight. Looking good."

"Hey, still does, nobody's denying that. So who's she next to? That guy Smokey, we decided?"

"I don't know. I don't remember. She was Pep Club, French Club, I think, some other stuff. She wasn't that involved, I'd forgotten that."

"Well, she's involved now, Mojo, that's for sure. Pep Band, French Club, Medium Security Holding Tank, Dykes' Playmate of the Month, et cetera."

"Come on, Wink, I can't hear that stuff. It drives me crazy. She tells me she loves her husband. Then there's this jerk Zumrad. Drives me crazy."

"Joe, you already are crazy. You know what you're doing here, *gumbah?* Having her there when Slabb told us about the new 'topsy? You're nuts."

"Yeah, I know I am. I just can't help it. Wink, I tell you, I'm gonna keep this one in the air."

"How long for?"

"For forever, if it takes."

They both had been around Homicide long enough to know how things worked. After a couple of days, each thing went one of two ways. Cases either sank to the bottom from their own lack of weight, or they got bound over to the DA. Sometimes the DA or one of his investigators had an angle to work, so things went different, but mostly it was either let them sink or bind them over, that was it. Clear it, let the DA plea-bargain it on down to something the quiff never did to begin with, not as bad as the thing he really *did* do.

They also knew there were always enough people you could pressure, then their friends and enemies to pressure, then their known accomplices, then their KAs' friends and enemies, then all the paper, so you could keep a case in the air as long as it took. If the brass'd let you. Brass, though, they just wanted it cleared, that's all.

"Look, Joe, congratulations in making this thing a murder. That was good work, I mean it. But it don't work out, let's decide now we move on, all right?" Wink asked him.

"No, not this one. This one, I feel like I'll just keep coming and coming."

"Jesus, Joe."

"Him out there, he knows it, he finds it out. This one, I just keep coming on it."

"Him, you said, not her, huh?"

"Him, her, I just keep coming, Wink. Hey, you know what your old friend Sherlock Holmes said, right? Said, 'The game is afoot.'"

"Hey, paisan, that foot is no game. Sheeney's getting pissed on it, wants it cleared quick."

"Sure, sure we do, but not today. This afternoon, we work on this thing here. We free?"

"Nothing comes up, we are. As free as we can be."

So they worked on the case that afternoon. First they took turns reading Sharon's new autopsy report. Toxology, probables, sexual activity, external, internal, cardiovascular, liver and biliary, hemis and lymphatic, endocrine, urinary, digestive, the "manner, cause, and circumstance of decedent's death"—all of it said just one thing now: a hypodermic needle full of insulin drilled into the left eye.

Then lists of things to do. Check the neighbors closer, canvass who's in, who's out that night, phone-call records, in and out, any other ways to go. Snitches? Probably not, not up there on Money Hill. Nice, easy neighborhood to canvass, but you'd get shit for snitches.

Then, on the phone, on the computer. MO for such a crime—nothing there. R and I, DMV, on Audie again, on the jerk—Chester

Zumrad. Nothing. Hospitals, clinics, drugstores, too many of them. Too much insulin to organize. AFIP, FBI in Washington—what are we looking for anyway? Who you gonna trust?

Call forensics, call criminalistics, yeah, we had Audrey's prints all over her own house, big deal, Wright's prints all over there too, big surprise, nobody else's that anyone knew. Cleaners, visitors, workers, what? Who knows?

LaLuna didn't think she could have done it. Who you gonna trust? And he couldn't get it out of his head—Chester killed him. More than just a dumb hunch maybe, couldn't it be right? Chester probably killed him, couldn't it be? Don't you think? Killed for her? Killed to get her? Killed to kill?

"Let's split up," LaLuna told Winky. "I'll take the boyfriend, you go see this business partner maybe. Marmasette, Felix."

"Marmasette?" Winky looked up to ask. "Isn't that like one of those animals you see running across the Africa plains on 'National Geographic,' Channel thirteen? Nice name."

LaLuna found Chester Zumrad at home, half packing for a trip, half looking at a book of pictures of poor people with no teeth in France.

LaLuna looked over at the black-and-white pictures, twisted his head to see them on the table there, facing Chester. Ponytail, earring, smug-ass look to the guy. LaLuna told Chester, "Those are sad, kids look hungry, huh? Starving and everything? What's that, during the war?"

"Now, mostly. Brilliant shots, aren't they? They're the work of a genius with a camera, Luis Julius D'Vio. A society's portraits."

"Yeah, well," LaLuna said, "good luck to him. Maybe he'll save some kids with them."

Chester looked at him, told him he didn't understand. "The man has one responsibility," Chester told him, "one purpose and one duty. To take good photographs. Do you understand?"

"Yeah," LaLuna told him. "I'm just saying, be nice if he got some kids fed too, right? People see these, guilt comes into play, they chip in a couple bucks."

"Jacob Riis, Officer, ever hear that name?"

"I heard of his beach, yeah."

"His beach, huh? Riis was a photographer, New York, immigrant, turn of the century, decided to chronicle the plight of the urban poor. The first time much of America was ever made to stare into the face of hunger, in the face. His work began a cycle of social reform we still are caught up with today."

"Yeah, well, good for him, that's what I'm saying."

"No, officer, bad for him. Now they call him a journalist. The man was either an artist—a photographer, that is—or a journalist, or a social reformer. I like to think he knew, thought of himself, as the first, the artist. If so, then it's either incorrect or inappropriate or demeaning for him to enter the social process, do you see? I like to believe that was not his purpose and he knew it, despite the popular myths about the man."

"OK now, could I ask you some questions?"

"Oh, I see, you're of the Sam Kinison school of philosophy, then."

"Who now?"

"Come on, you know him, he was on television, for Christ's sake, Officer. Sam Kinison, the screaming comedian."

"I don't know him. Why we talking?"

"Oh, his first splashy routine. Screaming Sam used to talk about those video documentaries of the starving children in Biafra, and he'd scream"—here Chester's voice got loud and raspy, phony-funny-Jew-ish— "'Why don't the cameraman give 'em a sandwich!' You've heard him."

"No," LaLuna said, "but now that you bring it up, why not put down the camera, break out lunch?"

"It's been fun playing this game with you, Officer."

"Yeah, I agree. About these questions, I don't want to waste your time here."

"You already have, I'm afraid. Should Jane Goodall have fed the gorillas, then?"

"Come on, what?"

"Should wildlife photographers bring peanuts and milk shakes to give to their quarry?"

"Look, all I began this with, Chester, maybe somebody should be looking after these French kids with the sunken cheeks, that's all. If it's not 1946 now."

Chester pointed at a picture from his book. There wasn't even a kid in it. He held his finger on it and said, "Specimens. Subjects."

LaLuna said, "No, maybe people. Buildings. Eyeballs."

"What? What the hell?"

When LaLuna told him about Wright's left eyeball, Chester said, "That's interesting," meaning that it wasn't. Good job of not reacting to it. Maybe planned.

LaLuna told himself to be careful, that he couldn't be god-damned sure. No, he was right that first time, when he had first seen this *spaccone* in the park with Audrey. This guy was a damned murderer, the killer of Audrey's husband. LaLuna knew that for sure. Told himself to watch his step but couldn't help being sure about it. This guy.

"Look, Chester," LaLuna told him, unhooking his thumbs from his pockets, the coffee table holding the picture book between them, "there's a lot of implications here."

"Chet, please, Officer, Sergeant, whatever."

"Your license, it says Chester, OK? That's official, of course."

"Get me for any outstanding traffic tickets? Warrants? Anything?"

"Look, Chet, Mr. Zumrad, Chester, I'm just trying to impress you with the fact that this is a homicide investigation, as of right now. We'd like your cooperation, obviously."

"Sergeant, you've obviously got it. What can I do?"

"For now, could you submit to being fingerprinted? It's maybe a little degrading for you, I realize, but very painless. It'd help."

"All right, of course. Could be an experience. How do I do that?"

"Just come down when you get a chance. Tell them at the desk what for. Takes five minutes, no ink on your clothes or anything, the people are very good."

"I'm sure. But hey, where do you stand on this case? Has anybody been charged with anything? I'm worried about Audrey, of course, as I'm sure we all are, correct? What's happening?"

"Well, we're just investigating things. We'll turn them over to the DA and his office. They decide. No, nobody's been charged with anything, not by a long shot."

"If Milton was injected, do you have the needle?"

"We'd love to, but no."

"Sergeant, mind if I ask you a question from TV cop shows? Am I a suspect?"

"I'll give you the TV show answer to that."

"I know," Chester said. "Everybody is, right?"

"That's right," LaLuna told him.

"The Pink Panther," Chester said to himself. Then, "Look, Joe— Audrey told me your name is Joe? High school, right? Uh-huh. Joe, it's already been admitted I'm having an affair with Audrey. It's been ongoing. My fingerprints will be all over that house, things like that."

"You went there?"

"On occasion, sure I did, yes. Joe, I've already planned a very important business trip for later today. There's no problem with that, I suppose?"

"Nope, none that I know."

"No 'Don't leave town'?"

The cop didn't smile. "No, nothing like that." Then he asked, "How well did you know the victim?"

"As Audrey's husband I knew him. Not well. He wasn't just a victim in that part of it. I knew him."

"And he knew? You?"

"He knew me as Audrey's lover. Yes."

"Sounds very nice."

"Oh, come on, Joe, you see worse on your job every day, right? You know that you do."

"Yeah. Yeah, I do."

"Anything else?" Chester's eyes went back to the French picture book. LaLuna rubbed his nose. Geez, Chet, I hope I'm not keeping you from anything.

LaLuna said, "Audie's your alibi."

"Audie, is it?"

"Audrey."

"Yes, that's right. Audrey's my alibi, and I'm hers, right?"

"She said you guys split up for a while after Chuck Berry. You had to meet somebody."

"What? Well. Yes, that's right. A business contact of mine."

"Would you give me his name? I can contact him?"

"I'd rather not."

"Why not?"

"Business."

"So you won't give me his name, then?"

"If I have to, I will. *When* I have to, I will. Now, no, I won't."

"Why not?"

"Business."

"Chester, let me ask, do you love Audrey Wright?"

"Yes, do you?"

"Chester, did you kill Milton Wright?"

"No, did you?"

Chester's knees knocked over the coffee table, sent the picture book flying, as LaLuna lifted him quick off the couch, holding him in air, just using his hands and elbows. Chester twisted, said Jesus a couple of times, struggled a bit, then just hung there.

LaLuna tried to tell him, "Listen, you shit punk, this is goddamned serious," but Zumrad had started laughing by then, shaking his head, his ponytail flipping in the breeze, and the shit punk was saying, "Easy, Joe, easy, big boy—this won't look good on your efficiency report. Come on now, put me down. Down, big boy."

LaLuna put him down and said he was sorry.

"I was kidding," Chester said, grinning. "There's a lot easier ways of rekindling your old high school dates than killing their husbands, right? Jesus. I was kidding you, Joe."

LaLuna apologized again and left.

He could tell he wasn't covering very well when he and Winky compared interviews later, back in the Room. Wink was sharp, saw things, but he didn't ask LaLuna about what all had happened.

"How'd yours go?" LaLuna asked him.

"Kind of crazy," Wink said. "I knock on this really nice house, this white Tudory place, up on French Hill, and this voice up above me yells down, he answers. The front door, where I'm knocking, gold knocker shaped like a lovely tit, has two white pillars around it, the place is so nice, and there's a little half-circle balcony over it, somebody yelling down from there. I tell him I'm Sergeant Hraska from Homicide, tells me look out, here comes a mattress, and sure enough, this huge gray mattress, must have been queen-size at least, comes sailing off the balcony, almost hits me, because I had stuck my head out from under the balcony to talk to this guy. The mattress hits like a brick wall—those things are heavy, it could have killed me—and I jump back, tell the guy to watch it, ask if I can come in, ask him some questions, you know. Well, he's a persistent bastard, he tells me he's got to get these mattresses out, the trash pickups coming any minute. So anyway, the whole time I'm interviewing the guy, he's throwing mattresses out the window. Must of been seven, eight of them. After the first couple, I go up there, help him hit the bedrooms, help him toss the mattresses, see? I don't know why they'd get rid of all of them the same time. No cum spots on them or anything I could see. They're just goddamn rich, I suppose. I should've asked him I could keep some. Get rid of my lumps."

LaLuna asked, "Anybody else around?"

Wink said, "Didn't see nobody. He lives with his wife and daughters, three or four, I think. Lots of mattresses. Lots. Guy's hair is dyed blond, unbelievable. Looks like a wonked-up, five-hundred-pound, five-hundred-year-old beach boy, for Christ sake."

LaLuna asked, "You get anything?"

Wink said, "Well, the guy is apparently a fairly sneaky guy. Him and Wright's been partners"—Wink flipped open his little spiral notepad—"eleven years. Marmasette never really cared for the guy, though, from what I saw. I think it was Wright the businessman, this guy Felix the scientist, who thinks he can do the business end too. You know, he keeps telling me they were partners, equals, right? But there's no such thing in business, or anywheres, for that matter. There's never been two bosses equal. There's a boss and, at best, there's an underboss. Least with our friends in the Families, they recognize that fact of human nature and they honor it. With them you call one guy boss, you call the guy under him the underboss. If the underboss wants to get to be boss, he's gotta get somebody to yank an untraceable garrote around his neck while the poor guy is eating his *mustaciolli* in some crummy little clam bar in Brooklyn, am I right? Then the underboss becomes the boss. Not before."

LaLuna asked, "You think there's a chance it happened like that here?"

Wink said, "Could be, I suppose. Stranger things have happened. Guy's a scientist, after all. He didn't react, I asked him if he was diabetic. Who the hell knows? He tried this one veneer on me, that of the understanding, rational guy, concerned, authentic. But the guy's really about as authentic as a dildo, I do believe. And of course, just like everybody else, cops talk to him about murder, he was a lot shakier than he let on."

"Yeah, Chester too. What else?"

Wink said, "He obviously nibbles some coke along the line. I think from his eyes moving that he keeps it in the upstairs bedroom, probably right in the night table drawer there."

LaLuna said, "Probably in the mattresses."

"Yeah, probably. I probably helped the guy mule a couple tons of C off to the retailer level."

"You think he does anything else? Crack? Injections?"

"Who knows, you know."

"Well," LaLuna said, "we hit judicial, try to get searches on these guys, both their places."

"Yeah. No chance, of course, you ask me," Wink told him. "Guys wouldn't be stashing hypos around anyway; both a little too smart, naturally, you don't think?"

LaLuna agreed, asked again, "What else?"

"That's about it. He told me the company's working on something called the—let's see—the Radio Frequency Remote Set Fuze. What the hell is that thing? I tried to get old Felix to explain to me how in the hell a radar filaments and conductor factory, whatever the hell that is also, also gets into making flea collars, but he shrugs me off. You know, the big-shot scientist can't explain technical stuff to the little man in the street. Felix also told me he was a vegetarian the last year, two years. Which is strange in itself for a fat guy, huh? How many fat veggies you gonna see? This guy on the outside looks like he'd eat anything with a vowel in the name. So maybe he's lying, I don't know. Maybe he's a veggie around people, eats steers on the hoof alone, I couldn't tell you. But anyway, he says he doesn't eat anything that had eyeballs. I told him, that's funny, that's all I ever eat is eyeballs."

"Oh, how he must have laughed at that."

"Yeah, well, you do what you can. Eyeballs."

"Yeah, eyeballs. Well, look," LaLuna told him, "make the file nice on this guy. We may be using it a lot."

"Yeah, I already did. Started a nice jacket right when I got back, but I got a fax from the state of the incorporation or partnership registration papers to their business, Vor-Tech Industries—they all have a tech in the title now, don't they? By the way, Audrey gets Wright's half, gets everything of Wright's, right?"

"Yeah. I don't have the will, but that's right. I think what she gets, the money, the ownership—no control, though, I don't think. They'd both be crazy, set the partnership up that way to begin with, she don't know business, Audie."

"Anyway, I go over to make a copy of the Vor-Tech papers, for the guy's jacket. So I'm standing there, reproducing, and the copier machine it's leaking water. I swear, gallons of buckets all over the floor. You can see it from here, I think. Somebody better clean that up. It's a real mess."

"Hey, it must be from somewhere else. Copy machines, they don't hold any water."

"Yeah, well, somebody better go tell the copier machine that."

LaLuna grinned, pretended things weren't changing.

TWELVE

Mogie Hattes had been gently rousted by a quiet, polite, grease-ball Guinea cop who Mogie didn't even think was affiliated with Bunco at all.

The cop had stopped Mogie on the sidewalk there, coming out of Beachcrest Dry Cleaners. Mogie had picked up some stuff for the ladies—wool skirts, his checkered pants from Italy, his red plaid vest that Ellen said made him look like a bartender. He loved that vest.

The ladies were at work, so he had picked the cleaning up and was hauling the wire hangers and the hanging plastic bags back to the Cadillac, when this greaseball cop took his elbow and said, "Excuse me, you have a minute?"

Polite. No need for the cop to flash his ticket, this guy's haircut was his badge, and so Mogie said yes, he did, what could he do for him?

Cop said his name was LaLuna and would Mogie care for some ice cream.

Well, it turned out not to be ice cream at all but that frozen yogurt or custard shit that all the rich bitches ate so as not to get any fatter than they already were. But hell, this guy LaLuna was buying, so Mogie ordered up a lemon, the flavor on the board that he hated most, just to keep him in a bad mood while LaLuna did whatever he had planned for him.

Mogie kept reminding himself there wasn't even any cholesterol in this cold crap. With all of these diets around, the biggest selling factor about food in the country was that it had no nutritional value. The less actual food in food, calories, the better. None at all, the best.

Not an ounce of cholesterol in this crap, he kept telling himself. That kept him tuned.

Mogie got up to hang the plastic bags on the coatrack, so the stuff wouldn't get wrinkled being folded over the back of the booth. When he got back and sat down, LaLuna let him know that he knew about the radio station thing in Missouri. What did this cop care about that?

"That was a business venture gone bad, Officer," Mogie explained. "We've all had them."

"The charges were what, Interstate trade? Conspiracy to defraud? Use of the mails? I can't remember it all."

"That was a bad business venture, that's all. The charges just blew over, nothing ever happened. It's almost a formality in dealings like that. You sue me, I sue you. You charge me, I charge you. We've all had ups and downs in business. Me maybe more than most, but what can I say? We all have them. It's happened to you, I bet, LaLuna, hasn't it?"

The cop didn't answer. Quiet.

Mogie went on. "Police, from what I know about them, the smart ones always have some business ventures going on the side. You know, bars, maybe a real estate license, yogurt shops, whatever. We all need something for those retirement years. I was in the service, twenty years to retire. Just like most police departments. What's it here, twenty too? Twenty also? You know, you retire, you're still a young man. It's good to have some things going. Don't vegetate. You have something like that, I'm sure. And sometimes they just go sour, like mine did in Missouri. Do you have something like that?"

"No."

"No, you don't? A smart young guy like you? I'm surprised. Why not?"

"They go sour," LaLuna the cop told him.

Mogie smiled and said, "Hey, I'll give you an example of the vicissitudes of business. You want a story on that? I had money in a place in Minneapolis. Lunch, mostly. Well, we had location, we had financing, wholesalers, suppliers, we had the staff, we had it all. Everything worked. Business started out great, hand over fist. Then, maybe two, three months in, the lunch crowd just dies on us. They're nowhere to be found. Nothing. It's killing us. You want to know what it was killed us? Shows you how strange things can go. It turned out a local cesspool crew—you know, the guys who show up with a tank truck to pump out your backyard septic tank—well, they loved our place, came every lunch they were in the area, which was about five times a week, it seemed. Now, their truck on the side says something nice like 'Scavenger' or 'Hygiene' or something, but everybody knows, and not just by the looks either, everybody knows it's a cesspool-pumping truck. These guys took their time ordering and eating too. I mean, what's the draw for them to get them back to work, you know? So for an hour, hour and a half each day, our customers drive up, see the truck, say, 'Not today, José, looks like they're having cesspool trouble,' and they drive on to the Pizza Hut or somewhere. Well, it killed us, and the ironic thing is, we didn't realize what was happening until we were well into Chapter Nine, filing for bankruptcy. We're in the cesspool ourselves, you know? It goes to show, huh?"

The cop said yeah and started bringing up Mrs. Smith. Mrs. Smith from Poughkeepsie.

"Now that," Mogie explained, "that was an example of a relationship gone sour. A wonderful lady, Mrs. Smith, driven crazy by medication and TV game shows. Given the choice, a business deal soured or a relationship, a relationship with a lady, give me the sour business every time. What sticks worse, what *stinks* worse, right?"

Mogie licked the lemon yogurt.

"There were charges there too." The cop had gotten chocolate. There was a chocolate yogurt now, for Christ sake. What next?

"LaLuna, you know about me. Why the interest? But you always bring up the bad. Bring up my service years next time, why not? Bring up my Vietnam time. Bring up my honorable discharge. Why bring up Mrs. Smith? It was a bad relationship, that's all. Don't we all have them? Don't you?"

Cop didn't answer.

"Sure we do," Mogie told him. "LaLuna, why the interest? What have you been working on?"

"A severed foot," cop seemed to say.

"What?"

Nothing.

"Come on. What do you want? What's this about anyway? We're both of us busy men. What is it for you, LaLuna? Luna, tell me true."

"What I'd like, I'd like you to go."

"Go?" Mogie asked. "Go where? Go out of here, this place? If that's it, I'm gone. Keep my yogurt."

"Go out of here," cop told him. "Go out of town, go out of the state. Go. Make me happy."

"LaLuna, come on now. You know a lot about me, you know that I can't just do that. I'm working on business deals and personal relationships here. I can't just go, just to make a cop happy, can I?"

"Yup."

"Or what?" Mogie asked him. "Pardon me for asking, but if not, what's going to happen?"

Every cop Mogie had ever met would have paused there, skipped a beat or two. He would have shifted around, waited, looked at the ceiling, taken a lick of the chocolate, hung on to his belt buckle, act big, make the answer seem important and threatening and cold.

Instead, this LaLuna just leaned forward and told him, "I don't know. I don't know what'll happen." It was like he really meant it. The poor guy really didn't know.

"I'm usually so calm," cop was telling him. "You ask, you'll find that out. But lately, I've been getting very jumpy. Very edgy, on edge. A lot of things are going on right now with me. So I tell you the truth. You don't go, I don't know what will happen."

Meaning it, every word. Not even threatening that much, just telling him he didn't know.

"Well, I tell you, Luna," Mogie said, "I got things going on too."

"Will any of the things we've talked about upset those things?" cop asked him. "Those plans of yours? If they came to light?"

"LaLuna, come on. Let me be honest, for crying out loud. I just perfectly explained to you about those things, with no lead time on my part. Out of the blue, you accosted me on the street. And you're a cop, for crying out loud. Please imagine, when I'm ready for it, with a little practice, with some work on the loose ends, to people who aren't policemen, to people who know me and like me and want to believe me. You see what I mean? Heck, Luna, *you* had to fight yourself not to believe me, and look who you are. See? Can you imagine someone more, how should I say, anxious to believe?"

"Gullible."

"Anxious to believe. Trusting. Somebody not so—I don't know the word—so cynical. The police are cynical, you can't deny it. They really are. Been on the job too long."

"There're elements, of course," the cop was saying, "that don't like lone operators around. The whole East is like that."

"No, no, no." Mogie shook his finger and smiled. "You can't convince me, Officer, that the Five Families are concerned about little Mogie Hattes and what he's been up to. You stretching now, or what?"

"Yeah, maybe so, a little," the cop said, "but I didn't mean Families."

"I don't think I need fear La Cosa Nostra at this stage of my career. And scammers, they tend to live and let live, don't you think? If, indeed, that's what I am."

"Just go," LaLuna said. "Just go," he told him again, getting up to go.

Mogie watched him, finished the lemon, went over and bought a quart to bring home for the ladies.

Later that night, eating a bowl, he was thinking how nice it was that LaLuna had found out only the pretty good stuff about him. That's how it always seemed to work, though. That's what the wire held, just the pretty good, the not-too-bad stuff. Imagine if people were meant to find out the really bad things about each other. What a world that would make. What a mess for everybody. Whoever was in charge sure knew what he was doing, all right.

Mogie called into the kitchen, "Ellen, do you happen to know a policeman named Luna or LaLuna, something LaLuna?"

"LaLuna?" She was cleaning the bread box. "Yes. He's Sharon's friend Joe. Why?"

Well, now, Mogie figured, now it figures.

THIRTEEN

After the woman told Audrey that her husband had been murdered, the woman had given her a ride home.

Dr. Sharon Slabb asked her how she was doing, if she was all right, if she had been getting enough sleep at night. She was really asking this: what's it like to find your husband dead, and how much worse is it when you find out that someone came in, stuck a death needle into his eye? She was asking, in her own way, did you do it? Maybe have it done?

"When I have trouble sleeping at night, I get up and just get a cigarette," Audrey told her. Audrey took out a pack of Slims, there in Sharon Slabb's Cadillac.

"Do you mind?" Audrey asked her.

"No, I don't." Sharon Slabb kept her eyes on the road, didn't look over.

"Are you sure?" Audrey asked her. "It'll stink up the upholstery, I know. Nice car."

"I smoke sometimes. My mother and her boyfriend smoke a lot. So everything is already stinked up around." She gave a smile, made it look like her face was cracking.

Audrey said, "Yeah, can you imagine a product that says right on it here, 'This stuff'll kill you,' and we pick it up, and we say, 'Gee, this looks good. I'll have a bunch of these, please.' Anyway, human beings,

I suppose. Whatever gets you through the night, I suppose, is what Frank Sinatra says."

"I get up and turn on some music sometimes at night. Softly. I've got my own little stereo in my room."

"Oh, do you? You live alone, with your mother?"

"Yes, I do," Sharon Slabb said.

"And her boyfriend, you said?" Audrey asked.

"Oh, no, he doesn't live with us. He's over there a lot. It's a new thing for my mom. We haven't dated all that much."

The cigarette lighter hadn't taken the first time. It popped out again, and Audrey took it, used it. She said, "I use music too, at night, sometimes. Classical. Vivaldi. Schubert. The usual. Something like that."

Sharon Slabb said, "Judy Garland. We both like her."

"Your mom and you?"

"We both like her. Bette Midler sometimes, when she's being serious."

"Oh, I see. That's my house there," Audrey told her.

Before Audrey could thank her and get out, Sharon Slabb asked her, "Did you know Joe in high school, he said?"

"Yeah, we did. Isn't that crazy? Bad way for a reunion. When he picked me up today, was driving me over to the diner, I thought we were seventeen, he was so nervous, except it was burgers and fries and how my husband died, when we got there. That sort of rhymed, huh?"

"I didn't want to tell you any of that. To your face. I feel sorry. Joe decided on it."

"I know. It's OK."

Sharon Slabb said, "I'm very sorry for you. This is so terrible. I never have to deal with the people that my business affects. This is just so awfully terrible."

Audrey had a hard time believing that this gentle little mouse took up a scalpel for a living, cut up dead people into parts, had cut up Milton. Twice.

"Sharon—can I call you that? When do I get the body back, do you know? You're done with it, right? Milton's family wants to know. Me too, of course."

"I don't know. When we're done with it, my boss, Dr. Bobby Dekar, Robert Dekar, releases the bodies, through the police. I'll give you his number. At work. It's the same as mine. What was Joe like, anyway, back in high school?"

"Joe? I don't know. Not like now."

"Was he sad? Like he is now? He always to me looks so sad now. Now, that's really something, coming from me, the queen of the sad faces."

Audrey told her, "He was always quiet. He actually talks more now. But he was more serious than sad, I think. Back then."

Sharon said, "He lost two children, you know."

"No."

"Yes. Through accident and disease, I believe. Those sad puppy-dog eyes he has."

Audrey said, "Oh, he always had those. Always the basset hound eyes. But that's just physical, I think, some of it. Nobody's perfectly happy, don't you think?"

"I don't know. Joe's face. There is a real relationship between physiognomy and emotion. Definitely."

"People look like the life they've lived, by the time you're forty, right?"

"Yes. That's been said. So you, Audrey, must have been living a very nice life." Sharon blushed at the neck.

Audrey thanked her.

"That doesn't mean you look forty, I didn't mean. Just."

"Oh, that's all right. I know I'm forty. I'm not going to start battling that. I have enough things to battle. Well, listen, thank you for the lift."

Sharon shook her hand and held on. "I meant what I said about being sorry. About your husband. About what I found. You'll be strong. You'll live with this."

Audrey thanked her again, got out, and reminded herself to take her own car next time.

Inside her house, her mother-in-law and sister-in-law came on bitchy right away—where have you been so long?—and asked if there was any news about Milton, when can we get the body? Audrey asked if anyone had called. One. Chet Zumrad. The name came off her sister-in-law's mouth like a cream puff gone rancid. Audrey went upstairs to call back.

She convinced herself that the line was clear from downstairs, and then she told Chet about the needle. The moment she did that, she decided in person would have been better; she could have read her lover's face.

"God," he said. "Do they have any suspicions who it was?"

"I don't know," she told him. "I'm sure they think it's probably me. Men get killed by their wives, I guess. Joe just told me. Actually, the lady doctor who's the coroner told us both. A weirdo. He didn't talk about arresting me or anything. But don't you think that's what they'll be thinking—me?"

"Or me," Chet said. "Men get killed by their wives' lovers too. Audrey, what the hell is going on here anyway?"

"Can *you* tell *me,* Chet?"

"Oh, come on, Audrey. God, what the fuck."

"All right, I'm sorry. But God, Milton was murdered, Chet. You're asking me what the hell is going on? They've proved that somebody walked into my house while I was out with you and injected my husband. Oh, my God, it sounds stupid to say. It sounds just awful. Chet, Chet, Chet, please ..."

"It's all right, baby, please. Come on. It's all right."

"Chet, this coroner, she looks so weird. Please, can we meet? I can't even be at home when I'm home now, with Milton's family here. Oh, God, they're horrible, and they don't even know the truth of it yet. Why the hell should I be the one to have to tell them? They'll love it, Chet, just love it. It will validate everything they want validated. Can we meet? Can we meet, please?"

"Of course we can, baby, but not now, I'm afraid. The timing just stinks, is just awful, but I have to go away. Business."

"When?"

"Tomorrow. Late flight. Tomorrow night."

"Chet, you never go away. What's going on? Your business, it's here, Chet. You never go away."

"Audrey, sure I do. Try to stop crying. The bitches in your house are going to hear you, then you'll feel worse. Just breathe, baby, just breathe deep. Come on."

"Chet, where are you going? Why are you going?"

"To Boston, honey. Then Chicago. And San Francisco, I think, probably. You knew this was happening, would happen, babe. I'm getting bigger than to be working out of the trunk of my car. I've been doing it like that seven years now. It's time I'm picking up a national thing with it. It's the only way to survive. It's the best, sweetheart. I keep my autonomy with this deal but still get national tie-ins. It's the only way. It's good for me, babe; I've gotta do it."

"Not now, Chet. I need you."

"Now or never, baby. I'm sorry. I'll call you before I go."

"You'll have women, won't you? You'll fuck women just like you always do, but in Boston and Chicago and wherever now. You'll be doing that, and I'll be here with my husband dead and my house taken over and the police talking about me."

"Baby, let me call you before I take off. We'll talk about lawyers then."

But he called her sooner than that; he called the next afternoon. He said, "Audrey, that guy LaLuna, the cop, just came by here."

Audrey asked him so what, what did he expect?

"I just don't like the feeling I get. It makes me uneasy. I've never been questioned in something like this before. He told me about the needle. It was eerie. He even tried to muscle me, I swear."

Audrey heard a short buzz on the line. Her first thought, the cunts downstairs, listening in. Then she realized and said, "Chet, I've got call waiting; hang on." She tapped the button and asked, "Hello?"

It was Felix Marmasette. He said, "God, Audrey, are you all right? There was a cop here today, a horrible little guy. He told me about Milton. Injection crap. Are you all right there?"

"Yes, Felix, I'm getting by, I suppose."

"Good. Good. He kept asking questions about me and Milton and business and you. What do they think, Audrey? What the hell do they think?"

"I don't know, Felix. I don't know what the hell they think."

"Oh, God, Audrey, this is just awful. First Milton dies, and now it turns out it happened like this? Audrey, you know, of course, someone doesn't just come in off the street and kill like this. It's devastating, it's devastating and it's scary. I can tell you this because I trust you, right? Each other? Audrey, I know you loved Milton. I know you two had an open marriage, wide open, but it was all right. I told the little policeman that, of course, Audrey. I mean, there was no secret there, about that."

"No, Felix, it was all right."

"Audrey, I know you loved your husband. I told the cop that. He asked me questions about the business too. I was so cool about it. I don't know how I did it. Don't worry about the business, Audrey; I'm taking care of everything. Sometime, I'll come over for signatures. Just some signatures, that's all. Is Robinson still your lawyer? Your personal lawyer for you and Milton? He's a good man, if he is. He can be trusted, Robinson."

"I don't know, Felix; I guess so, I guess he is. My mother-in-law, Milton's mother, is doing a lot of paperwork. Felix, I have a call waiting on the other line."

"All right, Audrey. I'll get the legal stuff that I can in order. Audrey, let me know if there's anything else I can do. I'll be seeing you. Let me know what I can do to help you out."

He told her that, let me know if I can help, and then he hung up to call his own lawyers.

Then Chet again. He said, "Audrey, let me know if I can do anything."

He told her that, and then he flew off to Boston.

He had been following her a long time, all day really, too long for any good to come out of it.

Just the doing of it felt good, though, with just the right mix of evil and business—for him, for her. She didn't know it, of course, and even if she did manage to spot him tailing her, he could probably get her thinking any way he wanted to about it. He figured he could, if it came to that, pretty sure he could pull that off. So he kept his tail on her all day—it even had a good sound to it, didn't it? Keep his tail on her—and she didn't even know.

She had gotten back from Ridgeport four days ago, flown up there and back, even though it was only a couple of hours by car. She had put Milton L. Wright into the ground and then landed back here with just a carry-on and one Cassini case, sans husband, sans in-laws. A woman newly unattached.

And so today he was slipping out of his car and crouching behind parked trucks and leaning behind building corners and ducking behind buses and trees and troops of people on the street. This morning he had watched her walk into the jeweler's, LeGrande's, him knowing he was doing everything right because she was walking like a woman unaware of being watched. She had been a long time in there—why a jeweler?—and she had walked out carrying a white paper bag no bigger than an envelope. She had bought herself something nice in there. He had figured that much—the delicate white bag, the shine on her face as she was walking out. Baby, I'm dead now, Milton was telling her, g'head, get yourself something pretty, get yourself something nice.

The tail watched her, standing there perfectly still behind a street peddler's pretzel cart, and he felt like calling over to her: G'head, put it on, I want to see, I want to see you, how you look with it on.

Then, after the jeweler's, a paper store; walked out with a brown bag about the same size as the jeweler's bag. An expensive purchase first, then a cheap one. The cheap one took her just as long. She had seemed just as absorbed by it. Maybe that came from being rich: made all purchases equal, weightless.

But maybe the jeweler's hadn't been for her. Maybe she had picked up a card there in the paper store, just a card to go with the jewelry. No. No, look how she's holding it, keeping it close. Letting herself play with it, not even slipping it into her purse just yet. Nah, the jewelry was for her, all right.

Then, after the paper store, wasting time. A walk to nowhere, a drive nowhere, almost lost her on East Avenue, the drive too aimless to follow easily, too random, you really needed a three- or four-car tail. But this operation was his, his alone. Him and her. Not too close, not too far back. She had almost gotten away from him, but she didn't. He picked up a sight of her at a light. Hooked a right, eased it into her lane, caught up gently, enjoying it all. She didn't know. She was just wasting time for something.

For a lunch date. She went into Tommy Maestro's at ten minutes to one, made a solo entrance. He parked across the street, couldn't catch sight of her in there. Alone?

At one sharp, a fat guy with blond, almost white hair walked into Maestro's. So she'd been alone in there, probably drinking at the bar, puffing, maybe waiting at the table, waiting for her lunch date to show up.

There followed a crushingly long seventy minutes. The only longer seventy minutes he had ever spent in his life, it seemed to him, was once at the Ice Capades, with a toothache. And maybe a couple evenings with insurance men had been longer than this. Talking coverage, reading off the policy, talking monotone. Deadly.

Finally, Fat Blondie had come back out, alone, not happy. Somehow looked like he should have washed up after his meal, disheveled, things undone, not an *après*-dinner look to the guy at all. Then it was her coming out of there, thirty seconds later, pissed. Had she brought the small bags—jewelry and paper store—into Maestro's? He hadn't noticed. If so, where were they? In her purse? Not with that fat wonker, let's hope.

Then some more wasting time, all driving now. Was she getting wise? Trying to lose him? Nah, she didn't know. He was the only one who knew. He still liked that.

Three o'clock—First Body Perfect, an aerobics/tanning salon. Had her dark-blue gym bag in the trunk, pulled it out in the parking lot. Leotards, leotards—yeah, God, make it leotards. First Body Perfect an old white cinder-block building—not a window in the place. Probably for the best. Probably safer that way for all concerned. "Hey, ladies, who's that guy peering in the front window there?"

Back out on the sidewalk again at four-twenty, her hair still wet, different shirt, same shade of tan she had worn into the place.

Suddenly, he almost lost her again, by dreaming, because of thinking, too much going on, blowing him out of focus. Wet hair, jewelry, and Fat Blondie, and suddenly something happening, or maybe not.

He was trying to figure it out. Could there be someone else tailing her? There was maybe, he couldn't be sure, another tail, who maybe dropped a roll of film, and there was shuffling and damn garbage cans to trip over, so he couldn't quite get a fix on the strange car that was pulling out. When did he pick up on that? How long into the tail? How does all that work? How does that fit in, the film roll and the little gray Omni or something and the shuffling and the drop and the pickup? If he hadn't tripped, garbage cans flying, he might've got the guy.

Out of breath, patting the yellow roll in his jacket pocket, he lost her for real, damn it, but she was probably just heading home, so he had gunned it, mad now, got to her place just in time to spot her disappearing into her fat-cat, overstuffed house.

Then, back to the street, him parked across and three houses down, waiting. Time to bag it, buddy. Wrong neighborhood for his car for too long. She's gone anyway, done for the day, and he's getting sloppy, too much to care for, to think about. She's eating now, watching TV, drinking, kicking back, stockings on the rug, getting stoned, see you tomorrow, cowboy. G'won home.

But he couldn't make the break. He'd been enjoying it all too damn much. She doesn't know, still, I'm out here.

Then, a little before eight, the sun going down, he got glad that he couldn't go home, couldn't leave her. She appeared again, like a comet, like twenty thousand dollars' worth of fireworks, dressed in jeans and a thick gray sweatshirt with a hood and Italian writing on it. She took the parkways south.

To the beach. Not deserted, but pretty close. West End at sundown. Too good to be true. Thanks, God. The only other thing I could ask, long as I live is—better than leotards—and it was happening: there go the jeans, bathing suit underneath. Red and two-pieced. I owe you a retreat, my dear Lord, minimum.

He walked up to her blanket with his shoes off, tucked under one arm, hands in his pants pockets. The sand had gotten cold, felt wet on his feet. The sun was just about done, cutting a few last long shadows from across the inlet to the west. His shadow cut her there, between the two pieces of red cotton. Her right arm had fallen across her eyes, as if to protect her from the sun. A beach pose learned at noontimes, not needed now.

He said to her, "Hello, Audie."

Her arm came down, both her elbows propped her up quick, she squinted up at him and said, "LaLuna, you scared the shit out of me."

He stood there until she asked him to sit down, on her blanket with her.

"How'd you know I was out here?"

"Your maid told me."

"I don't have a maid."

"Your answering service."

"Don't have one."

"I been following you all day."

"You fuck."

"I'm sorry."

She started packing up, beach bag, big straw hat that had been folded up inside, sweatshirt. "Look, Joe, if I'm a goddamned suspect—and you're treating me like one—then treat me like one, for

Christ sake. You can't have it both ways. You're not my friend and my arresting officer both, buddy."

"Audrey, I said I was sorry, I am. I'm not following you because I think you're gonna go into the discount medical supply store, get a couple gross of hypodermic needles. Honest I'm not."

"What then? You know already everything you have to, all right? You already know I've been seeing Chet. You know he's gone for a while. That's the only incriminating thing I do these days, Joe. I screw a guy who's not my husband. So what are you looking for, LaLuna, anyway? What else?"

"Different things, I guess. Little things. Things we don't even know yet. Things you and I don't even figure until they've been brought out, see?"

"What things?" she asked him, looking at him hard, like there would be sun in her eyes, but there was none. "What kind of stuff are you talking about anyway?"

"Who knows? Maybe like Marmasette. I'm sure, Wink's description, that was him you had lunch with today, am I right?"

"Yeah, that was Felix, so all right."

"Could I ask you what he wanted?"

"Why do you think he wanted something? Couldn't I ask him out for lunch? We had lunch."

"Could I ask you what he wanted?"

"Joe, there are a lot of business things. A lot. I don't understand them all. Felix is being really good, really nice, supportive as hell here."

She slapped at a mosquito on her thigh, a thigh that had been tanned professionally, a First Body Perfect tan. She said, "Did you know he came up to Milton's service? Flew up for the day. More than that prick Chet did. More than you did. The only friendly face I saw all day that day."

"That's good. Of course, it was the guy's partner, it's the least he could do, I think. I was working. Did he get into anything else? Felix? At lunch?"

"Why you asking, Sergeant?"

"I don't know, he came out of the restaurant, he looked burned a bit, I thought. You too. Just an idea."

"Yeah, well, that's pretty good. Yeah, there were some things I didn't just go along with. Nothing important."

"Business things?"

"Sure, business, what else?"

"Tell me about them?"

"No. They're not important anyway. Too hard to explain. Nothing. Meetings and proxies and voting blocks and stocks."

"Any nonbusiness?"

"What, you in the restaurant, Joe? Had a camera or tape recorder there or something?"

"No." LaLuna grinned. "Why? I get something?"

"Because he grabbed my leg, the cocksucker, above the knee." She laughed a little, sounded good doing it. "Tried to make like it was part of the punch line to some stupid story he told me. Like trying to cheer me up. Milton lukewarm, not quite cold, tepid, partner Felix groping for a feel. Hey, does this widow look that damn desperate?" She laughed again.

"Want me to kill him for you?"

"OK," she said. "That'd be nice. That'd be great, actually." Then, "Joe, listen, I've done a lot since the last time we saw each other, you know? I mean, other than this thing, since high school, I mean. I've been through a lot. I've done many things that I'm perfectly glad you don't know about. Not legal—illegal things. I don't mean that you're a cop. I just mean, you used to think of me a certain way, back then. So now I'm just glad you don't know everything I am. You know? You understand?"

"Yeah, I think I do. I understand. Anyway, you check your house again? Anything?"

"Joe, I'm talking about me. I'm tired, it hurts all the time for me. Anyway, I told you, there's nothing missing in the house. I checked. There's no sign anybody broke in anyway, right?"

"Huh."

"So Milton must've let somebody in, right? Don't you think? I lock up when I leave, so right? Agree?"

"Probably so, yeah."

"That's somebody he knew then, right?"

"Probably. I guess so."

"So somebody killed him he knew. So anyway, why the hell you been following me all day, Chief? Want to catch me screwing a duck?"

"Audrey, I'd like to see that very much, yes, but first, one last Marmasette question."

"Yeah, I guess I'd rather a duck than Marmasette, but anyway, what?"

"What did the guy eat in there?"

"What, Marmasette? In the restaurant? Sure he ate, it was lunch. Just salad. Why?"

"Just asking."

"So you were gonna tell me why you spend your days, on the tax-payers' dole, following a merry but bereaved widow around town all day, weren't you?"

"Well, I already gave you one reason. To pick up on stuff, stuff like this Marmasette, what was going on with your husband. Also be on hand to stuff Marmasette's hand down a Cuisinart he touches your leg again. You look great, by the way. I got a couple other reasons too, though, following you."

"Like what?"

"One I just touched on. Protection, of a sort."

"What for? Who from?"

"Audie, don't get scared. I'm pretty sure somebody else was following you today."

"You're going nuts, LaLuna. Plain, flathead nuts."

"Yeah, no, really. You know anyone owns a little gray Omni, dull gray, lousy little car, junk?"

"I don't even know what that is. Somebody in that was following me around?"

"Yeah. I think so. I just happened to notice it a couple times. Just a thought. Out of the corner of my eye. I didn't manage a good glimpse, but I'm pretty sure."

"No, you're wrong, Joe. There's a million little gray Omnis around. They were each one different ones."

"I don't think so. Anyway, you said you don't even know what a lit-tle gray Omni is, so how you suddenly know there's a million of them around?"

"It just sounds like it. It doesn't sound like the type car you'd say, 'Yeah, he just bought a little gray Omni, one of only eleven that were ever made'—you know what I mean?"

"Sure," LaLuna said. "Anyway, you're right on that."

"So there was no one else, you're imagining, I'm sure. So what's the other reason?" she asked.

LaLuna jerked his chin at her, like to ask, "Huh?"

"You all out of reasons for following me? You got any others, better make it good."

She was looking right at him, not backing off. He looked out to the waves.

"I don't know how good it is," he told her, "but listen. I don't know why, but since your husband died, since I came out there to your place and saw you again, I've been up a lot, thinking about things. I guess I have things I've thought to say. I've been trying hard for the words. But. But they won't fit together right."

"Joe, what?" she asked him. "You nervous?"

"So I guess," he said, "first, let me tell you a couple things. First thing, that this no way is going to come out right. The words of my thoughts will be wrong, I know that already, going in. Second, this is no pass, OK? Maybe halfway through it'll begin to sound like that, but I'm not trying now to hit on you or anything, all right? Honest."

"I don't remember you so unsure, Joe," she said.

"Who, me? Sure, I was always that way. Anyway, what I want to say is, if I didn't have a wife at home, which I do, but if I didn't have her, OK, I'd set myself, in love, up for you, that it would be like high school. I mean"—he started grinning at her now, shaking his head—"I mean I'd be out there doing your yardwork, and going to the store for your hairspray stuff, and helping you with your headaches, you know, and simonizing your car. I'd be doing all that, you know?"

She hesitated, seemed to be considering, said, "It'd be nice, Joe, it really would." Then she seemed to decide something, said, "Joe, we're both upper forties—you're upper forties too, right? I'm getting old even for the role I *have* been playing, never mind the one you've been talking about, trying to put me in. Too old, too much gone by."

"Yeah, but still," he said, "I wanted you to know all that. And so anyway, to get back to the beginning, the reason I've been following you, reason number what—three?—is that I enjoy it. You know, call me a weirdo pervert, a damned voyeur, or what's the word, but I've just enjoyed just the looking at you. Seeing you. That's a big reason of it."

"Yeah, that's sweet, Joe, it is."

"Yeah, that's what you say to a guy when there's not much else to say, I guess. That it's sweet of him. To care." He looked around at the ocean. "So, do you come out here a lot? To the beach? Alone? At night?"

She grinned and said, "Only when I want to be alone with a man."

LaLuna grinned back and wondered: So who was the first? Who was the first guy to wonder what the hell was going on, and who the hell was stalking who around here anyway? It didn't matter, because female skin can be so damningly beautiful, looking soft, smooth, and tan, First Body Perfect tan, and the only thing better than that is a First Body Perfect tan that's been mixed with a touch of dying sunlight, and, a little later, mixed with dying sunlight and new moonlight, and, a little bit after that, even, just mixed with the moon alone, bouncing off the Atlantic Ocean. There was nothing anywhere better-looking than female skin such as that.

Later, back home, LaLuna's wife had him check her rash, thought it might be starting to blister up some. The doctor had said be on the lookout for that.

"Without my protein, it's bound to happen, he said," she told him.

"I don't see much," LaLuna told her, rubbing his fingertips across the little red bumps on her back. "It looks OK to me."

"It's awful, I spent my whole day just sitting around trying not to scratch. It's funny, all these years we thought it would be my blood that would take me, now it turns out it'll be my skin. I'll end up looking like that man on the show on Channel Thirteen, the 'Singing Detective' guy. I'll look just like that. Goodbye. Horrible."

"No, that's not gonna—just don't scratch. It won't happen. That's psoriasis," LaLuna told his wife. "That's not you. This is something completely different from that, what you've got. That's blisters and welts and dried and flakes. You don't have that."

"I have casserole," she said. "It's a tuna. You have a little bit. Hey, by the way, I ordered something for you, can't talk about it, you'll like, have the tuna fish."

"No, geez, I ate," he told her. "I just want to take my shoes off."

"You have some."

He left the room, called out, "How about Carl, he been out yet? Madeline, should I put Carl out?"

"Yeah, put him out," she called.

"I should put him out?"

"Put him out. Watch him, though. Keep an eye on him, he'll run away, get into trouble."

Carl hadn't tried running away, or gotten into any trouble, for about five years now. Thirty-five years, dog time.

Later, as LaLuna ate some tuna fish casserole, Madeline told him about a trip to Yellowstone National Park that her family had taken when she was thirteen. She remembered every detail. They had stayed at the hotel at Yellowstone National Park, because her father didn't like to camp out. Dad didn't like sleeping on the ground.

"Is that dirt on your pants?" she asked LaLuna, surprised, pointing.

"No, sand," he said. "I had to go to the beach. For a case."

"You had to go to the beach?"

"Yeah, I did."

"I haven't been to the beach for years. Which one? That's how I'll end up, though, to change the subject, looking like a circus freak. How's the tuna?"

Still later on, eating cheese in a closet at the end of the extra-long telephone cord, LaLuna listened to Wink telling him, "Mojo, nothing, nothing at all here. Neighbors didn't see nothing that night, either out or in, they probably never would, it's that kind of neighborhood. Phone-call checks don't give nothing. The insulin trail is dead— there's just too much of it, too many places. Computer files, all just bullshit. And there ain't no stooges of yours or of mine gonna know anything about what goes on Money Hill. No way. So, where to, paisan? Give it over to Philbrick and forget about it? Time to let it sink, this Polack'd tell you, you ask. Let's not spend any Bobby Lewis nights over this stinker of a case, huh? You get anything today?"

"This one don't sink, we don't let it. Yeah, I did get something,"

LaLuna whispered into the receiver. "It was funny, strange."

"Yeah, what? You whispering?"

"Madeline's asleep. I tailed her today, Audie, you know that? Well, I keep thinking I'm seeing the same car, a little gray Omni, out of the corner of my eye. I remember one of the neighbors saying about a little gray car the night of Wright's kill, we canvassed a bit, you remember that?"

"No. Yeah, you sure, though? About seeing one?"

"No, but I think so. Three, four times, it is. Maybe, I say—*maybe*, now."

"Maybe somebody else on her tail, you're saying?"

"Yeah, it seems. Hers or mine, and nobody wants me."

"What, Joe—you spot a tail, you couldn't nail this guy? Come on."

"Well, if it's true, if it's really true and there, then the guy's quite good, I can't quite whack him. But listen, she was at this gym working out, place on Essex Street, and I'm bored, jumpy, so I decide circle the building. Nothing. Then I circle a couple buildings across the street."

"What for?"

"'Cause I'm bored, 'cause I thought there might be a tail, 'cause I'm a good cop—what do you think?"

"So what do you get from that?"

"Well, something really good. *Maybe,* I'm saying. I get three quarters of the way, the far wall, it's a little dingy set of stores—stamp collectors' place, I don't know what else—and before I can make it around the corner, I hear a little four-cylinder squealing out, in a rush, just taking off."

"So what?"

"Well, maybe it's the Omni, I'm not sure."

"Hey, Joe baby, maybe, maybe, maybe. Maybe you gotta excuse me, Billy Graham just came on the tube from Australia, it's more interesting than this shit you're throwing at me here. Come on."

"No, wait a minute, Wink, you haven't heard. I look around, I look on the ground, there's a film canister there. On the ground."

"A what?"

"A little roll, thirty-five-millimeter film, you know the kind."

"What are you talking about here?"

"Hey, listen, there's a roll of film. It's on the ground, right at the corner of the stamp store, perfect spot to be shooting."

"Joe, you on Mars? Hello? You on Mars? What the hell you talking?"

"Wink, listen. Maybe the tail's shooting film, right? Of Audrey, of whatever. So he's changing the film, he looks up, sees me gone, he gets jumpy, figures I might have spotted him, I'm coming around there, he gets out, he leaves so quick he drops film. Could be, right?"

"Yeah, right, Joe, could be. Could be also space aliens, with Elvis Presley shooting that film. Could be E.T., Judge Crater. You gone nuts. You know that, of course, right? Because as long as you realize that, there is hope that your mind can be reclaimed. As long as you have the truth enough to say to yourself now, many times over, 'I'm a wonking madman, I'm fucking nuts, my brain has turned into *baccalà*.' Et cetera, Joe, and et cetera, OK?"

LaLuna said, "Partner, I'm glad you're behind me on this. For a while I thought you might just shrug it off, think I'm onto the wrong track. Anyway, not a *baccalà* brain—nothing's *that* hard, my friend. Kielbasa brain maybe, but not *baccalà*."

"Yeah."

"So tomorrow I'll have the lab develop it, they should have it for us noon."

"Do better at a wonking Photomat, my friend. Same-day service."

"Probably. That other thing too I thought of," LaLuna said. "Try to remember the neighbors, we canvassed the street? Gray?"

"What? The car?" Wink asked.

"Yeah, the car. I'm sure somebody, some neighbor, said a little gray car, told us one was parked around that night, didn't know its purpose. Don't you remember?"

"No, I don't."

"I'll check my notes, see if it's in there."

"If so, so what?"

"So, same car? Maybe. So then we run DMV, see who of our little friends here owns a little gray Omni, Chevette, Fiesta, that crap."

"Huh."

"So, partner mine, what d'you think? We having any fun?"

"Hey, it's all fun and games, till somebody gets their eye poked.

Anyway, there's nothing else, I'll see you tomorrow, then, I'll pick you up. I gotta go now, I think Billy Graham's gonna do a tap-dance routine or something. Better than the shit you been shoveling. In the meantime, do me a favor, Joey. Check yourself into Creedmore. Have them throw away the wonking key. Please. For the sake of humanity in general, do that much for me, please."

Before he hung up, LaLuna said, "Hey, Hraska, again I thank you for all your support."

ig Bob Bell, chief of detectives, had either had a stroke in the spring of 1985 or *not* had a stroke in the spring of 1985. As was often asked around the Room, "A guy like that, how the hell could you tell?"

LaLuna sat across Big Bob's desk from him, LaLuna forcing himself not to look at Big Bob's left ring finger, which was chopped off at the knuckle but still held a gold wedding band. Big Bob, called also "Ole Nine and a Half" by his men, or "Señor Nine Digits," had once tried to unclog his power mower by hand. At retirement parties, Big Bob would make a few stupid remarks, and all the men would clap with their left ring fingers curled down. He never caught on, even though clapping that way had a sort of hollow sound to it.

The rest of Big Bob's fingers were the size of hot dogs. When Big Bob would stop somebody in the Room to talk, Wink would position himself over Big Bob's shoulder and make like he was chewing his fingers, like they were franks with mustard. You had to not laugh. Wink always said hot dog rolls, they should come in packages of nine and a half, in Big Bob's honor.

"Lieutenant Sheeney asked me to have you in here," Big Bob was telling LaLuna. "He, by the way, thinks the world of you, as you know."

"Thanks, Bob. I know he does."

It was not usual procedure for Big Bob to call a detective into his office, which was downstairs a flight from the Room. Sheeney ran Homicide, and the other heads basically knew what they were doing. Big Bob of course did not, so it tended to work out fine.

"It's no secret, Joe, that the plan is to move Sheeney over to Major Crimes, as soon as it gets going, everybody's heard that one, right?"

"Yeah, that's been the word upstairs."

"Sure. And he, of course, will take you with him. As the associate. He's been good to you, you appreciate it, Sheeney's been your rabbi for what, how many years now, Joe?"

"Eighteen, I guess, you could say. Since I came on the department. Right out of the academy. He was my first supervisor."

"Right. And he's got maybe twenty-six, twenty-seven in, something like that. He don't even know he'll go for thirty or not. Depends on retirement, Social Security, his kids, stuff like that. He don't even know, he gets there. He might be out in a couple years. Hard to tell with Sheeney."

"Right."

LaLuna looked at the big stump of a hot dog, ringed. Couldn't help it. Why was he here?

"It's also no secret, Joe, we'd love you taking over Major Crimes—once that's happening, once it's in existence—once Sheeney buys a grapefruit shirt and goes off to Florida. We been grooming you for that move. Of course, what is said here, it isn't gospel. Make you no promises and I'll make you no lies. But still and all, that's been the plan all along. And don't worry, Big Bob'll be around long enough to see to it. Big Bob retires when the cows go home."

LaLuna shifted his ass on the hard seat, shifted his glance. Why am I here?

"So anyways, Sheeney asked me to have a little talk with you, 'cause he's been concerned lately. Well, he didn't really come right out, but he hinted around some. I'd be glad to. I told you already, he really cares."

"I understand."

"Joe, you know what makes guys like you, me invaluable to this department? It's this. It's we know how to relax. We got the secret. It's a stressful job, Joe, I don't gotta tell you that. The guys succeed are the guys who know how to forget about it, go home, don't get the ulcers, am I right?"

"Yeah, you are."

"You take me. I got a little workshop down the cellar. A bandsaw, a table saw, a lathe, a couple jigsaws. You know, saws. What I do, Joe, I go home, I have a beer, I go down my cellar, and I do odd things."

Odd things, Bob? Odd *jobs* maybe. It was the stroke talking. Or maybe not. Maybe Big Bob really does go home, goes down the cellar, does odd *things*.

"And you, Joe, you have always had the same technique. You never let things get to you. That's what makes you so unvaluable a policeman to this department. Many things, but that's a main one. You stay cool. Everybody knows how you can clear homicides like nobody's business. You do it and you stay cool at it. That's excellent."

"Thanks."

"How many years you got in, you say, Joe?"

"Eighteen. Eleven in Homicide."

"Eleven in Homicide. All those years of walking in on one kill scene or another, huh? All that blood, and human faces you could hardly recognize as such, the barf and the blood, all those missing limbs, chopped off God knows how many kinds of different ways."

LaLuna didn't look at the stump.

Big Bob went on. "A lot of destruction there, huh, Joe? And the way you survived it all, a smart young bugger like yourself, and lived to tell the tale, was by not letting it get to you, like the water on a duck's ass, no concern, be a snob, forget about it, no dents. No dents, Joe."

Big Bob paused a minute to let his words sink in. LaLuna didn't say anything.

Big Bob leaned forward, folding his arms on his desk, and he said, "That's why we've been concerned for you, Joe, as of late. You begin to look, of course, might I say, like shit. Lieutenant Sheeney, this one case seems to be rattling you a bit, this thing about the needle in the guy's eye, wasn't it?"

"Yeah, it—"

"Hey, we, everybody together, believe that you did a fine service by placing the whole thing as a homicide to begin with. That's police work, to be sure. But. You knew the girl, in high school? Right?"

"Yeah, I did."

"What you got on it? She stick the needle in her husband's eye-ball?"

"I don't think so. She's pretty well alibied. We've gone all the usual ways—prints, stooges, neighbors, MOs, paper chases. It's been tough. Nice residential neighborhood, easy to canvass, but nothing doing. I got a couple other ideas, other people, on it."

"Yeah, that's good, you got some other ideas, but the idea is, Joe, just who the hell was it stuck the needle in the guy's eye anyway? Who's the mack on this?"

"We don't know yet."

"We don't know? Joe, I don't know I've ever heard of this before. We got a domestic homicide, we don't know who did it? What the hell is this case, a Julia Christie or something?"

Agatha, Bob.

LaLuna said, "The way we reconstruct—forensics, the ME been a big help—is that the victim was home alone, in bed, in pajamas. Between nine and eleven maybe, maybe later, he went down, let somebody in. Presumed to be somebody he knew, was familiar with. Walking back through the house—'Hello, how's it going, what's new?'—the mack somehow suddenly gets the victim down on the rug, in the hallway. Only little bruises on the shoulder, hip, so he got him down real easy. Leads us to think it was a big assailant—the victim's not small. Maybe the guy knew jujitsu, judo, or something. Quick, he's got him down on the rug, on his back, pins his head there with his legs—there's big bruises both sides of the head where he kept him pinned. Quick, the needle's out, pop, insulin in the eye. Left eye, right-handed mack probably. Stuff starts working almost at once. The mack gets up, maybe strolls around the house now, knowing the guy is gone. No strange fingerprints, even smudges, nothing missing from the place, there were wads of cash left around, nothing disturbed. The victim manages to flop over on his stomach and die. The mack strolls back, hauls him to bed, props him up there. Clean, clean job. It's strange and interesting, don't you think?"

"Yuck. Listen, I heard the guy used to stick his wanger in a milking machine, that right?"

"Well, not then. I don't know. There was one there. Wife says it's mostly a joke."

"Whee, imagine the feel of that, huh, Joe? What kind of feel would that be anyway?"

"I don't know, Bob."

"Just clear the case, Joe, OK? For Big Bob, do it, just now."

"I'm trying, Captain, I am."

"Oh, come on, Joe, come on, don't get upset with me. It's no big thing, it's just one more homicide. Don't get involved. Sleep at night, you look bad. Did Sheeney tell me pictures or something?"

"That's right. Somebody's been following the wife around, taking pictures of her. Let me go get them a minute, I'll show them to you."

"No, Joe, sit down. I'm sure she's a lovely woman. I got no time for pictures."

"So anyway, I don't know, Bob. Prints, I told you, I think, nowhere, nothing. Plus there's nobody submitting to a polygraph, of course. We been trying to find a judge for search warrants, I've written so many affidavits, asking, maybe even taps, wires on two guys we think might be implicated. So far, no luck. I have to admit, I see what the judge tells us on it. It's a long shot, three-point shot. Still, if it's the only thing left to go with, maybe, I was thinking, you got some contacts at judicial, maybe you put in a good word for searches, even taps maybe."

"Joe, how you doing with that Mondello thing, the thing with the crutch?"

"Cleared. It's over to Strickland."

"Oh, that's great, Joe. That's what Captain Bob wants to hear. And the Boy Scout, that's been all done for a while, Sheeney told me that already. And, Joe, how about—I almost hesitate to ask this—how about the foot?"

"Nothing yet on the foot, Bob."

"That's too bad, really. Why don't you direct your attention to that one for a while. We gotta be careful, the newspapers here. They been quiet lately, but you never know with those guys. Try to make it, maybe, somebody was just passing through. You know, some butcher sort of got off the Expressway, dumped the foot, went on down to Kansas or somewhere. Not our deal."

"Yeah, maybe."

"And the needle in the eye, Joe, just clear it. Pack it up, send it on over to Strickland, forget about it. The papers are still quiet. Go out, take your wife to the movies. There's a good Arnold Schwarz'n'hammer playing now."

Wink had said that he once overheard Big Bob, alone in his office, singing the Simon and Garfunkel classic "Bridge Over Taras Bulba."

"Yeah, old Arnold, he takes a guy's head off, says something funny," Bob was saying, "tells a joke about it, like 'Don't lose your head over this, buddy.' Meanwhile, he's ripping the guy's head right off. Those things are not quite true to life, but they're fun, right? They keep us young. A Kraut like that with the name of Schwarzanigger. Who knows what the hell happens in this world. Goddamn Arnold. The Robocop, huh? Huh, Joe?"

"Yeah, I guess so."

"Sure. On another matter, Joe. Not on the same level, but still. With the tragic death of Detective Mallarny, Sheeney tells me you're running the World Series Pool."

"Yeah, that's right. I guess I am."

"And twenty's always been the magic number there, isn't it?"

"Yeah. It's just a good number works out with the draft. Just about enough players to make everybody happy. Any more than that, somebody gets stuck with some real dogs, they start complaining."

"I see. Well, you know, Joe, I've never mentioned this, except maybe to Mallarny, back when he was still living, but I've always felt a little bad about not being included there. I mean, I know it's Homicide, I know some guys up there, clerks and secretaries and stuff, are anxious to get in, but still, if I'm chief, which I am, then I'm chief of Homicide too, which sort of makes me Homicide, so it would really be nice to be included there. You see?"

"Uh-huh."

"And of course, now Mallarny's dead, he's not only not running the pool, he's also not *in* it either, which, if I see right, it frees up a spot."

"Yeah, I guess it does."

"If, Joe, it's not too soon to ask. It's a hard thing to time right, of course. I don't want to appear insensitive to the death of a fine Homicide officer. But of course, also, I don't want ten other tecs getting their names in before me, you see?".

"I see. I think I can work it out. I'm sure I can. It's early. People aren't even thinking about it yet. Nobody's asked."

"Oh, well, that's great, Joe, so fine. Anything you can do on it for me, OK? It would be appreciated."

"OK, Bob."

"Sure, Joe. I wouldn't worry about it. I'll check with you again come October, maybe come sooner than that."

"Sure."

"OK, then, Joe, I'm glad we talked. It's always a pleasure with you."

LaLuna thanked him and got up. Big Bob grabbed his missing finger and said, "Joe, you just clear up the needle eye thing for me, OK?"

LaLuna said, "Yes, I will. I just got a couple little things to clean up on it first."

"Sure, you g'head," Big Bob said. "I'm not rushing you. Am I? Am I? Nah."

Mogie was in his room, saying his rosary, when he had to go get the knock.

He got up from the little kitchenette table and looked at the beads, so he'd remember where he was. It was Third Sorrowful Mystery, third Hail Mary in. He stuck the beads in his right-hand vest pocket, patted them down, went to the door, and yelled, "Yeah?"

"Open the door, Mogie."

Oh, sweet bloody Jesus, it was the Guinea cop.

"You again? What'd you want?"

"Open up."

He let the cop in, led him across, sat him at the table, sat down opposite, and said again, "Yeah?" Didn't offer him anything.

The cop told him, "You're still here," like Mogie hadn't been living up to the cop's expectations.

"Aw, come on, Luna, we been through this. *I'm* still here, *you're* still here, we both of us still here, what?"

"I was kind of hoping we both agreed you'd leave, leave things alone."

"Come on. I ask you the last time, what's this all about? Sharon been telling you about me? She doesn't like her mother's dates? Hey, Luna, the lady could do worse, right? You seen her? She's no Carmen Miranda, you know. But we get along. Sharon shouldn't really have a say here in this, should she? I mean, it's her mother, it's not her."

"Sharon who?"

"Yeah, Sharon who, OK, that's good. Can't fool you. Look, Luna, I'd like to have you stay, I'm right in the middle of something right now, all right? You're interrupting."

"You gonna leave or what?"

"No, what, I'm not gonna leave—what for? I told you, I got business here, I told you last time. Look, get the hell out of here, you hear me? You got nothing for me, so get the hell out of here. You gonna rough me up? I gotta call a lawyer? Get out of here."

The cop reached in his pocket. He brought out a piece of paper. He said, "I got an arrest warrant."

"A bench warrant? Arrest? Where? For where?"

"Warren County, New York."

"Warren County? I never heard of Warren County. I never been in fucking Warren County."

"It's Lake George."

Mogie felt his face tighten a bit, felt his ears get a little hotter than they'd been. But all right, he knew from experience nobody could tell, nobody would see that. Aah, Mogie baby, you should have been on the stage, I swear.

He said, "Well, yeah, Lake George of course I heard of. Everybody heard of that."

Cop asked, "You been there?"

"Yeah, I think so. Everybody been there."

Cop said, "OK, then."

Mogie asked, "It seems to me I've had a business dealing or two there. Lake George. What you got—car theft, right?"

"Grand theft, auto."

"Well, shit, Luna, you been really doing your homework then, huh?"

"Ah, well, how many guys named Mogie Hattes there gonna be anyway? You never use another?"

"No, I don't. What for? I got nothing to hide. This car thing, it's a misunderstanding, that's all. I got nothing to hide, I'm telling you."

"You got Lake George, you got."

"Oh, come on, Luna, look. We both know this to be nothing,

right? Don't you have other things to be doing? OK, so you're sweet on Sharon Slabb, that's fine. She's a fine and intelligent young lady, and I'm sure you see her inner beauty. As is. I don't know what your plans are, I don't know if she's a thing on the side—I see your wedding ring there—and I'm not asking. So she tells you what, I come on to her when Mom's not around? The lady drinks and misinterprets, Officer, I swear she does. I never came on to her, laid a hand on her. And, to tell the truth, even if I did, would that be so bad? Would that be so bad for a woman her station in life? Would it?"

Cop said, "Who we talking about here?"

Mogie kept going. "Or maybe she thinks I'm scamming her mom, right? Gold-digging? Again, Officer, I put it to you, who's suffering in this business deal? I talk to the lady, we go to church together, I know you probably think that's old-fashioned, or part of the scam, but we do. We traveled to Atlantic City, and we both, the both of us, you understand, had a marvelous time there. We both were sure we spotted Myron Cohen in the lobby, until somebody told us he had passed on. But the thrill was still there. Mom and I, we enjoy. No harm done. Her last squeeze, you know, was no more than a molester of small blond children. I rescued her from all that. Some paramedic, 911, kind of guy. I got her out of that."

"Whose mother we talking about?"

"So, Luna, what's gonna happen here, huh? You take me in? It don't matter, you know. Not in the slightest. It's an afternoon out of my life, and I'm not working steady anyway. You won't be keeping me from anything, really. What, I'm gonna shit my pants at a holding tank? At getting fingerprinted? At the sound of the steel doors? Come on. Hey, when we got short in the service, we had an expression, we'd say, 'I got a year and a half, Sarge, I could do that standing on my head.' Listen, Luna, I could do this warrant standing on my head. We both of us, you and me, know it ain't possibly gonna lead anywheres. The very worst it will be, will be a lawyer's fee. But it's old and it's a technicality and nobody the hell cares at all about it up in Lake George, that's for sure. What, they got a posse out looking for me up there? So what's it gonna get you? I'll grease Ellen, she'll be steamed at Sharon, and that'll be it. You got no hold card here, buddy. Drop out."

Cop said, "You force my hand, Mogie. I told you I've got a lot of concerns to take care of."

Mogie said, "I force your hand. What? What, you're gonna rough me up? Is it worth trouble for your career? Come on, Luna, you're gonna put your career in jeopardy for Sharon Slabb? Come on, you can do better, huh, guy like you? You screw up your career, do it for someone has a personality, at least. Do it for someone with tits, at least. Do it for someone smiled one time, once in her life, at least. Your career for a dog? Come on, how good can she be?"

Cop said, "Mogie Hattes, now comes this duly sworn officer to place you under arrest."

Mogie said, "Oh, Christ, this is so dumb. OK, I'm under arrest, I got my rights to a lawyer, if I can't afford one, I know, I know. This is so dumb."

Cop said very quietly, very evenly, like he meant it, "Don't resist arrest, you've been duly warned."

Mogie looked at him. Cop didn't say a word.

Mogie asked, "What are you talking about? I'm not resisting, am I?"

"Don't resist arrest."

"What?"

Cop was crazy. He leaned back off the table, made a fist with his right hand, and he drove it hard into the right side of his own face, just below the cheekbone, right by the mouth. You could hear the thud of it hitting, crack, no cheap shot.

Mogie coughed in surprise, then stared at the crazy cop. The cheek was already turning purple. A lot of blood was coming out of the cop's mouth, made his teeth look whiter.

Mogie laughed, nervous. He said, "I think you got this a little backwards, don't you? Ain't *I* the one you're supposed to beat up?"

Cop ran his palm across his mouth, brought it down filled with blood, so much it was pouring out of the cup his hand made. Cop looked at his own blood in his hand there, pointed to it with his left hand, said, "I wish you hadn't done that."

Mogie's laugh dried up. He said, "Done what? Done what?"

This cop got up from the table, started coming around.

Mogie asked him, louder, "Done what?"

Felix Marmasette, using his big flat hand and the back of her thigh, finished himself off, rolled off her, burped, farted, and tried to excuse himself.

He lay on his back, looking up at the ceiling, baby-plump legs over the footboard and off the bed, from his knees on down. Him just breathing. After a while he reached over for a cosmetics magazine that had gotten thrown on the rug.

"All right," he said. "All right. How's your brother Ronnie?"

He was holding the magazine above him, leafing through it ten, fifteen pages at a clump. He always asked about her brother Ronnie after he was through.

Some men should die. Audrey knew this. Some men should know nothing but a hot, sharp point full of something deadly going into their eye, the whole way in, all the way up to the stem of it. Couldn't it be that a mistake had been made? Couldn't it be that the wrong co-CEO of Vor-Tech Industries had taken the sharp needle?

"He's doing all right," she told him. "His wife got him into a program. Up in New Hampshire. It's supposed to be a good one, I don't know."

"They can afford that?" Marmasette asked, not looking away from the models in the magazine.

"It's social agencies, I think, doing it. They don't have any money themselves."

"I didn't think so," Marmasette told her. "You help them out at all?"

"Some," she said. You mean other than this, you slimy sucker? You mean do I help them out other than my bimonthly debasement at your hands, at your tongue? She tried to think of a word rotten enough for this man who was half-lying on her bed, looking at her magazine. There was none.

"They're pretty proud," she told him. "They don't like to take much of anything. She's a secretary or something at a Ford place."

"That's good," Marmasette said. "It's good to have pride. You want to go wash up?"

She told him yeah and left. In the bathroom, she swore to God that if she could find a needle in there in the medicine chest, or a knife, or an ice pick, or a six-inch shard of glass, then she would go back to her bedroom holding the weapon behind her, wink at the pig, and as he winked back, drive the weapon into his one unblinking eye.

She took a shower, let the steam hit over her for ten minutes, kept her eyes closed, her mouth open. When she got back in there, he started getting dressed and asking her for something. She could always tell because he was so bad at it, so dull and brutal about it.

He had first brought it up when she opened the door and let him in, but she had interrupted, told him again that LaLuna might be around. She had told him that over the phone too. He told her again, don't worry.

Without saying it, they'd both decided to make Milton's murder a nonfact, to ignore it like a couple of highbrows, like talking about some new restaurant while ice rain slapped you in the face.

Now he was sitting on the edge of her bed, pulling his pants on, grunting with the effort of it. Getting around to asking her for something.

"Listen, I did everything but sign over Milton's holdings. What the hell you want else?" she asked him, her voice more tired than anything. "I've done it all, Felix, haven't I?"

"You've been great," he told her, "just wonderful. Legally, contractually, I couldn't ask you for more. What's happened is this, though. Milton, for all of his shitty ways of treating people, has a following within the company. Still does, still there, still loyal. They wouldn't have to do much more than just shuffle their feet, act dumb, to scuttle everything I'll be trying to do with Vor-Tech now. They know, I know. It's a tricky time for us. Defense is history, at least for a while; everybody knows that, everybody's scrambling. It won't be just flea repellent leading us into the twenty-first century, I can tell you that. Everybody's hurting in our field, even the big boys. Not just us. I'll need a tight ship, and even with that, who knows. Just a couple insubordinate subordinates trying to rip me in the back, and we all turn to shit, including the part you own."

"I don't understand it," she told him. She was at her dressing table, using her cleaning cream, hundred-dollar stuff from Sweden. She was working it in around her eyes, down to her neck. It felt good, so it didn't matter so much if it worked or not.

"You're the boss now," she continued. "I've got some silent stock, that's all, so what? I don't know from a business end. What do you want from me?"

He rolled onto one cheek of his ass, there on the bed, rolled back onto the magazine, on a model's face. He was putting on socks.

He said, "Tacit support, really, is all. That's all I'll need. In the marketplace, a smile's more important than a signature sometimes. I need your lovely smile behind me. Organizational quarterly meetings, Christmas parties, the Labor Day picnic, those things. That's all. A couple personal appearances, you on my arm, it diffuses anything the rebels have going."

"No, it won't. That's ridiculous."

"Yes, it will. I don't mean so they think I'm humping you or any-thing. You're right, that would blow up in my face real bad. I mean, just some quiet things to show you're behind my moves. In favor. I know how it works. I can bring that off. Trust me. I'll tell you what to do. You just follow my lead. I'm saying please, Audrey, now."

"Dry cleaning bills?"

"What?"

"If I have to spend an entire party with you, Felix, I'll soil myself for sure. One way or another, one end or another, I'll lose it. I guaran-tee."

"You're flattering me, baby. Look, Audrey, I don't care about you or your sense of humor or your wardrobe or anything else. Well, not quite true, I do care about you. Don't believe it, that's all right. Just do it, all right? I'll let you know. Are we straight on this, or are we not, now?"

She turned and looked at him. Put her jar of cream down. Time to dig in. She told him that it wasn't in the contract.

"Audrey, there never was a horse couldn't be rode, and there never was a cowboy couldn't be throwed."

"And there never was a contract couldn't be broken. You've told me that already."

"And I was right when I said that," he said, "especially when the contract is a two-party, back-room deal written on a scrap of notebook paper by two people who should have known better. Two people working in the very shadows of their everyday life."

"Yes," she said, "that's a contract that can be broken by party of the first part, party of the second part, right? What's party of the first part going to do—take the other party to Wapner, on television?"

"I don't think so," he said. "You know what party of the first part will do. No, baby, I don't see it in the cards, the dissolution of this contract. I see what we have here as more lasting even than the sacred marriage contract. Till death do us part. Death or impotence, whatever comes first."

"In your case, how do we tell?"

He smiled, hesitated a moment, then looked at her and asked, "This is horrible to say, but did you know I used to hurt people during sex? I'm sorry, it's awful, it's true. It was something took me. I don't know how I ever made myself stop doing that, except that I knew it was repulsive and wrong. And I tell myself, don't bring it up, Felix, it's not an addendum to consider right there. I swear it's not. Don't worry about old Felix, Audrey."

She dipped into the cream. Didn't scare her. She held her whitened fingertips to one spot on her cheek for a moment, and she asked, "You have someone taking pictures of me?"

He looked at her like he didn't understand, so she asked him again.

"What do you mean, a photographer?"

"A guy with a camera, I don't know."

"No. Why? What?"

"I just've got a reason to believe somebody's been following me around, taking pictures."

"What makes you think that—you saw him?"

"I got reason to believe, that's all."

"Well, it hasn't been me, sweetie."

"I know. But I thought maybe you hired someone."

"Why would I do that? Am I a pervert or something? No, I'm not. Do I ever have you latch us onto the old Milton and Audrey milking machine? You're good-looking, but if I want poster pictures for my room, I can get a bit better at the mall for four bucks, I'm afraid I'd have to tell you. Paula Abdul. Hey, you know what we have here, baby, is a two-party deal. That's the sum of it. That's what makes it exciting. No third parties with a camera. Not a bad idea, though, I guess, pictures. Maybe next time I'll bring along the old Minolta. You know, with a tripod and that time-lapse button they have on them. Get shots they don't sell at the mall. Or these homegrown X videos, VHS. I'm kidding."

She stood up and went over to him. He was trying his silk tie in front of Milton's mirror. She stood behind him, off to one side.

She asked, "Hear anything from Seaman VanKleef's family?"

He smiled again. "Old news, Audrey. Old, old news. We all know none of Vor-Tech's products were ever implicated in that tragedy. I can't even give you credit for a nice try there, baby."

She tilted her head, raised her voice. "I don't know, it just seemed to me that Milton was always so much more concerned with quality control at the company, so much more than you were."

He said, "Fishing. Not close. No cigar. Sorry. Try again?"

She said, "The Marmasette girls?"

He shook his head. "No, I'm afraid not. What, with Milton? Seems to me that's an old try; I've heard that before from you, I believe. Wouldn't hurt me, even if true. Hurt *you* maybe, Milton's rep, not me. Look, Audrey, one of my daughters worships the devil, the two others worship anything in pants. If I were to decide to knock off everyone they've been involved with, it'd be full-time. I'd have to retire from Vor-Tech, which I don't want to do. Why, if I ever decided to track down the men the Marmasette daughters have been personally involved with, I'd have to travel throughout the country, abroad, parts of the Orient, parts of hell. No. This is nothing. Not like Ronnie."

"I don't know. It just seems to me, Felix, these are the type things—leads, they'd call them—that could keep Sergeant LaLuna busy for weeks, months."

"They probably would. So he'd keep busy; fine with me. He'd never get anywhere, certainly not to me. The main reason? I didn't kill anybody. I certainly didn't kill Milton. Look, this is such a waste, Audrey. We've already plumbed the depths of each of our sordid lives. We've got a deal, works fairly well for us, doesn't it? Can't we both just live with the contract, make both our lives a bit simpler, something we both really need at this point?"

Audrey didn't say it—I'm not the one keeps raising the stakes; you are.

"We all set then, baby?" he asked, looking in the mirror at her. "We OK on this business thing for Vor-Tech? I'll let you know the specifics. Painless."

She didn't answer him.

He said, "Audrey, you think of me like a monster, I know that, I know you do. Maybe you're right. Maybe I am. Maybe I was. But not the way I see it now, I am now. You know what I am, girl? I am just a man, a man trying to deal with his own mortality. Just like everybody else is, see? Self-centered? Sure, I guess so. Affection-starved, gluttonous, into self-gratification? Guilty. But I admit it, at least, and I play by the rules I've helped set up. That's not so bad, is it? Is it, Audrey?"

"Pig," she told him, "you get to me once every two months. That's the deal. Find yourself your own dates for the damned company picnics."

He let his shoulders rise and fall in a sign to her, him still looking in the mirror.

She had kept a handful of her Swedish cream. She wiped it now across the front of his white shirt and his blue dotted tie. He stood there taking it without flinching, like the fat one of Laurel and Hardy would have done.

He looked down at the smear and then reached for a handkerchief. "Hey, sweets, come on now, that's like a hundred dollars, what you did just there."

He pulled the wadded-up handkerchief across his shirtfront, making it worse, and he asked her, "So how's your brother Ronnie doing?"

Mogie was hurting all over.

He had to lean forward a bit off the hard back of the pew to ease the pain. Even with the black padding they had added over the curved wooden back, probably done just recently, it still hurt the sides of his ribs and his back if he put on any pressure at all. He dropped himself slow, down to the kneeler, put his face into the cup of his hands, pretended to pray, and thought to God about how much he just kept hurting.

Back at St. Fletcher's, maybe sixth grade, some big kids on the playground had held him down, run their bikes over him a couple of times. He hurt like that now—the same rancid and painful mix of shame and fear and bruises and frustration. Piss on that.

The Guinea cop'd been like that, in-crowd cool.

Mogie had heard himself squealing, had tried to cover himself up, tried to wrap himself in his own arms and shoulders, hunching, but it was either his head or his ribs left out exposed, and he had finally decided to let the ribs go, as the Guinea cop had used the refrigerator door on him too many times to count. Mogie didn't cry, through it all.

He was crying now, though. With his hands over his face there in the pew, touching skin only with the fingertips so the wounds wouldn't get pressed on, his ribs letting him breathe in only a little bit of air at a time—the worthlessness of who he was brought home by the cuts his tongue could feel inside his mouth—he cried in choking little sobs that he hoped nobody would notice.

You know, they did this to Jesus too.

But a song he had heard once answered that with "Yeah, but you're not Him."

Hail Mary, full of grace, the Lord is with thee.

He had almost cried there in the Jew lawyer's place too. Couldn't help it. The secretary sitting him down like she was used to dealing with scummy little guys who looked to be in the saddest of sad shape, crusted-over pain hanging all over them like manure. The shyster comes out with shirtsleeves folded up to look like Bobby Kennedy— they all of them wanted to look like Bobby Kennedy—telling him that the Guinea cop had checked himself into North Shore emergency. They had the report: facial lacerations, a tooth gone, maybe a chipped bone, X-rays weren't clear on that.

Resisting arrest, assault on an officer, battery. Mogie the cop-attacker. Assailant. *Hallowed be thy name.* No. *Hail Mary, full of grace, hallowed be thy name.* No. *The lord is with thee.* How many times had he said this? Probably more times than he had ever said anything else in his whole life. And he still didn't get it right? He was upset, that's why. Anybody would be. Jesus.

Shyster had kept Mogie hidden, in case anybody who was hot shit had walked into the office there, and the lawyer had given Mogie the plan without really saying it—forget it, cut your losses, fold up your tents, head off into the night.

Yeah, but my ribs, they still hurt me like an ax went into me there, Jew boy. I tried to brush my teeth this morning, I spit out red water still, God damn it. I still hurt all over.

The only *good* hurt he had was the knuckles and the side of his right hand. That rage had felt good, righteous, Jesus with the Money Changers kind of rage. He couldn't get her off her feet, though, she kept leaning against that damned off-white kitchen wall, not covering up in a shell, like he had tried to do with the Guinea cop, but instead just flailing at him with open palms, like swatting flies, really begging, even though her words were cursing him.

"Fuck, Jesus, Mogie, please! Fuck, Jesus, Mogie, please?"

And his hands came back to him red with somebody else's blood for a change.

He had looked at her quick as he was leaving out the door, after he had left her in the kitchen for a couple minutes, gone upstairs to get some sports jackets he had kept over there. Mom standing there still against the wall, hair matted wet red against her forehead—how can you cut up a forehead with just a punch?—her eyes swollen and looking for forgiveness, her nose running red and yellow.

He had one of the sports jackets on a wooden hanger. He got it all tangled up before he could rip the hanger free and fling it at her, missing, not by much, her not even bothering to try to get out of the way. Fuck you and your ugly, weird, corpse-screwing daughter too, lady.

Blessed art thou among women, and blessed is the fruit of thy womb.

Mogie sat back easy into the pew, stroked his eyes and nose with his handkerchief. He looked around at the coin-driven fake red electric candles, then he gazed up at the statue of Our Jesus on the Cross.

Now what to do?

Back at St. Fletcher's, the candles had been real, and the Stations of the Cross were carved into marble or stone, to come out of the walls at you, 3-D, instead of just cheap fucking latex paint, like these here.

Yeah, but now what?

His enemies would be punished in hell, don't worry about that part of it. Lawyer had struck the deal—get out, make a clean break. Stick the shyster-Jew-cock boy with his bill; he'd never see that money. Let him eat it. Serve him right; he won't go broke. Too busy shystering widows to chase Mogie out of state for a couple bucks. End of year, declare the loss, the Jew'd make out better *not* getting the money from Mogie.

The Guinea cop would be burned in hell for eternity, that's sure, and Mom's face was nice and all crushed up, just right. And Sharon, well, fuck her anyway—let her live with her stiffs and let her come home each night smelling like formaldehyde for the next fifty years of her hollow, stinking, wasted life. Her formaldehyde smell turning to booze smell each night, then into formaldehyde for good some year.

Yeah, sometimes it's best to just get out, leave it lie, start all over, clean sweep. Everybody learns that sometime, sooner or later. Only difference is, some people learn it, are still too dumb to act on it. Not Mogie.

Sometimes you hold 'em, sometimes you fold 'em, according to Kenny Rogers.

One thing's for sure, though. Steal a nice car to get out of town, drive it into the dirt. Maybe a town car, that what they call them now? BMW or something nice. Hard to do, although not impossible. Road cars. Mercedes. That's what the TV commercials called them now. Road cars. Christ, so what's everything else, then? Goddamn air cars? Ocean cars?

What's the little Jap import so hard to get? Two seats, big backlog of orders? Always red. Migotta? Milatta? No, too easy to spot; wouldn't make the Triborough Bridge before he'd see a blue light in the rearview mirror. "I hope you don't resist arrest, sir."

Maybe something classy, then. Quiet. Gray or black and big. Tan. No, cream-colored. A cream town car. New plates for every state you go through. Paint job over the Jersey line maybe. Powder blue. I wonder they still got powder blue for cars. Maybe two-tone, if they still got that too. Or vinyl on top.

That's it. Leave this jungle with a nice new town car. Put that baby on cruise control, climate control at seventy-two degrees, seventy-two miles an hour, drive it into the ground. Fuck the peasants.

Still hurt, though. Jesus.

Holy Mary, Mother of God, pray for us sinners, now and at the hour of our death, amen.

Leaving the church, Mogie did something he hadn't done since he was a little kid, him and Jason Droppo back at St. Fletcher's, Friday afternoon, after Stations.

Spit in the poor box.

All things happened for the best. In the long run they did, at least. Sometimes you couldn't see it just then, blinded by the immediate fog of your feelings and by the scrapings of damp and lonely emotions upon your skin, but looking back, years later, you could finally make yourself see that it had all been for the best. God knows.

Sharon's dad had died her junior year in high school. Emphysema mostly, with some other complications mixed in; two or three packs a day, Camels, unfiltered, thirty years of French inhaling, had finally done the job, managed to strangle Dad from the inside at last. And the loss of him had crushed Sharon entirely.

Dad, what about the driving lessons? You promised me. Mom can't, she's just not equipped. Especially with stick. You said you'd teach me stick. What about the prom? Remember you promised the boat ride, remember, a cruise?

But looking back, Sharon knew that the coin had two sides to it. She and her mom had finally gotten to know each other then, had come together to share, in his death, Dad's memory, instead of their angling and bickering and screaming for his time and his attention during his life. They had started out, and for years had remained, just "those two" or "you two"—Can't you two agree on anything, stop fighting over everything?—and in time they had become "the girls." Not "my girls"—he was dead and gone from them and always would be—but at least they were now "the girls," and they shared things, more than just the Saturday morning food-shopping trips. Many things. And they drove together to these many things in a Cadillac, Caddies which came only with automatic.

Sharon had fallen in love with Len Bixby her junior year in college—the only time that had happened. Then Len had left for his one-year mission, his ministry, somewhere in Southeast Asia. Indonesia? She couldn't remember the name of his church, but he said everyone was required to do it. And then, as far as she knew, he had never come back.

Dates to the movies had become kisses at the airport had become letters every week had become nothing. And as far as she knew, he had never, ever come back. She couldn't get up the courage to drive by his church, stop in, ask someone about him: What happened to Len Bixby, sir, does anybody know what happened to him? They probably wouldn't tell her much anyway. She had never gotten up the courage to go by where his family had rented that old gray house on Spruce Street. Someone had said they moved away a long time ago.

But that loss had led eventually to medical school. First it was just the College Boards, to keep from thinking about things too much, but you might as well do something with these scores now, these scores are very good, Sharon, and so Sharon had become Sharon Lucille Slabb, M.D., M.E.

Corpse-cutter, but still, wouldn't it be great to find out Len's address somewhere and write to him with an M.D. after her name?

So see, that had worked out too.

And this would work out too.

Sure it didn't seem like it now—too many horrible memories crowded too close together—but they'd fade. Slowly, they'd fade, all right.

It was the look on her mom's face—the shame and the anger and the disappointment—more than the puffiness and the discoloration, that Sharon had to deal with in her mind and in her memory just now. I'm not even playing in this game, Mom. I just go to work and come back home. Why me? Does this really have to do with me, your daughter?

This apartment could be nice. She could make it into something. They had done a professional job of painting it, covering right up to the natural woodwork around the windows, with no splotches or missed spots that she could see.

What she'd have to consider, though, once things got settled, a condo. Why lose all that rent; she knew that much. Even a girl who had never made a mortgage payment or paid a rent bill in her life knew that much. It was a sin, wasn't it, that a thirty-five-year-old Columbia graduate had never paid a bill other than some silly purchases that didn't matter, had never done a budget, never checked a utilities bill. It would be fun to learn.

Maybe Sprint would call her up, try to take her business away from AT&T. That's what happened to young single girls on television. Young single girls with gold cards and reservations at restaurants and laughing, hair-flinging faces of freedom. So it would all work out. Leave her old clothes at her house, her mom's house, and charge a whole new wardrobe. Who could help her with that? She'd need help there.

First, though, before the clothes, furniture.

She hadn't yet made much of a dent in furnishing this place. She was sitting in the kitchen, a white case of Seagram's V.O. as her chair, two more cases piled up as her kitchen table. That's it, so far. I love what you've done with the place, Sharon; do you know if Mr. Jim Beam is open to try his hand at doing my place sometime soon?

And kitchen utensils, she needed those badly. She had tried to cook an egg this morning, sunny side up, but halfway through didn't have a spatula, so had used a plastic fork on it. She had ended up half-frying, half-scrambling the damned thing, brown on the edges and messy all over. And the fork melted a tong. The egg tasted OK, but she'd need kitchen things and garbage pails and curtains, maybe shades. Get herself away from the feeling of camping out.

Get back to her place, somehow, and get the PS/2 and the printer. That was about all she needed from the old place. And buy a good stereo, with compact disk. Fifth Dimension and Karen Carpenter and Carly Simon disks. Yes, Garland too, if they were out on CD; she didn't know. Probably.

Sharon had gotten home that night, tired and ready for a drink, and her mother, her face unrecognizable, had flung open the door and screamed at her to get out of her house, and Mom had thrown a spring jacket at her and then nearly fallen over, bending and twisting at the knees and shoulders. A whole new level for Mom, way down below Blitzkrieg, or maybe it was Blitzkrieg after the blooding, Blitzkrieg from a bunker, fighting to hold on to her life, herself.

What horrible thing had happened, and why had it happened now? Her mother's face was swollen to twice its size, puffed into blue and purple and red and amber, abrasions and contusions, beaten about the head and shoulders by an easy-to-figure-out-who assailant. And tears and snot and blood and "Get out of my house and don't come back. He's gone, he's gone, he's left."

"Mom, who's gone? Mogie's gone? What did he say? He did this? What happened, Mom? I've got to get you to the hospital. Sit down, sit down. Breathe. Try to breathe, Mom."

"Do you hear me?" her mother had said, like a mother with a kid in a store who was grabbing a toy and wouldn't let go, and her mom had kicked at her then, holding on to the knob at the bottom of the stair railing as her foot lashed out at her one child.

Her mom would ask her to come back, naturally. A month, a week, Mom'd call and talk to her awhile and tell her about the neighbors and some strange dog that's been going potty on her lawn, and then she'd ask her back. Tired of shopping by herself, eating by herself, watching TV and drinking by herself, she'd realize what she had done to her innocent daughter, and she would ask her back, beg if she had to.

Tough shit. Sharon wasn't going back anywhere. Sitting here on her whiskey-carton kitchen set, Sharon condemned her mother to a lifetime of singles Monopoly and Uno-99 games, and getting done with videos only to turn to an empty chair to talk about the show as it rewound in the machine.

Sharon sighed twice, letting her shoulders rise and fall like a shell she was wearing. She got up, walked to look out the kitchen window, looked at the spot on the wall where the phone would hang, looked into the other room, then sat back down.

She used her nails to rip open the top half of her kitchen table, even though it was still only 10:00 A.M.

Y ou remember *Mary Poppins?*" LaLuna was asking Audie, taking little side looks at her there on the bench. "Didn't I take you to see that, back when first it came out?"

She told him no, she didn't think so. She remembered it, but only on television.

"Yeah, I'm sure, I think I did," he said. "I remember sneaking in, looking around, making sure nobody I knew was around, seeing me going into the movie house to see *Mary Poppins*. Could've been big trouble for me, my circle of friends back then. I think so. You were with me. It was the Beacon in Port, I think, even."

"You know, we went to see *Hud* together, though," she said. "That was good."

"Oh, yeah, great movie, great movie," he agreed. "Paul Newman, he had so many great lines in that movie." He looked up and said, "I don't remember any of them, though. One was something about dying, or getting out of life. But I just don't remember."

They were sitting on a bench in front of a stream that neither of them had known was there. LaLuna held a little stick he had picked up.

"You happen to know if Myron Cohen is still alive?" he asked her.

"Who?" she asked.

"Myron Cohen, the little Jewish guy, tells stories, used to be on Ed Sullivan all the time, raised up one eyebrow when he talked?

Somebody told me he wasn't alive anymore. I just wondered about it."

She said she didn't know, and she looked at the water. It wasn't much, but it had a current and it made a constant and gentle noise for them.

They had started out the afternoon at her house, seated properly in Audie's oversimplified living room, LaLuna going over stuff with her again, trying to dig out something, anything. For over an hour, maybe an hour and a half. Hashing and rehashing all the stuff, trying not to get her annoyed or bored or upset. Just keeping her calm as he was probing and looking for anything at all. It was all getting so old, he knew that.

She had asked him what was new on it, and he had answered along the lines of the guy he kept calling "your boyfriend Chet." Or sometimes "Chester." She kept shaking her head at that, kept telling him that Chester should be cleared off his list, it was just ridiculous.

"We've been looking into him," he told her, "running some background checks, stuff. Trying for an insulin connection, or at least some sort of a medical tie-in, needles, syringes, anything at all."

"You won't get anything, Joe," she told him. "You knew Chet, you'd know. Leave him alone, for everybody's sake. It's not him. He's not involved, except with me. Leave him be."

"Why not? I keep thinking that way, cop's instinct. We're close to some drug connections with the guy, minor stuff for certain, I admit, but it could tie in. An Article Fifteen in the service, drug connected. Who knows where that might lead. He's got some seedy associates too, through the years. Maybe you don't know these things about him. This isn't a crusade, Audrey, a witch hunt; it's a good, solid homicide investigation, boring as it is."

"Joe, what are you finding—that Chet did some blow in the army years ago, for Christ sake? Joe, I told you a hundred times, I did coke, Milton did a lot of coke and stuff. Shit, the dope connection makes me out a better suspect than Chet ever is. Check *me* out, Joe, not him."

"We do. Don't worry, we do."

Audie had gotten up, put out her cigarette, gone to a desk, opened a drawer, looked through some papers there.

"He's cold, this guy," LaLuna went on. "I've talked to him."

"Cold, you said? Why?"

"OK, you know the story, this guy Don Slayton?" Audrey looked at him from the papers in her hand, shook her head. LaLuna said, "Slayton was a guy Chester brought in from California, got him a nice job, charged him the fee for it."

"That's what he does. And?" she asked.

"And two weeks on the job, something doesn't work out, the guy's dumped. That's all right, that happens. Then the guy's wife comes down with cancer, they're off the medical, all of a sudden they're hurting. Well, your Chester not only doesn't let him off the hook for the fee, something like two months, six months salary, which he's not getting anyway, and not only does Chester take them to court, but he *enjoys* it. Talked to Slayton, told me wonking Chester *enjoyed* the whole thing. Guy had to sell his house."

"That's business, Joe. Yeah, I said business. And I know Chet has legal outs for the client when the job doesn't work out. I don't know what happened there, but I bet you didn't get Chet's version. You talk about him like—look, he doesn't enjoy kicking women and kids out on the street, Joe, honestly."

"Oh, no? You know he owns the Linda Arms?"

"The what?"

"Linda Arms, fleabag motel, guy's a slumlord. I've also heard when there's a woman owing rent, he collects with his pants down, makes the kids stay out in the living room watching TV, he collects."

Audrey grinned. "Yeah, he did tell me about that."

Joe said, "He *told* you? See? He tells you about that?"

"Joe, sometimes he does stuff to, I don't know, he thinks he's punishing me, he's punishing himself. We laugh about it."

"Yeah, g'head, Audie, laugh about it. You gotta feel sorry for the guy, he punishes himself so much, collects rent in the bedroom, tells his woman about it."

"Ow, I'm his woman."

"He ever hit you?"

"No."

"A slow no, right there. Too slow."

"We both got drunk one time, went at each other. Hey, I gave as good as I got."

"Yeah, so you're saying the guy's mean, he just ain't tough."

"Joe, get off it, please, a rest? Just because Chet doesn't fulfill your ideals of Italian-American manhood."

LaLuna hesitated, stopped, finally said, "I'm sorry, Audrey, I just can't get out of my head this guy killed your husband. I bet anything on it. I'll prove it soon, I hope."

"Why?" Audie asked him. "Why would he?"

"For you, I tell you." LaLuna smiled, trying to show her it was the most natural thing in the world. "He wants you, your husband was in the way. That could be, huh?"

"Joe, he already *had* me. He had me all he wanted to. He and I often, if not always, young man, spent our time together—what's the term of endearment you cops are using for it now?—wonking each other?"

"Yeah, right. But listen, a guy like that, he figures, I have what I want sure, but not entirely, though. Guys want somebody, they want them entirely."

"He hasn't exactly been around dangling a wedding band in front of the widow, you know, if that's what you mean. Matter of fact, he hasn't been around much at all."

"Give him some time. What are you looking for there anyway, with those papers?"

"Nothing important. And where do you fit Chet in with the pictures somebody's taking of me?"

"Maybe he took them. Maybe it's him."

"Joe, he's been out of town, out of the state. I've been telling you that."

"Yeah, he's been telling you that. Very easy to fake that too, of course. Very easy to do."

"Why, Joe? He wants any pictures of me, I'd give them to him, he just asks. He doesn't have to sneak around with a telescopic lens or something."

"Audie, remember that thrill I got, I told you about, following you around that day without you knowing? Biggest thrill of my life. It's disgusting probably, but I got a thrill off it. Well, maybe he gets the same thrill taking candids of you. Who knows. Christ, maybe he's a psycho. Stranger things than that I've come across. A lot worse. Aw, hell, who knows, maybe we're all psychos, we're all a bunch of psychos taking secret pictures of each other. I don't know."

"You act like one sometimes, Joe, I swear you do. For what people tell me is a good cop, you sure are going one way, the wrong way, on this."

"I been carrying these wonderful thoughts of you with me for years now."

She said, "That has to turn out bad. That'll disappoint you every time. Joe, this would be real nice if we could be sophomores again, sure. But, Joe, you know what I am? All I am is a middle-aged woman, still looking for a morality. Any morality. To live by. You have yours, Joe, but I don't have one. You follow? I'd love to love you, Joe; I can't. Joe, can you tell me, what do I live by?"

"I don't know. By the beach?"

"Yeah, funny." Again she started shuffling the pack of papers she had taken out of the drawer, looking quickly at each one.

"Hey, I'm sorry," LaLuna told her. "Look, anyway, we've been trying to trace the film roll I found. They got little serial numbers on them mean dates, but it's just about impossible. I have to admit, though, even though what I said before, your boy's business trip does seem to check out."

"You checked that?"

"Yeah, we did. We've checked a lot of stuff. Hey, come on, what's with the papers there? You looking for something particular, or not?"

"They were lousy pictures anyway. It's just my Midas guarantee I'm searching for," she said. "My Volvo's been sounding like a truck. I think it might be the muffler, the tailpipe, but I know Milton had it done, maybe a year or so ago."

LaLuna offered to take a look under the Volvo. They went out to the driveway, he put one gray pants leg to the blacktop. He looked back up and told her he spotted what looked like a small hole right where the pipe went into the front of one of the mufflers. On the driver's side. He told her, start it up. She did, and that seemed to be the case, all right. LaLuna offered to come along with her, down to Midas, since he wanted to keep talking to her.

"You're not too busy? On the clock now, remember."

He told her he was never too busy.

At a light about a block away from Midas, she asked him to reach onto the back seat, get her handbag, get her shades out for her. As he did, she touched the bruises on his face, gently, and asked about them again. He had told her once, now he told her again that he had gotten his face caught in a refrigerator door, and he just laughed it off.

"New kind of diet?" she asked.

Wink had laughed at his bruises too, when he first saw the damage done. He had heard about it already, around the Room, before LaLuna came back.

"*No más, no más,*" Wink had called out, trying to hold up his mitts like Roberto Duran. "*No más,*" he echoed himself, checking out the other detectives.

Audie had looked sad at the stoplight, as if the damage on his face meant something to him, as if it bothered him. Which it didn't.

Midas took them right in, that was nice, but the work took a little longer than they thought. Maybe because a foreign muffler. LaLuna used the phone, checked in. After they'd hit the coffeepot there in the waiting room, been through most of the magazines that were new enough to look through, they took a walk. He couldn't talk to her in the waiting room, so he suggested the walk.

He led her out around the big yellow-and-brown garage, saw a footpath beaten into the weeds down over a little bank, and they took it on down, just to see where it went.

They found the little stream at the bottom, and even a bench there to sit on. Probably put there by the Midas folks, trying to treat their customers right.

Nice day, nice look to the surface of the water.

LaLuna thought he might know this stream. It was a little gully-filling run of water with no name to it that he knew. But he thought it might be the same stream that they used to go down to and drink beer, back when they were in high school. The boys and him. Not right here, but a leveled-off spot along the stream, closer toward the stores. No reason they had chosen that place, just a place like any other, except that if you had beer somebody had got for you, the water's edge was where you went to drink it. Friday, Saturday nights, somebody would be there to help you share it.

LaLuna bet it was the same stream they were looking at now,

maybe a couple miles upriver. He didn't mention it to Audie; he
didn't think she was ever there back then. She touched his face again,
the bruises, and they started talking about the movies they had been
to together, those years back. Maybe *Mary Poppins* and definitely
Hud.

Then, he didn't know why, he said to her, "Sometimes I think you
maybe did kill him, Audie, killed him so that I'd come out to your
place."

She answered, "Maybe you always thought a little too much of
yourself, Joe. Maybe, huh?"

He said, "No. Maybe I always thought a little too much of you,
though. I know I been doing that now. Lately."

She waited awhile, like counting beats, and then she said, "We're
different people now, Joe, right? We've covered that already? You
know that. I told you. Remember Mr. Kilko, in biology, what he
taught us? Every seven years the body completely replaces all its
cells. So we're different from what we used to be, completely different, what, four times over? Four times seven?"

"I never had Kilko," LaLuna said. "I don't know who I had for
bio. I think I took it, I guess I had to, but I don't remember that stuff
too well. But anyway, what I wanted to say, no, we're not so different.
We're not so different at all, really, hey."

Audie smiled at him. "So where's your sideburns, Joe? Where's
your corduroy jacket, then, huh?"

LaLuna smiled too. "Well, maybe I still got them. At home somewhere."

Audie said, "And maybe *you* killed him. So that you could come
over my house and play."

LaLuna said, "Maybe I did."

The Volvo was finished when they got back up the bank. New
pipes, muffler was OK, all on guarantee except a couple bucks for
labor. She thanked the guy in the brown hat, she thanked LaLuna for
coming along with her to get it done.

As Audie was waiting to pull out into traffic, he asked her, "You
still got that ring?"

She looked at him. She didn't understand.

"It was a big blue ring," he explained to her, pointing to his own hand, "I gave you back then. Something they'd call onyx or something, something like that. Big, big ugly thing. Blue with swirls of yellow or white in the stone of it, I think. Looked like Indians would have made it or something. I was just wondering."

She put the Volvo into park, even though she was right there at the entrance to Midas. "Joe," she told him, "I'm sorry. I don't even remember any ring."

"Don't matter, don't matter," he assured her, waving a hand. "That's OK. I probably spent about under a buck on it anyway, it was nothing. It's just one of the crazy things you think about. When you're thinking."

"Joe," she said, "I'm sorry. Joe, I swear, now you look even sadder than usual. I should've lied to you about it, God damn it."

He got an idea then.

"OK, look," he told her, "I'm gonna prove you something. C'mon, I want to show you something. You got a little more time? For me?"

She said she did, she had all day.

"Pull out here, then," he told her. "Right. Stay to the right. I've got something to show you."

Twenty-five minutes later, she pulled the Volvo up to a faded clapboard house that LaLuna knew she didn't recognize.

"It's my uncle's," he told her. "Used to be. Here, park in the driveway, or else on the lawn, it's all right. Nobody's home. C'mon around back. I'm gonna show you something now."

In the backyard, a twenty-by-fifty of yellow weeds and small stumps and abandoned swing sets, there were four junker vehicles. The weeds had grown up around their bumpers and axles, dead leaves on the hoods. Their windshields were all gone, and you got a nesting feeling about the interiors, like these were nature's vehicles now.

LaLuna took Audie over to the skeleton of a red truck in the back corner of the yard, under a dogwood. He had her stand there, looking at it. A Chevy.

After a while, her eyebrows came down a bit, gave her face some expression, like she was getting it.

"Can you read the door?" he asked her.

"No," she said. "Can't make it out."

"Yeah," he told her. He brushed the door with his palm a little bit. "Yeah. There. Right there on the door."

She started to smile. "I still can't make it out, but LaLuna-Lawns?" she asked him.

"Hey," he said, "LaLuna-Lawns."

"Oh, God," she told him, "oh, God. You know, I still root for the football Giants."

He told her she'd damn well better, and they smiled about things awhile, looked over the truck. Then they stopped and there wasn't much else to say about it. So LaLuna went over to the bed of the truck, put his hand on the corner, feeling dark-red paint flaking, and he asked Audrey McKenna there, "You care to climb in?"

She told him she didn't think so. She didn't think so.

"See?" he asked her. "What do you think? Pretty good shape for something hasn't run in twenty years maybe? This could be a timeless classic."

She said yeah.

"You sure you don't want to climb in?"

"No, I'm sure," she told him. "We'd cave through. But let's go back to my house; that'd be OK with me." She said that. It'd be OK with her.

Talk was tough on the ride back. It seemed a long time, and the Volvo, its conditioner on, closed them in. He tried to make talk about his job, all the years and cases he'd been on. He thought he might be whining, getting annoying, so he just shut the hell up about it.

In her bedroom, she came to within an arm's length of him and she said, "Unbutton my shirt, Joe. You still like your job?"

He started with the buttons, fumbling some; it had been a while. She helped him out.

"Sometimes I like it," he said, looking at the buttons, at nothing else. "I used to. I used to a lot. But sometimes now there's just too many people dying. Just too many."

"That should make you feel better, though," she told him. "I mean, the fact that you help. Help people from getting killed. What would we be like without cops, without Homicide?"

"No, I don't help," he said. He kissed a button as it came open. "I don't stop anything. I just get some of the people locked up who killed other people. I don't have anything to do with stopping any of it, or slowing any of it down, even. Besides, you've seen firsthand the kind of job we do, on this case for your husband. Nothing."

Her shirt was open, and so he was telling her how beautiful she was, had been for so many years. God, oh me.

The next half hour was just a glittering fog of working angles, planning and working hungry angles for the limbs and flesh of them, like the perfect pool game where all the balls and all the sticks were covered in sweet-smelling velvet, and juiced up with about ten thousand volts of blood-soaked electricity, the balls and sticks rubbing their way across the top of the felt that covered the hard slate of the table.

And any good pool shooter plans ahead, got to—three, four shots—so that's what LaLuna tried to do, but most of the time the ecstasy of their bare-assed dance just took him over, creamed him and bathed his brain, so that he couldn't think of anything at all, except, Hang on, Pancho, just hang on.

And when he wasn't whispering to her, he was talking to no one, but still saying a couple of million times through clenched teeth, "Worth it, loves, the wait." Thirty years for thirty minutes, and worth every second of it.

Better yet, better still than all the think time that had gone before it, the thirty years of daydreams and night dreams that had put the two of them together, dreams of the two of them locked together, nudes on a staircase, phantom-locked bodies in the dunes at West End Beach, the two of them locked together at his house, at her house, in cars, trucks front and back, airplanes, in covered wagons while Indians were attacking, in prison camps and Jell-O-filled swimming pools, standing up, sitting on moss, propped up on a urinal, under a desk, in the monkey house at midnight, between innings in the dugout, in space suits, shower stalls, jockstraps, bolo vests, and silk.

And better, sweet Audrey, for real this time, better than all of that because you are, my love.

After, she had gotten another shirt out of her closet, pulled on some jeans; she went over to her little table there, and she started putting on some white face cream. She pulled her head back to get the stuff on her neck, get it on even and smooth, and LaLuna wanted to start up all over again. He didn't, though, because he didn't want to scare her off. He was still in her bed.

"Joe, I've got to give you a theoretical," she said to him, looking at him in the mirror. "Please."

"A what?"

"Something in theory," she said. "Suppose I need help with something. Somewhere back there, when we were going good, I was screaming that I need you, and suppose now I really do?"

"For what? For love again?" He pulled his mouth down, using the look that said: Not bad, not a bad idea.

"No," she told him. "Well, yeah, that too sometime, but I've been having trouble since Milton died, with something, somebody else."

"Chester, that cocksucker?" he asked her.

"No," she said. "Just forget Chet, please, Joe. He's for me. He always has been. He's on my side."

"Audrey, your side in what?"

"My side in everything."

"What, then? Who we talking about?"

"Someone else. Something else. It's a legal thing. It's pretty bad. It's my family."

"What?" he asked, propped up in bed like her husband had been, two weeks ago, his lifeless head against her headboard. "What?" LaLuna asked her.

She told him to forget it. She came over and sat beside him, put her hands on his shoulders, moaned sort of, and rotated his shoulders, first left, then right, left, right, shaking him in rhythm. He started a motorboat sound in his throat that vibrated with her moving his shoulders.

She came at him again, and then he lifted her, all of her, knees down, onto his bare and breathing chest, and he closed his eyes and opened his mouth and he waited. Waited for whatever fabulous favor she would grant him next.

The phone rang. He was closer, so he quietly picked it up, gave it over to her, still kneeling.

She said hello, listened a second, then gave him back the receiver. He didn't like this.

The phone said, "Joe? Hraska. Yeah, listen, I thought you might be there. Listen, I don't know how to say this. Listen, they just found Lou Duva, dead."

TWENTY ONE

Pearley was back from loony leave—his daughter hadn't painted her body in a little over a month—and he decided they should take the ten-eight call on LaLuna's wife being down.

Actually, it wasn't their call at all. They hadn't acknowledged it, and they weren't even near the ten-nine location. But Pearley kept hearing the squawks, squawks ElRay could barely make out—he was still so bad on the box it wasn't funny—and Pearley had finally sniffed twice and told him, "Kiddo, something's happening here. Hold on a minute."

Pearley had driven the cruiser over to a call box on DePlains, used it a few minutes, climbed back into the cruiser, and told ElRay about LaLuna's wife being found dead. "Let's you, me go see," Pearley told him, pulling out.

"Backup needed?" ElRay asked him, feeling dumb.

The nice thing about Pearley—it was grand to have him back on the job, it really was—was that he never made you feel quite as dumb as he could. He'd make you feel dumb, all right, but you always knew that if he wanted to, he *could* make you feel ten times dumber than he did.

"No, kid," Pearley said, "we're not needed, by any means. But we'll go do some rubbernecking, what do you say? Everybody'll be over there. You want everybody else get back, be talking about this thing, you, me feeling like an asshole about it, not know what's going on? C'mon, we'll go over there."

Pearley read his look and told him, "Hey, don't worry about it. Everybody'll be too busy, too interested, to bother with us, try to throw us back to the street. We'll skip a winding this time around, don't matter to nobody. Patrol's patrol, but everybody'll be there."

Pearley either knew where LaLuna lived or he had gotten it from somebody on the phone. On the drive over, Pearley started telling him that this should be good, 'cause everybody'd been talking how LaLuna'd been wonking a babe on one of his cases.

"I worked a homicide with him when you were gone," ElRay told him. "A guy dead in bed up on Money Hill."

"That's the one," Pearley yelled. "That's the one he's been supposedly wonking."

"God, really?" ElRay asked. "There seemed to be something funny going on even then, I thought."

"Yeah, I'm sure," Pearley told him, flipping on the top light. "Funny is right."

Pearley was right. Everybody in the whole damn department, guys not even on duty, plus people ElRay had never seen before, were crawling all over the neat little Cape with the big bay window. A few blues were trying to look busy. Most were just gossiping facts or telling stories. Somebody said that LaLuna was upstairs, but nobody they talked to had seen him yet. Everybody wondered how the guy was reacting.

A guy in a tweed coat that ElRay didn't know was standing right on the flowers on the front lawn, drinking coffee. ElRay felt like a grave robber and told Pearley to fuck this, let's get going.

Pearley wanted to know what was wrong.

"C'mon," ElRay said. "Hey, Pearley, this is a cop, one of our own here."

"Aww, shit," Pearly answered by way of explanation. They hung around a couple of hours.

The body was already covered in white, so they didn't get to see much there. Instead, they talked to Jock Dugan about it. He said he had been the first on the scene, but you couldn't really trust that, not with Dugan.

Dugan told Pearley that LaLuna's old lady, who really *was* as ugly as everybody said she was, had been found there at the foot of the stairs in a white kind of housedress-robe.

An ice cream man, one of these guys buys his own truck and makes home deliveries with a million different ice cream sandwiches and stuff, had found her, late afternoon. He came by there every second Thursday, standing order, but she changed a few items each time. She was always there, always home, sickly. So this time she didn't answer the door, the guy figured she was in the shower or something, so he went on in. He'd done it before. Had to find out what she wanted that week.

"Well, he found her, all right," Dugan said to Pearley. "Dead on the rug."

Pearley went over and shot the shit with the ice cream guy awhile, unofficially, came back and reported stuff to ElRay, and then asked him, "You don't think this ice cream guy was wanging her, huh? Both of them just too ugly, don't you think? Imagine the resulting offspring of a union like *that*."

ElRay turned away from him, and Pearley told him to loosen up, live longer.

Dugan came back by them, and he stood next to Pearley. Dugan wanted to talk some more about it, be the spigothead of information for a while. He told Pearly, "You should have seen how the body was lying there, though. Like she was doing the damned lambada, the forbidden dance, before she keeled over. I hope they got shots of that. Wasn't a pretty sight, no matter how you looked at her, you know? Dead or alive, a dog. Had an old picture of the football Giants right there with her. Somebody said she was planning to give it to her man. He's a fanatic on the old Giants."

ElRay asked him, "Were there any bruises you saw on her, around the head or anything?"

"What the hell you talking about?" Dugan asked him, loud. "I look like Joe Medical Exam, for Christ sake?"

ElRay kept quiet. Pearley said, "Hey, hey, Jocko, you know what a fucking bruise looks like?"

Dugan said, "Yeah, I know."

Pearley said, "You have seen bruises some, during your long and fine career on the force, right?"

Dugan said, "Yeah, I seen bruises."

Pearley stepped closer to him and said, "All the boy's asking you,

you seen any bruises on the stiff, that's all. You being the reporting uniform, first on the scene, huh?"

Dugan said, "I already told him I didn't see any, didn't I? Didn't I tell him that already?"

Pearley said, "Well, that's all. That's easy, then, isn't it?"

The partners moved on, talking to other people here and there, uniforms, suits. A few knew something, most would just bullshit or recite lines. Nobody knew about any marks on the body; Pearley never asked ElRay why he was interested. They found out there had been no forced entry, nothing robbed, it looked like; suspicion was just a natural death, that's all.

"I'll tell you the interesting thing to come," Pearley told ElRay when they were standing alone, back by their cruiser. "Who does Sheeney give it to? Huh? If it's a case? You can't do it normally. Hraska got the call—that's his partner, right? So who does Sheeney put on it, huh? I mean, everybody's got implications with LaLuna, so do you go out of town, or do you give it to someone knows the guy? Fascinating? Lookit Hraska there. Lookit wonking little Winky Dink there, running around."

Hraska, all five feet couple inches of him, was overseeing the meat wagon boys coming out of the house, pointing at something, then looking around for something else to do.

"Hraska, huh? Fucking Kojak or something, he thinks," Pearley said. "Big cheese pizza, trying to run the show. That won't last long. Sheeney will get his greasy ass the hell out of there. No partners allowed."

ElRay asked, "What's the story with that guy? He's kind of creepy. I noticed that when we were doing the Money Hill guy."

"Yeah, kind of creepy's a good word for Winky Dink—he's that, all right, and more. He's a weird one, that's for sure. Don't pass out drunk around that guy, you'll wake up with a hose up your ass so fast it's not funny. You heard about that, right? What he does? Those little fish monkeys in your system, all swimming around?"

ElRay just looked at the street, figured this was one of those conversations beyond questioning.

Pearley went on. "My wife and his wife, they used to pal around a little bit, back before mine took the big swim and his took off north.

Funny, she said she never talked about him, not even bitching and moaning about stuff, you know, like he'd use the electric razor over his fried eggs in the morning, little beard bits falling in like pepper. I mean, every wife bitches about everyday stuff like that, right? But not Mrs. Winky Dink. Nothing. Of course, then she up and left him, no trace, which is weird too. Smart, though, don't let him fool you. Won't ever get anywheres beyond where he is, because he's got a personality like Don Rickles on steroids, but without the laughs, big wonking mouth on the guy, but still, he's done all right for himself, detective sergeant, but that, of course, is because of LaLuna being his rabbi. Dwarfs with bad personalities, they don't go too far by themselves. But he's had LaLuna, good-looking guy, gets along well. Who knows what this will bring now, though. Who knows, maybe now he'll marry the guy. Retire, live happily ever after."

ElRay asked, "His rabbi? What do you mean—what's that?"

Pearley looked at him like he'd just asked who Martin Luther King was. Pearley said, "Kid, at times you amaze and disappoint your old pard here. You been on the job what, almost a year now?"

"Almost seven months, counting the academy."

"Yeah, seven wonking months, counting the academy, and you don't know how rabbis work yet? Kid, you and me both know you're an ambitious son of a bitch, which I think is great, just fine with me. There's nothing I'd like better to see twenty years from now, me retired, all my kids finally locked up somewheres safe, than for you, for me to turn on the news and see the broad there saying something about Chief of Police ElRay J. O'Keefe, the first black chief of color in the history of the department, told reporters today, blah, blah, blah. I'd be proud to know you then, proud to tell whoever it happens to be there drinking with me there in front of the TV screen that I was the one got you started, I showed the kid how to wash off his rainbow stripes and dry his ears."

"All right, Dad, you know me, I *do* want to get ahead. So I'm all ears—tell me about rabbis."

"Rabbis, kid, are the only way anybody gets up and ahead in this man's police force. What do *you* think—affirmative action's gonna do the trick for you? That stuff's dead, buddy. You better grab yourself a rabbi, quick. I can't believe I haven't told you this yet. It's my kid's fault. If she hadn't started climbing trees, makes me go on loony leave all the time, I would have covered all this already for you. Those were valuable weeks lost in the career of Patrolman O'Keefe. I hope it doesn't stand in the way of you being Chief O'Keefe. Uh-oh, there's another problem, kid. Chief O'Keefe, it sounds dumb, right? Rhymes too much, don't you think? You might have to consider a change. I don't know what a shiner-man like you is doing with an Irishman's name anyway. Why don't you take a President's name, like all the other blood guys do?"

"Kennedy maybe?"

The gurney carrying the body, bagged now, rolled past them. ElRay wondered what LaLuna was doing.

"No," Pearley said. "Maybe Jackson or Jefferson. What's with you and Irishmen? You black Irish?"

"That's a good one, Pearley; never heard that before, about black Irish? Write it down for me? Pearley, I'll tell you, I've lost interest and I'm starting to go to sleep here. Let's roll, there's nothing to do here. Let's go make a wind, go get something to eat."

"Wait, hold on. I ain't told you yet what a rabbi is yet."

"I've lost interest. I'll just struggle on without that knowledge."

"Oh, no you won't. Can't be done. You see, the reason you don't miss it, you've had a rabbi in your career so far, son, and it's been me. Trouble is, you got a rabbi dresses in blue, got more black marks in his file than Himmler. Going nowhere. Which means you gotta latch onto someone new, you want to get anywhere at all. What you gotta do, my boy, is get yourself a rabbi, high up, and then just keep kissing ass until your lips bleed. I'll miss you, my son; go ye forward in peace and prosperity."

"Pearley, here's an idea," ElRay said, only half joking. "How about getting ahead by hard work and dedication and a shitload of citations for bravery and duty and stuff?"

"Oh, yeah, and a buck gets you a Lotto. Listen, home fry, ain't nobody on this job, or ain't nobody in this world for that matter, ain't at least just a little bit tainted. That's why you need a rabbi. Look, see Sheeney is LaLuna's rabbi, huh? Been that way for years. This death turns out suspicious—I'm sure it won't, the wife's been sick for years—but if it does, Sheeney has to decide if LaLuna keeps riding, all the way to Major Crimes after Sheeney retires, or if it's time the rabbi cuts him loose, see? It'll be very interesting."

"Yeah," ElRay said. "Nobody ever said this job wouldn't be that."

Pearley took them back inside LaLuna's house then, so he could make fun of the chalk outline. A guy from Crime Lab was there doing a schematic plat of the downstairs. Pearley mocked the guy's artistic style. Pearley did all this quietly, of course. After all, the husband was still upstairs somewhere.

With only a half hour left on the shift, ElRay finally got Pearley into the cruiser and out of there. As they were driving back to punch out, ElRay asked Pearley who had been *his* rabbi, back when he was young.

"You shitting me now?" Pearley looked away from the traffic to ask him. "Shitting? Now who the hell in his right mind would want to be a rabbi to a guy like me? I know *I* sure as hell wouldn't. Would you?"

ElRay said no.

Since she had left her mother's place, Sharon had successfully furnished the apartment, set up a Yamaha stereo system with one hundred watts per channel, gotten delivery on a brand-new kitchen set from Bill's House of Kitchens and Bath, and drank up her entire former kitchen set.

It was late, after a long day. She was eating bratwurst for the third time that week when the phone rang. Her mother had hated bratwurst.

This could be her mother's ring this time. Sharon thought it could be, might be, each time the phone rang, but it never was. Maybe this time, though. In reality, it probably was somebody asking for Mr. Anthony. People kept calling her up here, asking to speak to Mr. Anthony, who was someone she didn't even know. He must have been the one who had this number before her.

Fourth ring, bratwurst swallowed, she picked up the receiver. It wasn't her mom, and it wasn't someone for Mr. Anthony, and she didn't recognize the voice even for a moment after it told her, "Sharon, this is Audrey Wright."

Sharon didn't know what to answer, said, "Oh, it is."

Audrey's voice said, "Listen, I was thinking about you. Then I saw Ma Rothe's in town. Isn't that great?"

"Who?"

"Ma Rothe—you know, Mamma Rothe. Remember, you drove me home, you said how much you liked her singing?"

"I'm afraid I don't know her."

"You don't? You sure? I thought I heard. Anyway, though, she does a lot of Judy Garland. Now, you did tell me Judy Garland, right?"

"Right, that's true, I do."

"Oh, so, great. Listen, I have tickets. Ma Rothe's at a place in Queens, little place. I've got two tickets. Come on?"

"Us?"

"What? Us? Sure, that's what I'm saying. C'mon, it'll be fun."

"Well, tomorrow I'm working."

"Well, that's tomorrow. Tomorrow I'm flying to Niagara Falls. That's all right, Ma won't mind."

It wasn't that much later, with Sharon still wondering, when she heard Audrey there at her door. Sharon was still fumbling around, looking for a decent sweater to wear over. Had just finished a shower and her hair. She got into Audrey's Volvo, Audrey told her she was looking just great.

But it was Audrey herself looking great. With a big white bulky sweater, probably wool, high neck, hair pulled back, little white earrings showing. She said she was going to Niagara Falls tomorrow to see a friend's photography exhibit.

On the ride, neither of them mentioned Joe, or his wife, but the fact of it was riding with them there in the car. What do you say? Sharon tried to talk about her job, her boss. Audrey asked about her mom. Sharon didn't answer.

They had driven around Queens for almost an hour, looking for the place, finally found it. The Arabi, looked like just a small bar on an old, busy street corner. Venetian blinds behind a beer sign, aluminum siding and torn awning for a front. An old-fashioned, stand-up sign on the sidewalk said, "Blues Lady Tonite Ma Rothe."

Cover charge was ten bucks at the door; a woman in a black leather jacket and a white face took it from Audrey.

"You had tickets," Sharon said, looking around.

"That's just to get you to come. Come on, you'll love her, live she's just great. You have any albums?"

"I don't know her."

"Put the money away—I've got it, silly. Remember, I'm taking you."

Inside was small, dark, smoky, tiny wrought-iron chairs around tabletops the size of a pizza, different levels of floor surrounding a round stage covered in a pure white light. Two black men in black pants, white shirts open at the collar, onstage playing a piano and a bass, looking a bit bored.

Sharon stood at the entrance, let her eyes get used to the dark, said, "There's all women."

Audrey laughed and said, "Girls' night out. Most men are goons, don't appreciate Mamma's work, no way, no how."

Sharon looked at her, doubtful, confused.

"There's guys, if you need them, there, see?" Audrey said, pointing with her elbow. "And the two musicians, right? They look like men to me. They're packing."

Audrey found a table for them.

Audrey ordered an old-fashioned, Sharon tried to go with a white wine. Audrey scolded her with an "Oh, come on now" look, so they made it two old-fashioneds. Sharon's nerves made her laugh to herself; it came out too loud; she said excuse me.

Almost through the third round of drinks, white light onstage turned icy red, a voice like a ringmaster's filled up the place, said, "Friends, lovers, lovers of the blues, Careno's Arabi Lounge proudly presents Miss Lady Blues herself, Ms. Ma Rothe!"

Applause, calls of "Ma, hey, Ma," a few women whistling like men, a beautiful black lady in a sequined black dress came onstage smiling wide, holding on to a wireless mike. Her lips were incredibly red, a diamond-studded hairband curled from one ear to the other. The piano and bass backed off, and Ma Rothe sang.

During the first song, second chorus, Audrey beckoned Sharon to lean over. Audrey's lips grazed Sharon's ear, said, "How old's she look?"

Sharon shrugged.

The lips came forward again. "Fifty. Can you believe it? Fifty, someone said."

Sharon shook her head.

Ma Rothe finished her first set: some songs she called "River road kind of blues"; the ballad "Somewhere" from *West Side Story;* a bunch of old-time jazzy-bluesy numbers Sharon thought sounded familiar; some scat singing "right outta Ella's songbook"; a raunchy number about a man's penis; and a medley of Stephen Sondheim.

Ma bowed, said, "Folks, gonna go oil these old pipes. Boss won't let me back on till you drink the till dry. So drink up, lushes. Be back now, hear?"

She laughed and left, to whistles and a half-standing ovation.

Audrey ordered more old-fashioneds, said, "What'd you think?"

"She's fine," Sharon said.

"So fine," Audrey agreed, and smiled at her and held it.

Two more rounds, Ma came back out in a similar dress, but white this time. Lips were blue.

Sometime during the second set, Audrey's lips had come forward again and said, "She really gets to me."

Sharon nodded.

Lips again: "Does she get to you?"

Sharon said, "Yes, I guess she does."

The lips said, "She's a great finisher too. A great, great finish. Wait'll we get there." Sharon felt the lips twitch a bit before they left.

Ma's face, neck, shoulders, were covered with sweat now. She kept her eyes closed, like a fighter who was on the stool, bleeding. She sang what she sort of pretended was her last song, "Imagine," then pretended she was heading off. Thanked the crowd, waved, bowed to the musicians, extended her hand to them, to the crowd, took a step away.

"'Mutton Leg Blues'!" somebody called from the dark back of the hot room.

Then everybody was yelling it. Audrey was yelling it.

Sharon leaned over, shouted, "What? What is it?"

Audrey shouted back to her, "'Mutton Leg.'"

Sharon shouted it too.

It seemed like everyone in the crowd sang along with "Mutton Leg," or else called out "Ma-aa!" during it, or else just closed eyes and swayed to the bass line. Ma leaned over as she sang, her head almost down to the level of her waist, the sweat frozen to her in the light that had turned blue sometime along the way.

Ma gave her left dress strap a flick with the hand that was holding the microphone. The strap fell. The crowd got louder. Ma leaned back awhile, sang some more, just improvising lyrics and harmony now, melody was in everybody's head to stay, didn't have to be physically present anymore. Then Ma leaned forward again, scat lyrics, flicked the other strap, crowd reaction, Ma leaned back again, the top of her dress gone, round brown breasts flowing as she did, bathed in the blue spotlight that bathed her and bathed her voice.

Sharon thought it was the most natural and beautiful and good thing in the world, the most natural and good thing that could have happened to them, to anyone, ever.

She looked over at Audrey, who was laughing kindly at her, with her. Even with all this going on, Audrey still showing *her*, Sharon Slabb, showing her *attention*. Just a little attention, and it meant so much. Everyone in the room was kissing. Sharon leaned toward Audrey a split second before Audrey started toward her. A half old-fashioned fell to the floor. They laughed. Sharon was the first to open her mouth a little bit, like she used to for Len, before he had gone to Southeast Asia on his mission and never come back to her.

Len had been a gentle person, like her dad, but she could never keep him tender for very long, never long enough. After a while together, he would always reach too quickly, grab too hard, use his muscle instead of skin, instead of flesh.

Sharon wasn't used to old-fashioneds, and she had gotten back to Audrey's house with a headache. Audrey gave her something for it, wouldn't tell her what it was. It smelled funny, like chloral hydrate, but she trusted gentle Audrey, and whatever it was, it seemed to help. Audrey massaged the headache away, fingertips on temples, Sharon's muscles going limp.

Audrey stayed gentle for hours, bathed her in hours of sweet tenderness. Together they rolled through colored clouds of softness and delicacy, Audrey using femininity and attention on her like an instrument. There was no stiffness, no muscle, no bone, just "It's OK, it's OK," and more lovely and intoxicating tenderness and attention.

It was the difference between a gentle leaning, swaying, and stiff, cold poking. The difference between a caress and an incision.

Finally, the liquor and the time caught up with her. She moaned to have it over, moaned for the future, both the good and the bad of it, as it seemed right now.

They were entwined, and Sharon almost felt herself asleep in Audrey's arms, the smell of luxury face cream all around her.

She could still hear Audrey, crying softly, far away, not telling her "It's OK, it's OK" anymore, but crying and telling her now, "Nobody's going to be part of us, of this, honey. Nobody. Not your mother, not your boss. Not anybody. Just you, honey. And me. We get it all for ourselves, baby, our sweet selves. And you, please, because you're going to check the eyes. Check her eyes for me, my baby, her eyes. Please. Check the eyes."

TWENTY THREE

The secretary had brought him into Marmasette's office, had him sit down there and wait. The CEO was probably off taking a whiz somewhere; no private bath here. Ten minutes. Must be emptying out a damn lot of fluids.

Chet used the time to check out the office, so he wouldn't have to do it after Marmasette got back, as they were talking. He could do it that way too, if he had to, but this would be easier.

A pretty straight place to get the handle on anyway. The St. Chicione lamps, stylish in their day, not now. The rug a good wool blend, but grown a little gritty around the edges, nicely vacuumed but not shampooed in a while. The rug showing a couple of brown spots; better check the ceiling for water leaks. The wet bar in the corner pretty well stocked, but just for looks, not a working fixture.

Chet figured Vor-Tech for a company three, maybe four years on the downhill side of glory, three, four years past its big crest, now looking desperately for a new wave to catch and ride. The defense market had blown off a lot bigger places than this. Ah, the whims of peace; it's a terrible thing indeed, an obscene price to have to pay.

Chet finished with the furnishings, leaned forward, grabbed and studied the gold-framed photo on the CEO's desk. The force-fed family-unity shot, standard *comme d'habitude,* de rigueur for the sensitive exec's desktop. The three daughters anxious for the one five-hundredth of a second to be over with, so that they could drop their

All-American little-girl smiles and get back to their partying and screwing and driving around town in daddy's Beemer. All of that was just beyond the frame there; Chet could make it out. Also there in the center of the shot, Mommy, frozen in fear, clinging hopelessly to this facade of a life, hoping the CEO wouldn't be too obvious in his lust for chippies or his disdain for her. Mommy holding on for a few more years, ten more maybe, then a settlement, a way out, anything.

Chet figured he was maybe being too hard on these Waltons with stock options. Probably not, though, probably not. Let's check out Papa in the picture. He's—

The door opened, the CEO came back into his office, Chet got to see the original instead of just the facsimile. Worse in living color than in the photo, much worse—older, more wrinkled. The hair, almost a distinguished gray within the frame, now just a bottle yellow that Chet remembered from the last time he'd seen the guy, at a party. Fatter and meaner than in the picture too. Wasn't aging well at all.

Chet stood up, they shook hands on the run as Marmasette circled his big chrome desk on his way back to the big red leather chair. He sat down, still holding on to Chet's shake. Chet felt like asking if they had just do-si-doed.

Marmasette put some pens in different places on the desktop, and he asked Chet how he was doing. In other words, get on with it, kid, I got me a floundering company to start bailing out here, buddy.

"We've met," Chet told him. "The Wrights' place, maybe it was Christmas, for the holidays, two or three years ago, it could be. You had on castanets from Mexico."

"Of course," Marmasette told him. "How could I forget that, you—the castanets, yes. It seems to me we spent an agreeable hour or so comparing common acquaintances in savings and loan."

Marmasette was one of those guys who could gaze at Chet's ponytail even while facing him. Physically impossible, but some pukes could pull it off. Chet was glad he had pulled the hair through a wide red ribbon this morning, had put on a Bullwinkle earring and an old black Harley tee-shirt under his black coat. These things were so much fun here in corporate America.

"I've been meaning for a long time to phone for an appointment with you, actually with you and Milton, before, but I'm glad I finally got the lead out of my ass and actually did it."

"Well, I don't mind at all, ever, spending some time with a friend, former friend, of Milton's. And of Audrey's, of course. Lovely woman, she."

"She is."

"How's she doing?" Marmasette asked him. "Getting along?"

"As far as I can see, fine," Chet said. "She's strong."

"She's very strong," Marmasette said. "A lot of inner, outer strength to her makeup there."

Chet started to smile, turned his head to an autographed picture on the wall behind the desk. Chet pointed at it and said, "LaMond, huh?"

Marmasette told him that it was. "I got it in Paris in '89, during the Tour. Snapped it, got it developed, enlarged, autographed, all right there."

"That was the year of his great finish, wasn't it?"

"The greatest," Marmasette told him. "What I believe and insiders say was the greatest ever—one of the greatest ever in *any* sporting event whatsoever, *I* think. I was very lucky to be there at the time. Ostensibly on business, but I had the time I'll always remember. You follow cycling, then, do you?"

Chet said, "I do. I try it a bit, way out on the Island, summers. I want to qualify for an event sometime. I met Fignon once. I didn't find him very pleasant at all, however."

"But a champion," Marmasette said. "Those men are small, hard, compact, everyday-sized champions. All heart and sinew to their makeup. Their dedication and conditioning is incredible, of course. They've no time for small talk, I suppose. You look at my body and you naturally assume, quite rightly, it belongs in the back of a Nazi touring car somewhere, but I get on a bike too, once in a while. I don't race, of course."

"We'll have to take a run at it some morning, you and me. It would be fun."

"Yes, sure it would."

"Felix, I'd ask you now what kind of bike you have, but I know that if I say or hear one word about a specific make speed bike, then there'll be no way I could stop discussing them for a half hour, and I value your time, I appreciate your agreeing to have me in here this morning."

Marmasette said, "Not at all. Then what can we do for each other?"

"Good question. Excellent question. My lead-in exactly. I don't know if Milton or Audrey ever told you, I'm involved with mid- and high-level corporate executive placement."

"Chet? Chet, you can say the word 'headhunter' in front of me. It doesn't offend me, if it doesn't offend you."

"It doesn't offend me at all," Chet said. "I just worry, when I tell it, people will picture me with a spear and a bone through my nose, sneaking through the Congo, looking for lunch meat."

"Well, that's so wrong?"

They both forced laughs. "What I'd like to do," Chet said, "is just establish contact here. Give you my phone and fax numbers, let you know I'm here. I've just gotten back from a business trip out west, the Coast and Chicago, and just between you and I, what I'm putting together is a national network here. In some ways, completely unique. Yours is a prototype company I'd like to build the future on. Being honest, I don't know very much about Vor-Tech, but from what I *do* know, it's apparently a very specialized market in a very specialized field. Defense and filaments and conductors and such shit? Well, I never do a very good job of understanding what it is the businesses I help really do, but I do an excellent job of finding them the people who can help them do it. Wow, don't ask me to repeat *that* sentence of mine, but you get the idea."

"Sure I do."

"Time becomes so important in these things. In all things in business. As you're aware, Felix, I know."

"I'm aware."

"Do you have any questions?" Chet asked him. He couldn't read him; the fat slob was being fairly cagey.

"Just an uncomfortable one," Marmasette said.

"And what's that?" Chet asked him, shifting, getting ready for it.

"The other-shoe-on-the-other-foot one," Marmasette said.

Chet told him he didn't understand.

"Not to be negative," Marmasette said, sitting back, "but you're absolutely right about the labor and personnel situation in this field. Give me the right engineers at the right time, and I could be IBM, I could be GE."

"So, then? Negative?"

"Well, Chet, isn't the negative simply the fact that every key person you find for me has left someone else? In the lurch or whatever? I'm not very good at sharing the people I use; are you? I mean, there simply are not too many people I want coming here that are just taking off their mortarboards and checking out of State University at Oswego or somewhere. I've never had anyone of any value work for me who was still paying off a college loan. Face it, you raid talent from businesses. Like mine. Make that mature, experienced talent. No offense. That's how your job runs. I'm right?"

"I think you'll like one ironclad policy of mine, Felix. And I'll continue it, no matter how national I get. It's this—I never raid from a customer. Use me once, just once, I guarantee I'll never place, help place, an employee of yours. Ever. Now. That's lifetime."

"That's good. That's a very good thing to explain to your clients. Very wise." He didn't say anything more.

Chet put his hand out, said, "Felix, listen, thanks for your time. I really appreciate it. I'll leave my information outside, with your girl there. Good of you to see me, really."

Marmasette swung his partner 'round his desk, square-dance style again, and they promenaded to the office door.

Marmasette stopped him at the door, thanked him, and asked him, "Chet, let me ask, personal, have they been bothering you with this murder thing on Milton? Like they have with me?"

For the second time during the appointment, Chet kept his smile in. Had almost missed, forced himself to keep his mouth shut, waited. Bingo.

"Yes. A couple interviews," Chet told him. "Just general annoyances, and of course that magical ability that law enforcement officers have for degrading normal people, people who aren't law enforcement officers—you know what I'm talking about?"

"Me too. A spittoon named Hraska, I think, and he had a partner, I think."

"LaLuna," Chet said. "He knew Audrey before. I think he thinks they're both still in high school and he's protecting her from the schoolyard bully or something. That's little me. They intimate that I'm in love with Audrey, which, I suppose, in a cop's mind, if I love someone, I kill their husbands. That makes sense. How about you?"

"They're pretty sure I killed Milton as some sort of a business move, apparently. Even though I didn't get anything out of the death at all. That doesn't seem to deter them. The whole thing is really beginning to stand in the way of my getting things done around here. Truly unfortunate."

"You get a lawyer?" Chet asked.

"I ran it by our company retainer," Marmasette said. "He's not criminal, but he had it checked out. He says it's apparently over, on the surface anyway. I mean, at least they're done with me for now. With us both, I'd presume. But I don't believe it. We're dealing with leeches, I believe. Once they get their fangs in, you have to burn the back of their heads with a cigarette. You? With a lawyer?"

"No, I didn't think there was a need then. Hopefully it is over. They've of course been all over Audrey's hair too. Suffer the poor and the innocent, goddamned helpless, bungling cops. Protect us all from bureaucracy."

"Righto. Amen."

"Felix, as long as we've brought it up, how would you feel comfortable about, sort of, covering each other's asses on this thing? If it comes to that. I mean, just you keeping me informed, and I you. I mean, if there are things still coming up that would concern us. I mean, if you trust me enough. I suppose I *could* be the one murdered poor old Milton."

"I'll bet against that. I'll bet on some kind of cool-assed psycho, sneakier than most, although the cops don't even seem willing to consider that line of it at all. And yes, to answer your question, I think it's an excellent idea we go all-for-one on this. After all, they've got us outnumbered, right? Can't hurt, right? We proud bikers stand united?"

"Right, I figure. I tell you, Felix, I pick up the phone these days, and I think I'll hear one of those weasels chewing on a cigar, writing down every word I say. They get you paranoid. They really do."

"Of course they do. They count on that. It's part of their attack. What they count upon," Felix told him, "is the secrets we all have, everybody has. They look at you, ask stupid questions, just hoping the secrets inside will rattle you, get you jumpy and saying things you shouldn't be saying."

"You're right. We all have our secrets."

Marmasette smiled. "And we're both smart cookies, Chet, so what do you say—I won't tell you mine, you don't tell me yours."

Chet smiled back at him. "I think that was the deal, even before we made the deal, wasn't it?"

Marmasette agreed, with a smile and a shrug.

Chet said, "Well, you know, I feel better just having been talking about this whole damn thing. I haven't been able to discuss it at all, even with Audrey very much. Thank you, fellow victim of the prosecution."

Marmasette said, "*Per*secution. So, my man, we've both been baring our souls here. You haven't told me how you really *do* feel about Audrey. Cops not counting. Wedding bells someday, when appropriate?"

Chet said, "We have our bumps—our relationship, it does. Ups and downs. But fuck it all, I'd like to spend the rest of my life with the woman. It's true, I could yell that from the rooftops, put it on the fax circuit. I usually don't say it, yet I know it when I think about it. It's true. Now you know too."

"Great, good to hear. But bumps you said, huh? The bumps and grinds of a meaningful relationship. I know. Well, that's just great for me to hear. We've said before that she's a very strong person, and she is. She's proved it with the loss of Milton too, of course. I'll tell you something, Chet. You're a businessman, you'll understand. I could use some of her strength down here in the business about now. She thinks she'd be better just staying out of my way, but I've been trying to talk her into throwing some of her support my way. I don't know how I'm doing on that score."

"Maybe I could advise her there," Chet said. "We talk. I could bring it up."

"That'd be great. I'd love to see you two kids get together for the rest of your lives," Marmasette said. "Invite me to the wedding, huh?"

They shook again. Marmasette suggested they seal their alliance—an alliance to battle thug cops, to win over strong women—with a drink.

There was dust on the bottle of Scotch that Marmasette brought out. No ice around either. Chet told himself he had known that.

They touched glasses and drank the burning stuff hot and straight. Chet thanked the CEO, put his empty glass down, and said at the door, "I hope this works out for everybody, Felix, especially for Audrey. She's a good woman and deserves the best for her life."

"Good and strong," Marmasette agreed as Chet was leaving. "Her damned legs are as strong as a biker's, I'm sure of that."

And as Chet left, he heard Marmasette laughing to himself about that.

The ribbon on the PS/2's printer was fading fast, so she made sure to check both copies before she put them in the mail. She didn't write reports away from the office all that much, but once in a while it became the convenient thing to do.

She had a blank NYFS-772 postmortem report, printed protocol type, saved there in the memory of her hard drive, so she could just call it up and fill in the blanks. That's what she had done on this one, before printing it up, twice.

She wanted to make absolutely sure she was finished with this, so she reread both copies that the machine had kicked out. Made sure it was all there.

The case number was A917-90, decedent named Madeline June LaLuna, female, maiden name Johnson, age forty-three.

Premises of examination: NHNL. Requesting authority: NHPD.

The external examination had been performed on a previously necropsied, unembalmed body of a well-nourished female Caucasian, measuring 62.5 inches and weighing, at time of death, based on the previous NYFS-772, 167 pounds, normal adiposity.

The facial area displayed deep furrows in the lower cheeks, around the eyes, and in the neck area, slight Campbell de Morgan's senile spots, all these apparently advanced for decedent's age.

The skin, especially that in the neck, upper back, and vaginal areas, showed an inflammation usually associated with manariasis, a lesser strand of the psoriasis group of epidermal conditions.

Both ears and temples were marked with areas of slight to advanced ecchymosis, these aberrations of the skin color probably having resulted from bleeding into the tissues from injury. The dark color of these bruises indicated the ecchymosis to be fresh trauma and not inflicted as postmortem wounds. No other patterns of injury were detected.

Unassisted visual, hand-held magnifying device, and polarized and TEM microscope examinations of the entire external of the body, revealed no unordinary puncture wounds nor immediately apparent lesions.

However, an internal examination of the eye bulbs, accessed by a reopening of the brain cavity, revealed a hemorrhagic track running through the left oculus area. A SEM microscope examination of both left and right eye regions revealed in the left eye a slight abnormality in the outer fibrous, middle vascular, and inner nerve layer, including the sclera and cornea and optic nerve. A corresponding abnormality was found in the ciliary muscles and in the muscle area behind the eye bulb. This abnormality seems to have been caused by the insertion of a surgically thin needle into the eye area and perhaps beyond and into the area behind.

Sharon's eyes kept checking, moving down the report.

The internal, clinical, anatomic pathology report stated that previous toxology examinations of the subject's liver, kidneys, stomach, stomach contents, urine, blood, and intestines revealed no abnormal chemical content. No evidence of recent sexual activity. The blood analysis test had been performed, as is standard operating procedure, with the UV and GC spectrometers.

However, an additional blood analysis, performed by the GC mass spectrometer in conjunction with the computerized data system, revealed the presence of the chemical synthetic Ermodemothan, to the extent of 0.3/100 ml, in the blood.

This presence, in turn, might very well be consistent with the dark-pink coloration of the hypostasis and the slight reddish discoloration of the esophagus and stomach.

Bobby Dekar hated any pathologistic interpretations in their reports. Screw Bobby.

There were other parts of the report, not as interesting, and both copies had been signed by Sharon Lucille Slabb, M.D., Forensic Pathologist.

She was finished, satisfied.

She put one copy of the report into a brown legal envelope and addressed it to Robert J. Dekar, M.D., Chief Medical Examiner, Town of North Homestead.

Attached to the report was a handwritten note that read: "Bobby, I redid the LaLuna necropsy, with no authority other than my own, and here is the report. This should in no way reflect on any unprofessional or less than acceptable performance by John Dreeve, who performed the original necropsy and report. I just happened to find some other things there. It happens. I just had certain things to look for. Thanks for understanding. Sharon."

She sent the other copy of the postmortem to Audrey Wright. The note with that one read: "I have redone the autopsy, as you asked, and I checked the eyes. Here is a copy of the report. I have sent the original to my boss, for proper handling and processing. Since I have now complied with your stated wishes to the very best of my ability, I must now assume that you will uphold your end of our bargain. I will consider myself blessed, and consider you a fair and just and honorable person, if you never mention my name in any context whatsoever ever again. Please destroy this note. Thank you. Ermodemothan is a poison."

Then she wrote to Joe LaLuna. No report, just a letter to a friend, almost six pages. Someone along the line might describe it as rambling, but who cared. She told Joe that he was the only honest person she knew, and that she trusted him, no matter what, and that she understood what he was trying to do for her and her mom with Mogie Hattes and she appreciated it.

She tried to tell him how much it hurt her that everyone around her seemed so bad. She told him secrets and bad things she'd been made aware of. People looked bad and were worse than they looked. Mogie, when her mom wasn't around, would lounge around their place with his pants and boxer shorts pulled down around his knees, exposing his business to Sharon. Captain Bell kept trying to make her go to a motel with him, and he would grab her everywhere, especially on her backside, whenever he could. And Joe's partner, Hraska, had gotten her drunk at a Christmas party and made her go with him to an interrogation room. He'd trapped her there, acted like a mongrel until she started kicking him. As for Buck Rodgers, the paramedic crew chief who had started to date her mom, they had received newspapers from San Diego that told about him being a child molester, papers probably obtained by Mogie Hattes. And yes, what they said about John Dreeve, what Joe had asked her about when they had their "date" in Zack's Blue, was true—John did awful things sometimes with the bodies in their cooler.

And there were other things, worse things even, which she said she wouldn't and couldn't tell him about. And she didn't even know why she was writing to him, except that he was the only one she knew who wouldn't just use people, use them for what he could, use them by what he knew about them, use them to find out even worse things about other people. And so on. He was the only one who didn't do that. Sometimes he seemed like he did, but she knew he didn't. Maybe her mother was like that too, but she couldn't write to her mother. So she thanked him and said she was sorry and she signed the letter and she read it over and hesitated. Then she went back and inserted a small "Love" above her signature.

Sharon took the three envelopes down to the lobby of her apartment house and mailed them. The super had a mail drop there, for the tenants' convenience.

Sharon went back upstairs. She remembered, almost surprised, that she was sober. Cold, stone, gum-swollen sober. She walked around a bit, put a few things in their places, ran a wet rag over her kitchen table and her face, and called up her mother.

After the fifth ring, Sharon was surprised to hear her mother's voice, previously recorded, talking about being out, talking about herself, not mentioning her daughter at all.

Sharon told her mother's voice, "It's me. Just wanted to check in with you. How's it going? I hope you're eating well and not just buying crap in the store. It's been a while since I talked to you, Mom, quite a little while."

Sharon hung up, went into the tiny bedroom, and sat down at a vanity table she had bought just last week. Her leather doctor's bag, which her mom had bought for her when she graduated Columbia Med, was on the floor, on the new woven rug by the table. She reached down and picked up the bag, put it on the table by her deodorants.

She took out her scalpel. It was a very good one, top of the line, also bought by her mom, part of a set for Christmas two years ago. It had a five-inch teakwood handle, perfect for grip. The handle twisted a bit at its far end, and it held a one-and-a-half-inch replaceable blade. This blade was new; she'd disposed of the one she had used on Joe's wife.

Sharon looked into the mirror, looked at her hand holding the scalpel. Steady. So the V.O. hadn't rotted away her nerve endings quite yet.

She made the initial incision, only skin, no muscle, at the left corner of the jaw, just below the earlobe. There was no pain at all. The knife must be drawn across the surface of the specimen, Doctor, never pressed, never thrust, never made to puncture tissue. Sharon's hand was still so steady, maybe she should have been a surgeon. Her mother had wanted her to be a surgeon, told her that her father would have been proud of that. It would have impressed Len too. And Joe.

The incision, paper thin and straight, went up the side of her face, in front of the ear, still just skin deep. The incision line had wavered a bit as it went from over the jaw to over the skull. The line the blade left was black, like a pencil, and it was followed a moment and an inch later by the blood spreading out from each side of it. They had made them do pigs in med school once, but other than that, she had never cut into anything alive.

Her right arm, the one with the scalpel, was making an awkward, square frame of her face as she drew the blade up and then over.

The pain hit, terrible and sudden, as the blade made a turn at her temple and began coming across the top of her forehead. She thought maybe she would have to work faster now, because the blood would obstruct her vision, but it flowed slowly, and it stopped before it got to her eyes, so it was only the pain forcing her to finish up the job.

At the other side of her forehead, as the blade turned down, her elbow was forced into a difficult angle and her stomach was lurching from the pain now and she had vomit in her mouth, so she made herself swallow and put the blade down on the table.

She looked into the mirror and counted to sixty through the hurt.

In that time, the skin from the corner of the incision, at the left temple, began to pull itself down and off a bit, by force of gravity or trauma. She worked on that. Her fingers took the skin and tried to separate it, a bit at a time, like you'd take off an old Band-Aid or a sunburn. But the fibers holding skin to muscle, skin to flesh, were strong. She picked the scalpel back up and tried to use it to flick away the skin from what was holding it up.

In sixth grade, at Halloween, she had mustered the courage to wear a gross-out mask that looked like this. The kids had loved it.

She wanted to think of other things now. Things like that. She knew that there were many things, either important or just nice or just interesting, that she should think of now, and remember, and sort out in her mind.

But the pain was too great, and she couldn't think of anything else. So she reached for the Nembutal bottle on her table. It would show up later in her liver. She reached for the Nembutal bottle, and with it, an exquisite freedom from all of her pain.

Big Bob was telling LaLuna his face looked like it was healing up pretty good, just a bad color to it still, but that always looked the worst on these things, and bruises were always the last to go, right?

LaLuna sat and nodded. He'd forgotten about his face and about Mogie Hattes and all those other things before.

"You get the teeth fixed up OK?" Big Bob asked him.

LaLuna said he did, yeah.

"So it's all taken care of, that's good. You need a bridge or caps or crowns or what?"

"Two crowns," LaLuna told him.

"That's good, I'm glad it's all taken care of. Job's a bitch, but you can't beat the dental, huh? You just can't. I wanted to ask you about all this crappy stuff at the funeral, but it was all so busy that day, you know?"

LaLuna nodded again.

Madeline's funeral had been quick, impersonal, just a series of formal motions orchestrated by the guys from Ferrara Brothers, professionals, owed LaLuna a couple of favors from a statutory rape thing a few years ago. So they had taken care of Madeline for him.

Just a few odd remnants were left of Madeline's family, his family, so that part had been easy. A couple of her maiden aunts he didn't know, his *Compare* Fred, wearing a pair of old Michael Jordan red-and-black sneakers. Louessa-Louise crying into wads of wet Kleenex.

Fat Joe chewing gum. Wink and a bunch of guys from the department, standing around. Madeline didn't have any friends. Later,
LaLuna dumped most of the people and snuck back to Zack's Blue
for a night.

Contributions were to be sent, in lieu of flowers, to the Police
Athletic League. They were trying to get a few bucks together to start
a boxing program for underprivileged street kids.

"There's no pain, then? Whatsoever? In the teeth? Anywheres?"

LaLuna told Big Bob nope.

"That's good," Big Bob told him. "Well, in that case," Bob said,
and he leaned forward and pushed his intercom button and shouted
to Aggie, his secretary, in the outer office. "OK, my dear, bring it on
in."

The intercom played no part in transferring the message. Big Bob
sat back and smiled at LaLuna.

Nothing happened for a while, so Big Bob said, "Aggie and me,
we got a little something for you, Joe."

Still nothing, so Big Bob asked, "And has all the personal affairs
of yours being taken care of? I mean, with the death and all? The
afterwards?"

"Sort of," LaLuna answered. "I found someone take care of the
dog."

Carl had been a pain in the ass since Madeline died. Whining,
complaining. LaLuna had to keep the poor thing in all day, a big dog.
Asked around, Winky, couple others; nobody could take him.

Walking across the parking lot of the pound—Carl just happy-
assed, sniffing everything, pissing everywhere, pulling at the leash
like he couldn't wait to get in there to the gas chamber—LaLuna had
heard somebody behind him call, "You Sergeant LaLuna, sir?"

LaLuna turned around. Guy in a fatigue jacket over a Prince
shirt, jeans, beard, Ray Charles glasses. He'd just gotten out of an old
black Firebird, was walking toward Carl and him. LaLuna told him
yeah, he was LaLuna.

"Nice dog, he yours?"

"Used to be. You want him?"

"Hey, Whitemeat, what I want him for? What's his name?"

"How you know me?"

"I don't. Talk to a guy at police, they said you was coming down here. I been waiting. Where you been?"

"I went home, got the dog. Who's asking?"

"What kind of dog that?"

"Everything. Collie, husky, shepherd, mutt—everything."

"Oh, yeah, you got papers prove that?"

"Yeah, sure. C'mon, Slick, busy here, what'd you want?"

"Oh, I gotta report something here to you, man. He eat much?"

"No, just what he can get his mouth on. Come on, crumb, I'm busy here, I said."

"Hey, Whitemeat, be easy, I don't want to disturb you. Just seems you bringing him in, you look like you don't want that at all, I could help you out some."

"How?"

"How? How how? What you mean, how? Take him, of course. You asked me if I wanted him. What his name?"

"What for? You gonna make him a gen-u-ine attack dog, you gonna be disappointed, friend."

"Hey, come on. You police, right? That make him a police dog, right? Good dog. My wife and me, see, we split the kids, week me, week her. Well, my week, kids could use a good dogger like that. They need something, at least. They good kids, he a good dog? Good for kids, you say?"

"He's a damned good dog."

"Well, then, Whitemeat, we got a deal?"

"What'd you wanna see me?"

"Oh, yeah, I almost forgot. Listen, Whitemeat, I'm the guy Chet Zumrad was with, the night you trying to put him killing a guy, his squeeze's man."

Funny guy, kept calling LaLuna Whitemeat. Guy was white.

Finally, Aggie came into Big Bob's office, carrying two big white soup bowls.

"Told you I had something for us," Big Bob said, grinning at him.

Aggie was a tall woman, losing hair above her ears, had been Big Bob's secretary since way before the summer of the stroke, or maybe not. She put a bowl in front of each of the men, on each side of Big Bob's desk. Then she put down two spoons, two paper napkins. LaLuna didn't look, knew what it was.

"G'head," Big Bob told him. "Ice cream."

LaLuna thanked him and picked up the bowl in one hand, palmed it.

"I wanted to be sure first it wasn't gonna freeze you, with the teeth, you know, gums. G'head, it's melting."

LaLuna and Bob ate ice cream. LaLuna bit his, Big Bob let his upper lip slide across the top of each spoonful. After a couple of spoons, Bob looked up at him and said, "Almondberry crunch. It's new. I like it. You like it?"

LaLuna tried to keep his eyes on his bowl, but Big Bob had put his down, held the stump of his finger out in front of LaLuna's face, forced him to look up into it.

"Y'know, Joe," he said, "once I lost my finger, I almost lost my mind."

Big Bob hung the stump in the air there awhile. Said, "Like I wasn't a complete man anymore, you understand?"

LaLuna didn't answer him.

"But," Big Bob went on, "in time, in time it passed, and I perse-vered. We, of course, all have had some days like that. It's life."

LaLuna ate.

"You saw the new autopsy on the missus, I know. A terrible thing, and tragic too. And, once again, nobody knows what the hell is going on with any of it at all. Who's the mack? We don't know. But the thing is, of course, the appearances of things. Which is often more impor-tant than the things itself, Joe. Which, as a cop, you already know this."

LaLuna knew now, had figured out why he had been called in this time. He had thought it would be Sheeney to tell him. So Sheeney had cut him loose.

Big Bob said, "We got lucky in one respect, though. We just got in a TDY from the city, a guy's been on drugs most of his career, worked with the DEAs in Florida on them and everything, he's here on some kind of exchange thing. Anyway, he's done homicide in the past, which is the main thing—I forget how many years, in the city—so he'll be taking over your wife's thing. He'll do an excellent job for us, Joe, first-rate, I can guarantee you on that."

LaLuna said, "OK."

"But getting back to the appearances, Joe, you of course know that Dr. Slabb's last autopsy, I guess I mean *really* her last one— tragedy on top of tragedy around here—the last report, it opened up some puzzling questions about the whole affair, I mean, thing. The MOs being so similar and all between the two. The whole thing, it's as crazy as shit, isn't it? It's just the craziest thing, ain't it, Joe? Everybody *I* know's just been asking what the hell is going on with this, and nobody knows. What the hell. We've never had a time like this so screwed up in the department since all that stuff from the Knapp Commission, seventies, spilled over all the way out here, the corruption and the graft and everything. Not that that's like this, Joe. I didn't mean to imitate that."

"So what happens to me, Captain?" LaLuna had finished the ice cream, put the bowl down, just wanted to get out.

"Joe, I know you're upset. Lieutenant Sheeney, naturally, is incontinent about this whole thing. As we all are. We are all behind you one hundred percent, to the death, on this, Joe, and always will be. There's not a man in this department has anything but the highest regard and no suspicion of any foul play of you."

"You need my badge and stuff, I guess, huh?"

"Just for a while, Joe, we do, just for a little while."

"You take them?"

LaLuna rolled forward in the seat, onto one hip.

"Nah, give them to Sheeney, you get back up there. He'll just hold on to them for you, Joe, that's all. Tuck them away somewheres safe for you. Cool things off awhile. Your salary, of course, remains intact, fully. As does all coverage and, I think, even retirement time in. So think about it like a vacation, Joe. You got people to go to? Florida or somewheres? We can send the check, keep you posted, be back up here in no time. You got people?"

"Not really."

"Well. Have a ball, then. Go south, Atlantic City, piss away some money. Have a big bake-off for yourself. Hell, you earned it. There's nothing you can do here anyways."

"Be tough to do."

"I know. I know it will, Joe, because you're a cop. You're a professional. Tough to turn your back on stuff, you got all this shit unsettled, this stuff with your own wife, and that other lady's husband that had you all upset before this, goddamned needles and everything, you still got that damned foot in the Dumpster still unsettled—I'm not complaining about that, of course, I know the whole thing is unsettled, but take my advice, Joe, just forget it awhile. You're a young guy, good-looking when you're not too beat up or looking like shit, go have some fun. Remember me and this, Joe," and Big Bob held up the stump again. "I came back from this. It just takes time is all."

Joe nodded and got up to go.

Big Bob called to his back, "Joe, before you leave. Geez, I almost hate to tell you this. Could you please give Winky Dink all the World Series Pool materials? Thanks a heap if you would, Joe."

TWENTY SIX

She was trying to touch his bruises, the ones she could see, on his face, as he kept grunting and driving her into the wall. They had already knocked a small sculpture by Noguchi off the hanging shelf, down onto the bedroom rug. She'd have to check on it later.

He finally grunted himself down into a couple of choked sobs. He pulled himself back off her, put his right hand on the wallpaper, and hunched over, his mouth open. He was finished, and his wife was still dead.

Audrey moved away, a prizefighter getting off the ropes, picked up the sculpture, looked, put it back on the shelf, and left the room.

She came back clean, carrying two cans of Torreine beer, German stuff still left in the refrigerator from Milton.

Joe was in her bed, sitting up, staring. Audrey thought: There's been some time-lapse aging going on with this poor guy. His arms dangled out onto the covers on each side of him, made him look like a scarecrow. His chest had sunk, his eyes had sunk, all in these last few weeks. His eyes would be surrounded by dark skin now even without the bruises. Once a puppy-dog face, now a scarecrow. Not just a scarecrow, she decided, a scarecrow with tuberculosis.

She gave him a beer, climbed in beside him, didn't touch.

They were there awhile. Then, still looking straight ahead, he said, "We really killed her, didn't we, Audie? We really just put her away, stuck her."

It occurred to her that things had gotten so confused in the past days, so crazy screwed up, that she couldn't even be sure who it was he was talking about. Put away *who,* which one of them? So she just waited.

After he didn't say anything for a long time, she asked, "Who you mean?"

"Both of them, I guess. I tell you Madeline had a Giants picture for me, '58 Giants? Ordered it on the sly for me, had it right there for me, the night she was killed. Both of them, I mean, I guess, but I was thinking when I said it, we killed her, I was thinking Sharon."

"Sharon? Joe, what are you talking about? You mean what here?"

"I mean I been watching. Watching here." He looked around the room.

She had taken only a sip from her can of beer; it was still heavy. She brought it high over her head and said, "God damn you."

He rolled away from her, stayed in bed, his back to her, holding his head. She beat his bare back with the can, spraying foam and mist, raising little round welts; she kept yelling for God to damn him.

He cupped his ears and kept saying, "C'mon, c'mon don't, c'mon don't, Audrey." Not loud, patient with her.

She got tired and threw the beer on the rug and leaned back on the headboard and cried. Her shoulders and chest kept jerking; she couldn't stop them. She thought he'd grab her then, try to hold her still, but he didn't. Didn't do anything.

Then he got out of bed, put her half-empty beer can upright on her rug, got back into the bed. Then he just lay there beside her, waiting for her to stop crying.

When she did, he gave her some tissues from the night table.

She said, "Cops and priests and cowboys and—and missionaries, all you two-bit do-gooders."

He said again that they had killed Sharon Slabb. Audrey had to wonder how smart he was. How much can a cop figure out from watching from somewhere out in the street as two women hold each other?

She didn't ask him. She just said, "I got what I wanted out of it. So what?"

She didn't get that by him, though. He asked her, "What was it you wanted anyway, Audrey?"

She started to cry again. "The worst of it is, I've done worse. I had to know about things, you and your wife, Joe. Sharon was capable of maybe letting me know if it was all right to love you. ..."

He sat there holding his beer with both hands on his belly, right above his crotch. He looked down at the can, his head tilted a little to her side of the bed.

She said, "Joe, there was a terrible, troubled, sad, sad soul. She hurt a lot deeper than anything I or we could inflict upon her. Her hurt went back however many years she was old. Who knows what horrible secrets she could've had, drove her to do what she did. Her troubles didn't begin with us, Joe."

"Yeah, they did," he said. "And even if they didn't begin with us, it ended with us."

He sipped his beer. She looked over at him and quietly called him an asshole.

After a while he asked her, "What's Marmasette got on you, baby, anyway?"

Her head jerked around left and right, her eyes trying to focus on something. She said, "You goddamned."

He moved his chin a little toward the phone by the tissue box. He said, "I shouldn't've. I tapped it. Completely illegal, no warrant, no authority, nothing. Doesn't matter now, I guess. But I shouldn't've done it."

"Oh, Christ," she said. She wished there were some new curse words. She grabbed his beer out of his hands and slammed his chest with the can. But the can was almost empty, not much spray this time, not much force or weight. He didn't even bother rolling away from her, just held up one weak hand, didn't care if she hit him or not. She wanted to break his ribs, but she was too tired. When she had finished, she gave the beer back to him. There was enough damned beer on the rug already. As it was, it would need a good shampoo and probably never stop stinking.

He asked her again what Marmasette had on her. He had learned some of it from his wiretaps, had put the skeleton of it together, wanted the flesh of it now.

The flesh was, three years ago there had been a party at Vor-Tech. Milton had gotten drunk and left with some deputy vice-president's wife. Word was this lady used to shave her crotch. So Audrey, abandoned there, had gotten drunk herself and left with the most despicable thing she could find around—old, blond, fat-boy Marmasette.

They'd come back here, to her house. She had hoped Milton and the slut would be here too, Virginia Woolf time, but they weren't. Probably were in some toilet somewhere, moaning and scratching and shaving each other.

Half done with horrible Marmasette and sweating—the central air had been constantly breaking down that summer—Audrey had heard a terrible pounding at the back door. She went down naked, Marmasette with her, about one third of him covered up by a burgundy robe of Milton's. She looked through the window in the kitchen door. She couldn't see who it was, but whoever it was didn't look good. It wasn't Milton, though, she knew that much, so she pushed Marmasette into the pantry. She had decided to get the slob hidden in the pantry half out of habit, half from embarrassment, half for fun; she couldn't really remember now. She figured she maybe would have hidden the slob even if it had been Milton at the door. She didn't know for sure.

Her brother Ronnie broke into the kitchen just then. He had seen her in there and couldn't wait, broke off the lock, using his shoulder. Ronnie was in a gray hooded sweatshirt, ripped. His hair was wet and dark with blood, it looked like, and he was shaking and crying, and he said, "Audrey, put some fucking clothes on, for God's sake."

She did and she got Ronnie seated at her kitchen table, Marmasette still there in the pantry.

Her brother Ronnie had been the prototype dope zombie, could have been the poster child for the tragic life wasted by drugs. Blow at twelve, coke just after that, designer shit and maybe crack full-time, heroin on weekends. He had never weighed much more than a hundred pounds in his whole life, most of that carried in the pupils of his eyes.

He sat there at the kitchen table and told his big sister that he needed money; he had just killed a cop in a mix-up. Jersey cop, over there. Cop deserved it, dirty, but that didn't matter to a guy with his track record. He would either be beholden to his sister for saving his weak ass, or he'd be dead. No other way, he told her. He couldn't do the time without dope, would never make it. They'd probably fry him anyway; that'd be a little better.

So Audrey'd given him about six thousand bucks she had in a wall safe, plus her Visa. Marmasette still in the pantry, trying not to giggle, he told her later.

Audrey didn't tell Joe about the cop-killing part of it. She called it, "Some trouble Ronnie got himself into."

Joe listened to her and said, "Yeah, I remember that kid. He used to steal your Rolling Stone, Bob Dylan records, make fun of them."

Audrey told him yeah, that was her brother Ronnie. Then she told him about the contracts Marmasette and she had made out for each other, cosigned, hidden away. Joe couldn't believe they had both signed things like that. They really had, she told him, had to, only way they could trust each other.

Joe asked her for her copy. She went and got it; it was hidden in a suitcase in the guest room. Joe took the contract, looked at it quickly, told her to forget the whole thing, that he would make it right for her with Marmasette. Told her to forget that shit punk; he probably was a damned killer too, on top of being a blackmailer.

"Joe," she said, "I have to tell you. You and me, we can't be on the same side anymore. If we ever were. Not since your wife and since Sharon's report. Sharon's killed herself and still didn't answer any questions for me. We're not on the same side at all, so don't worry about working on Felix Marmasette for me. I can work it out between us. I have so far."

"No," Joe told her, "it's OK. When I haven't been searching out your boyfriend Zumrad, paper-chasing him to death, I been chasing Marmasette. I'll manage to put enough together on him to straighten him up, get him off you. I'll make it right. It's easy, really. Guy probably hasn't paid his taxes in twenty years, who knows. There'll be enough to take care of the guy. You forget him. He calls, hang up on him, don't let him in. Guy's probably a damned killer anyway."

"Joe, please," she said. "I told you, believe me, we're not on the same side. Forget helping me about this. If I really wanted to fix it,

I'm sure I could, you know? Forget using your muscle or brains or whatever on him. Why you want to do that anyway?"

"Lot of reasons. For me, I've always been made to hate to see a lady in distress. I've always been like that."

"That gets you in trouble. Lady in distress usually means there's a dragon or something around."

"Well," Joe told her, "I help them out anyway. Saint who— George?"

He folded up the contract, got out of bed, and put it in the pocket of his jacket, which, before, he had thrown on the floor.

He was putting on his shoes when she saw a thought hit him right in his scarecrow face. He said, "Audrey. That time we made love, first time, right before Winky called me up. You started to ask me something. For something."

She told him she didn't remember.

He said, "You were gonna ask me for help with Marmasette."

She said, "I don't know. I don't really remember."

He said, "That wasn't the only reason I was up here. Was it?" He turned to her. "Was it?"

She said, "Sure, probably." She knew he couldn't believe that, and he didn't. He finished putting on his shoes.

He said, "So you still root for the Giants, huh? They've had some good years, but not players like back then. Katcavage, Modzelewski, Grier, Huff."

"The Giants are in Jersey now," she told him.

"Yeah," he said, "the Giants are in Jersey now."

He got up to go, she told him to sit down. He took a seat in a padded rose-colored chair, the only chair in the room. She'd never known anybody but herself to sit in it, and she told him that.

"This is no sitting room, I guess," he said.

"Joe," she told him, "this has to be it for us."

"What? You kicking me out, then?"

"Yeah," she said, "I am. Joe, so much has happened, things have gotten so crazy, I don't know what the hell's going on. I've always prided myself on living a completely unorthodox life, you know? That was fine with me, I wanted it, I worked at it, I got it. But I admit it, Joe, now I been feeling I'm in it way over my head. Too much shit.

Just too much shit, Joe. It would have been a nice concept, us together, Joe, but no way, no way it could work now. Innocence is no
deposit, no return. And I go over it in my mind and I go over it in my
mind again, and I just get more and more confused. And, Joe, knowing all the players like I do, the only thing I keep coming back to is
this. Take no offense, Joe, but I think, I'm pretty sure, you're a crazy,
goddamned murderer."

"Audie, you c'mon," he told her. "First of all, I never took chemistry. Never took the course in my whole damned life. So how can I
know Ermodemothan and insulin and lethal doses and shit like that?
Audrey girl, somebody smart's been killing people around here. Your
boyfriends and your suitors, your blackmailers, are smart. I'm not.
I'm just a dumb cop, Audrey. I couldn't kill anybody. What, you think
I killed my own wife?"

"Oh, well, Joe, I'm glad you cleared that up for me. 'My client is
innocent beyond a reasonable doubt, Your Honor, for you see, he
never took chemistry in high school.' Oh, well, if that's the case, let's
send the jury home."

"Audie. Audie, you want to hear my alibi for my wife? It's you. I
was with you the night Madeline died, right? It didn't make much of
an impression, huh?"

"Yeah, Joe, you were with me the night your wife died, and Chet
was with me the night my husband died. That doesn't seem to bother
you about nailing Chet, now does it?"

"Different circumstance."

"No, it's not. Joe, you *are* right about one thing, though. You are
stupid, my baby."

"Just a stupid guy who loves you."

"I *know* you love me, Joe. I *know* that much. I guess it's love, if
there's not a more twisted word for it. I know *that* much. You know
what? I think you love me so much you'd kill your wife for me. Even
though you already got me without killing for me. Kill my husband
for me, even though I didn't want it. Of course, I can't for the life of
me figure out *why* it is you love me, Joe. That's what it is keeps going
through my head. The why of it all. Joe, before this, you and me
hadn't seen each other more than two times in what, maybe thirty
years?"

"Five times."

"Five? You counted? Jesus Christ, Joe, you *are* nuts. My breasts aren't *that* nice, are they? I'm not all *that* sweet. I look in the mirror, Joe, I say, 'OK, pretty good, not bad for an old broad,' but shit, Joe, there's simply nothing that special here. Am I such a ballerina in bed? Come on."

"C'mon, don't shout. Don't talk like that either. All right? You all right?"

"*I'm* all right. *I'm* all right. *You're* the madman, Joe, *you* are."

"No, I'm not," he said, looking almost bored with it. "There's somebody going around shooting people in the eye with syringes. I don't happen to think it's either me *or* you. Professional opinion."

"Joe, you left behind professional opinion a long time ago. I know, I know," she said, "it's your archenemy villain Chet. Chet, the mad-dog killer, killing everybody to get Joe and Audrey together."

"To get Chester and Audrey together, could be?" Joe asked her.

She calmed herself, giving up. She said, "Chet told me he had his friend come in to see you, the guy he was with when he left me that night of Milton. Be reasonable, Joe, see the writing on this for one time."

"Well, yeah, for what it's worth. Guy's a friend, all right, maybe not trustworthy but loyal, all right. Nice circle your boyfriend runs with."

"Joe, I knew the first time I saw you you were a stubborn son of a bitch."

"Yeah, I am."

"Stubborn and confused, bad mix."

"Yeah, maybe that too," he said. "I been thinking about so many people lately. Madeline, and Sharon, people we went to school with, people I worked with. You know what? Lot of the time, I can't even remember who's died, who just moved away. That's the truth, Audie. I don't know the difference anymore."

They went into the kitchen and had two more Torreines. They sat for a while and didn't say much. Joe got up to go. He looked at her and said, "I miss my wife, Audie. Miss her completely. I didn't kill anybody."

She took him by the hand, patted the contract in his pocket, and pulled him back toward the bedroom. On the way there she told him, "Joe, I only think of you now as a crazy, cold-blooded killer. I mean it. I want you now to screw me to the bedroom wall one more time and then get out of my life forever. I mean it, Joe. I really do mean it."

TWENTY SEVEN

S he really means it," Joe was telling Hraska. "You can tell. She really does mean it."

"So what?"

They were sitting in a back booth at Zack's Blue. They hadn't been doing too much hanging around lately, but when they did, the problem was where. Big Bob and Sheeney didn't want Joe in the Room at all. Joe had gotten out with a brown Seagram's box half full of junk, and Hraska had copied every paper they had on the Wright and LaLuna kills for him and brought them over to his house. Everybody in the Room, including Sheeney, had known what Hraska was doing and what for, who for. Hraska didn't give a shit, though; nobody gave a shit.

But Joe didn't like hanging around home since Lou Duva had been killed, he'd put the house up, and nobody ever liked hanging around Hraska's pad, so it became a problem as to where.

Somewhere less public than Zack's Blue would have been better—guys never knew if they should come over to Joe, ask him how's it going, shoot the awkward shit or not. But what could you do? Zack's Blue beat the street, so the Blue was it.

At least they had a booth. Joe was dressed in a goddamned tee-shirt, tan Bermuda shorts, and a pair of loafers looked like they still had pennies in them from high school. Christ, Hraska wondered, how could a cop, any cop, even a suspended cop suspected of killing his wife, go out in public like this? Hraska was no clotheshorse himself, but this here was just an embarrassment.

So most cops in general, they weren't George Hamilton, but at least a jacket, Joe, maybe a tie. Joe, for Christ sake, short pants?

Even beyond the clothes, Hraska's partner looked terrible. Weary and worn out. It made Hraska feel bad for him. Had lost both his little kids in life, and here was Joe now, telling him not only he didn't have a job, a career, or a breathing wife, he didn't even have a girlfriend anymore. Guy needs a friend.

"She means it, Wink," he was saying. "She's out of it. Completely."

Here's a guy hadn't said three words since his wife was slayed while he was wonking another, not three words, and now he's repeating himself three times that Audrey's thrown him out.

"Well, so what?" Hraska said again. "I said, who gives a shit?"

Joe just looked at him, eerie, like it didn't matter anymore what Hraska said to him to try to cheer him up.

They were drinking beer from pitchers. Joe had been hitting it pretty good since Lou Duva. Hraska was trying to keep up today, trying to keep things light for his old buddy.

"Look, Joe," he said, pouring two, "you gotta admit, most of it is just the sex thing. That's the same with anybody. I don't care what anybody says, most of what goes on between the man and the woman, most of what everybody's caring about's the sex thing. Forget the talk shows, feeling and caring, it's true. And when you come right down to it, it's not a question of much, it's just a matter of tips, really."

"What?"

"Tips, I said, not tits. Tips and how you use them. You follow? Tips of fingers, tips of lips, tips of nipples, tips of dicks, tips of tits. God, I'm a poet, pal. I'm not drunk as of yet. You got yourself a poet for a partner. What I say? How'd I put it? Tips of dips, lips, what? It rhymed, poetically."

Joe told him yeah.

"Yeah, well, maybe you think of me as no expert, but I tell you, I used to wonk my wife Darlene quite often, and quite good. Constantly, as a matter of fact. It was the only thing I found would keep her mouth shut for ten minutes. No dirty remarks there, please, what I meant was, it kept her from talking for ten, maybe, minutes. Well, usually anyway. She could really talk, that lady, as you remember. Hey, but it came to sex, she sort of had a hair trigger, which was nice, when I could manage to get my trigger finger to it there. If not, well. 'Course, sexually, since she fled to Canada, I ain't been as active. But still."

Joe took a sip of beer, made a face like it didn't taste too good.

"Joe, all I'm saying is, you gotta live. This thing's destroying you, and if it's just sex, which I know you'll tell me it ain't, but whatever it all is, it can't destroy a good man, a good cop, OK?"

"OK, Wink. Thank you."

"Joe, couple of years ago, I don't know, maybe you don't even notice, I was down in the dumps. Maybe not as far down as you are right now, nothing like's happened to you happened to me, thank God, but I was down in the dumps anyway. Couldn't sleep at all at night. Bobby Lewis, hit single, 'I couldn't sleep at all last night,' right? Well, I'm spending many, many Bobby Lewis nights. One after the other one. So I'm up, middle of the night, watching David Letterman on the television. I swear to God, this is true, Joe, listen. He's got Stupid Human Tricks? You seen that? Well, I swear to God, Joe, guy comes on, they ask him what he's gonna do, he says he's gonna stop an electric fan with his tongue. This is a steel-bladed fan, Joe, no plastic crap. Steel blades. Well, the next thing you know, right after Letterman gets done telling the kids don't try this at home, the guy sticks his tongue in the fan blades, stops them dead. I swear to you. No blood, no nothing. Little by little, angle, angle it, he puts it in, he puts it in." Hraska had his tongue out now, showing Joe how it was done. "Before you know, guy's done it. He's stopped an electric fan, his tongue."

Joe told him he was glad to hear all this.

"Wait. The reason I tell you this, partner—I know it sounds dumb, but this one moment became to me like, like I don't know, I hate to say it, like an epiphany. You know what epiphany is, Joe?"

"No."

"The Church uses it, you've heard it. But it's not in the Church sense here. It means it's an eye-opener, something that shows you something so clear, you got it that clear for the rest of your life. That's what the guy, the fan, did for me. Because I realized that night, Joe—

and remember, I told you I been very depressed—that the human spirit can do anything, absolutely anything, as long as you take your time, you don't give up, keep courage, keep putting it in a little at a time. I for once saw the world, clear."

Joe looked over at the bar, told Tammy, who was working it, bring them over two electric fans. She yelled back, What? At least the guy was joking about things now. Good sign, Hraska figured.

"And this little inspiration lecture's been free of charge too, paisan. Think of it," he told Joe.

Joe thanked him, told Tammy he had said two more pitchers.

They drank quietly awhile. Joe said, "We got three places make Ermo."

"What?" Hraska asked him, looking up from a beer drop he was following down the side of a pitcher.

"The Ermodemothan, the stuff in Madeline—I've only found three places manufacture it. It's a poison, just slows down the body's metabolism rate, eventually to nothing at all. Some stamina athletes been known to try to cheat with it, slow up their metabolism, and it's in some pesticides."

"Oh, yeah?"

"And what else, what else—oh, the film roll I found, going nowhere. The little gray Omni, no one we care about owns one."

"This surprises me, truly."

"I think, I got time, I should do the rentals."

"What?"

"Rental places, maybe it was a rental. There's one of these rented wreck places'll give you Omnis, Chevettes, shit like that."

Hraska looked at Joe, took a drink, said, "Joe, c'mon, Shirley Ellis time."

Joe said, "You think so?"

"Yup. Shirley Ellis."

It was a little joke code they had of using rock-and-roll names. It had started back at Hoover, thirty years ago. They had been taking a quiz on a short story called "The Most Dangerous Game." Mr. Tooey, English, had asked them where it took place, the setting of the story. Answer was the Caribbean. Hraska mumbled to Joe, side of his mouth, "Mitchell Torok's territory." Mitchell had a hit single on the radio, "Down in the Caribbean (It's Not a Dream You're Seeing)." So Hraska said about Mitchell Torok, they both got that one right. Ever since then, "Mitchell Torok" meant the Caribbean to them, and "Bobby Lewis" meant they couldn't sleep at all last night.

And "Shirley Ellis" meant the Name Game. They had a tough case, lots of players, they'd use it, go over names one at a time, one after the other, help each other think, repeat, put things in their place. That was Shirley Ellis.

Joe nodded. That's all he'd been thinking about anyway, might as well play the game.

"We go motive, manner, means, opportunity?" Hraska asked him.

"Let's knock off manner, maybe means. We know they're both needles plunged into the eye. Means—don't have much."

"OK," Hraska said. "Motive and opportunity, then. Which killing first?"

"Let's go chronology," Joe said, "Milton Wright."

"OK, Milton Wright," Hraska said. He took a sip, pointed at Joe, and said, "You."

Joe said, "I didn't do it."

Hraska asked him, "We playing the game?"

Joe said, "OK. LaLuna's not involved in this first one. Fact."

Hraska said, "No. Fact: The second one makes LaLuna a player in the first one. Gotta do both together. MO, pal."

"OK," Joe said. "LaLuna. Motive?"

"Get to know Audrey again."

"Aw, come on."

"Hey, husband got killed, you went out there, you ended up wonking her. Been wanting to for years. It's all right there."

Joe smirked and sat back in the booth. Hraska asked, "Opportunity?"

"They called us in, right? We were on call that night, so I guess I was with Madeline."

"Huh, convenient. And you'll tell me he got the autopsy redone to bail out Audrey. All right, we move on. Audrey. Motive."

"What order of suspects you going in?"

"Start with the ones annoy you the most. Audrey McKenna Wright. Motive—to get rid of the guy, to inherit his gelt, to marry Chester."

"To meet me. Opportunity—she was with Chester."

"Yeah, and Chester was with her. And they were both of them with Chuck Berry. Let's strike Chuck off the list, though. I like him too much. Anyway, there were no chicken-walk prints found at the scene."

"Right."

"Joe, maybe neither one of them was at Chuck?"

"Had the ticket stubs, knew the songs."

"Well, hell, everybody knows the songs. Chuck's not about to sing 'People Who Need People,' you know?"

Joe said, "No tag teams here, we do Audrey alone. Audrey wouldn't have the strength. Taking the guy down on the rug, dragging him back to his bed. She couldn't do it."

Hraska's answer was, "Mojo, think. Your two favorite suspects are a little faggy guy and a fat veggie. Put each of them on an end, they couldn't lift up an ironing board. Audrey works out, you followed her there, told me that. Wright was stoned, Lou Duva was sick, it don't take much, my friend. Physical evidence says it was someone Wright knew. He knew his wife, inside and out."

"Madeline didn't know Audrey. Physical evidence says Madeline knew her killer too."

"We're not doing that one yet. We're just doing Wright. By the way, we ever check that crazy story Audrey told us the first night, her one-week marriage, guy died in 'Nam or something? Some little curly-headed squirt?"

"Yeah, it's apparently checking out."

"Huh."

"So we up to Chester yet? On Wright?" Joe asked. Hraska nodded. Joe said, "Chester—don't say Chester and Audrey, we can do daily doubles later on—just Chester alone for now. Motive—Audrey. Guy's still sniffing around her. Wants her bad. Opportunity—I wish you got to see the weasel who came in to alibi his time away from Audrey that night. Sleaze. Guy's name's Bugg. Bug named Bugg."

"Hey, listen to me, wop—sleazy alibi's still an alibi, right?"

"Guy was a tapeworm," Joe said.

"Hey, you gave him your dog, didn't you?"

"Won't stand up," Joe said. "I've started looking into Bugg, find the Bugg-Chester connection."

"OK, so don't get any bug juice on you."

"I broke into his place."

"Jesus Christ, Joe. Whose place, Bugg?"

Joe shook his head.

"Chester's place?"

"Yeah, I know. What they gonna do, take away my badge? Listen, old Chester had a ton of science books around, chemistry, chemicals, solutions and mixtures, shit like that."

"That's it," Hraska said, threw up his hands. "Guy's got books, let's book him, case closed."

"I hate that joke, Wink, I hear that joke all the time," Joe said. "Listen, I went through his checks too. Stubs and canceled. Eighty dollars and change to a scientific mail order house. American Pharmaceutical and Lab Supplies, something like that. I got it written."

"You trace it? Not that even you're dumb enough to ever use it, but."

"The place, they only keep records of written orders. Believe that? Chester must've phoned his in. Nothing."

"So we got nothing."

"Guy might have checked, Wink, knew there'd be no record of a phone-in."

"They sell that Ermo? Carry it?"

"Have to special-order. Said they could, somebody wanted it. No record of any, past year."

"Joe, I said nothing on this guy. Anybody could've ordered up a shitting truckload of insulin and that other shit they used on Lou, Ermo. We don't know. Joe, it's nothing, nothing, nothing, we got. To me, the most incriminating thing about Chester is the guy's name's Zumrad, nobody calls him Zum. You notice that, Mojo? You had a friend named Zumrad, God forbid, but wouldn't you call him Zum for short? But nobody does, I know of, now *that's* suspicious. The rest on Chester—we got nothing, not a thing, still *nada* after all this time. You understand me? I'm not saying he didn't do it, could be.

I'm saying we got a ways to go to get something. Next? Felix?"

"Wait a minute." Joe held up a hand. "I found a lot of camera equipment in Chester's place too. Thirty-five-millimeters, lenses, telescopics, foot and a half long, surveillance stuff. The camera, the one looked like the main one he uses, was set at 400 ASA."

"ASA, so?"

"That was the same ASA on the film I found, whatever shit punk was taking those pictures of Audrey."

"Jesus Christ, Joe. I said 'Jesus Christ, Joe' yet? Jesus Christ, Joe, that's so far a stretch, Patrick Ewing couldn't touch it. That evidence ain't circumstantial, Joe, it ain't even residential. Let's make a new rule: We can only use evidence from this one solar system, OK? Jesus Christ, Joe."

"Sometimes, Wink, I consider just taking the guy and beating the truth out of him."

"Yeah, let's see, a suspended homicide cop goes in, beats a confession out of a businessman, I'm sure that'd hold up. Maybe we could have him get Charles Bronson as his lawyer, instead of the ACLU, and Dirty Harry as the judge, *then* maybe it'd hold up."

"We tried so hard for search warrants, wiretaps."

"And you broke in and found nothing but shit anyway, so what's that tell you?"

Joe said, "It don't tell me the guy didn't do it."

Hraska said, "Nothing tells you that. You're beyond being told that. That's OK. Let's go on to Marmasette, the businessman. Felix the Cat."

"You're not gonna like this either," Joe told him. "I muscled Felix yesterday. Nothing physical. Intimidation."

Hraska just stared at him, beer glass stopped halfway up. Hraska said, "Joe, I can't tell you 'Jesus Christ, Joe' no more. I already told you that. I can't tell you how wonking crazy you have gone. I can't tell you you're pissing away any chance of keeping your career. You know all that. I can't say anything more. And when Winky Dink Hraska tells you he can't say anything more, you know you've fallen down a long, long way. It's a long, long shaft you've fallen down. The descent into insanity, it don't come pretty. So what's this about Marmasette?"

"He's been blackmailing Audrey. About something else altogether. I just convinced him not to, that's all. He thinks I'm still carrying my badge and ticket, so it was easy. Talked about digging up stuff, scared him."

"Yeah," Hraska told him. "I'm sure it was easy. How's it fit in to Wright?"

Joe said, "Maybe don't at all. But Felix could've killed Wright for control of the company, now he's getting Audrey out of any control of it. Plus he likes to be in Audrey's pants too."

"There's a list of guys we'd have to computerize to keep track of."

"His alibi for Wright is telephone records, working that night at his office."

"Who else, Joe? On Wright? Who else we got?"

"Just odds and ends; loose psychos, drifters, got some threatening phone calls once, back when it was in to be antimilitary, plus a couple crazy long shots I'll tell you about we get to Madeline."

"All right, let's get to Madeline. First off—Joe LaLuna."

"Wait a minute, we said we'd do daily doubles."

"What?" Hraska asked him. "Chester and Audrey on Wright? *You* and Audrey? How about you and Chester, you and Chester and Felix. The Three Musketeers. It just gets too damned confusing, Joe. Let's get more beer and just do singles tonight. It gets too confusing." Joe nodded.

"So," Hraska went on, waving to Tammy to get two more pitchers ready, "Joe LaLuna killed his wife to marry Audrey McKenna. Easy access, his own place, had the mutt locked in the basement, his master's voice. Easy."

"Madeline lots of times put Carl in the basement to answer the door. Dog'd listen to anybody. I was with Audrey when Madeline died."

"Yeah, and Audrey was with you. Chuck Berry was out of town that day, I do believe. Joe and Audrey both planned to kill their mates to marry each other."

The pitchers came. They were backing up a bit, but the two cops could play catch-up.

Joe went out of focus, said, "Night Madeline got killed, she had an old picture of the '58 Giants she got somewhere for me, I guess. Katcavage, Huff, all those guys. Probably saw it somewhere in a catalogue, mail-ordered. Maybe planned to give it to me when I got home that night. I don't know."

"Joe, c'mon. C'mon. Shirley Ellis time."

Joe looked back, said, "OK. No doubles. Too confusing."

Hraska said, "Right. OK, so Audrey did Madeline to get Joe, her handsome widower, or to get rid of Joe, to frame him, to marry Chester, her handsome fag bait. But would that work if she didn't know Joe'd be implicated?"

Joe said, "Chester did Madeline to frame Joe, get rid of him so he could marry Audrey. Same frame, different player."

"Oh, my sweet God," Hraska said, "it's too confusing. What is this, goddamned Colonel Mustard with a monkey wrench in the parlor?" He rubbed his eyes for about twenty seconds, took up a new pitcher, and drank from it straight for a long time, spilling, put it down and rubbed his eyes again, and said again that it was all too confusing.

When he was finished, Joe told him, "Felix killed Madeline, used the same MO, just to throw us off him killing Wright to get the company."

Hraska started moaning, his head dropping left and right, snapping back upright. "You know what's nice?" he asked Joe. "Drive-by killings. Let's transfer, you, me, to Los Angeles, Joe, what d'ya say? Out there, nothing's supposed to make any sense anyway. Nobody expects it to. Gang of spics get in a car with hydraulic lifters in the trunk, to lift up the car for no apparent purpose or reason, they drive by, kill another bunch of spics for no apparent purpose or reason. Nobody's expected to make any sense of it. It don't make any sense to begin with. So let's go out there. Must be very restful, I would think. Not like this shit here."

"Yeah. Wink, we might have a couple other players," Joe told him.

Joe took a postcard out of his pocket and put it on the table, by a beer spill. It was a picture of the Rocky Mountains. The message on the back said, "I heard about the terrible thing that happened 2 your wife. For me, you were right—sometime just splitting the scene is best. The west is lovely. Women—lonely. Banks—trusting." There was a sketch of a smiley face and the signature "MH." The card was addressed to Joe, at work.

"Who the hell is MH?" Hraska asked.

"Mogie Hattes," Joe said. "Slabb's mom says it's his handwriting."

"So he's a player? Who, the con man?"

"Maybe. In the second one. To get me back."

"A copycat?"

"He's smart. I don't know. I know he's smart."

"Doesn't help us on Wright, though, does it?"

"Nope," Joe agreed. "It doesn't help us on Wright at all. Far as we know, Mogie never even knew any of them. But what started this all off was Slabb, her telling us about the needle in the eye, right?"

"So?" Hraska asked. "So?"

"So maybe she made a mistake. Maybe nobody murdered Wright."

"She made a mistake?"

"An honest mistake."

"Yeah, that girl, her whole life was an honest mistake."

There was silence for a while. Both men drank more.

Finally, Hraska said, "We're both getting nothing an awful lot. That postcard from Hattes, says splitting the scene ain't such a bad idea sometimes? C'mon, Joe, you, me, we forget all this crap, go to California, start over. Joe, we began this evening, I believe, not with talk about the twin killings, not with talk of people plunging syringes into the eyes of other people, but rather with talk of sex. Talk of the joys and glories of sex. Let's have a beer and end the evening that same note. Let's talk about the first time we ever wonked a girl. No, we've covered that in the past, haven't we. Let's talk about instead, let's tell about the absolute *best* time we ever got wonked. The epitome of it."

Hraska did that. Joe didn't. They both drank some more.

Then Joe wouldn't talk anymore. About anything.

Hraska didn't care. No Bobby Lewis nights for him. He went home, took a salamander shit, and went to bed.

LaLuna stayed drunk for a long time, he thought maybe two or three days' worth. Mostly beer, any kind, some vodka he'd found in the closet, didn't remember buying. First the edges started coming off things around the house, turning fuzzy and losing their color, then smearing together just like the time and the days were.

It was around eleven, the late news was on, when he rolled over and saw the outline, a man standing above him in the dark. Not only the news, but LaLuna could hear his stereo on too, the Judds singing harmony. The tape player had an autoreverse, and he vaguely remembered listening to Wynonna and Naomi over and over again, his brain always starting up the next song as the old one was ending. Wyoming and Nairobi.

"It's all right, LaLuna, don't hurt me. I just came in, the door was open." The outline was talking to him.

"Zumrad? Chester? That you?" He had thought a lot about Chester, hadn't ever dreamed about him before. LaLuna found a gray sock on the bed, wadded it up, threw it at the shape with the ponytail. The sock ball hit, bounced off. Shape was real.

"Yes, Chet Zumrad. You awake? The door was open. I'm sorry, I knew you were in here. Nobody answered. I have to talk to you. You calm? This is awkward, but I have something I have to tell you. Please."

"I'm calm enough I didn't kill you, right, breaking in here? What do you want here? Get out of here, Chester."

"Something bad is happening," Chester told him. He was having a little trouble breathing. "Something to Audrey, right now. You're the only one I know. I know you hate me, you think I killed her husband and everything so confusing, but I can't go to the police, the regular police, for Audrey, on this."

LaLuna sat up more in bed; the room spun. Chester went over to a standing lamp by the dresser, put the light on. It hurt LaLuna's eyes. He bowed his head, held up a palm for shade, looked at Chester's feet, asked him what the hell, what the hell.

"It's a terrible, an awful thing. I'd go to anybody else in the world, except I know you're the only one there is. For this."

LaLuna said, "Get out of here. Sit down so I can see you."

Chester sat on the front edge of the brown wooden rocker. It rocked a bit as he sat, and LaLuna looked away. He looked back; his eyes slowly turned Chester into a shape he could deal with. LaLuna asked him, "What?"

Chester said, "I went over to Audrey's, I don't know, an hour and a half ago. Tonight. Going up the walk, up the back way, in the backyard, like I always do, Felix Marmasette came crashing out of the house, the kitchen screen, almost dragging Audrey by her arm with him. She was a little cut, I think, bruised at least, on the head there. Not drunk. Not drunk. I know her. I yelled at him what the hell was going on; he just looks at me. He had Audrey in one hand, that terrible milking machine thing that Audrey used to keep, in his other hand. What's going on here? He looks very crazy, and mad, and mean, like he hardly sees me at all, or doesn't care, or if he would just attack me if I tried to help her. To get her free from him. What the hell?"

"What Audrey's like? She screaming?" LaLuna asked.

"That's what's crazy," Chester said. "See, she's sober, straight, she's crying, she's hurting because he's really holding her by the arm, digging in, really dragging her, see, but still, it's almost like she's on *his* side. 'Get out of here, Chet, leave us alone.' Through her tears. And her feet are hardly touching the ground, legs swinging from him holding her up, like a doll, rag doll. God, it was awful. She keeps saying she's fine, that I've got no place here, but she's hurting and she's scared. I admit it, I stepped back, I let them pass me there."

LaLuna jumped up off the bed, caught his balance, asked, "Where'd he take her?"

"They took off in his Mercedes. I didn't know what to do. I thought maybe the cops, but Audrey didn't want that. I was confused."

"Where'd he take her? His house?" LaLuna was looking for his loafers.

"I know you and I were never together on everything. I know how much you hate me, I don't know why. I don't like you either, but we're both on the same side now, when it comes to Audrey, so I came over here finally. I didn't think of anything else I could do. You can keep things quiet, and help her. Please, LaLuna, help her out here. Bust that fat suck."

LaLuna grabbed Chester's ears and held on, and yelled over his screaming, "His house? His house? Where to?"

"No," Chester said, crying, "to a motel then. I followed them to. The Ho-Hum, on Regal Road, out on 23A, down from the Altmond's there. Should I come?"

LaLuna let go of his ears. "What room? Room?" Still yelling.

"I don't know," Chester said. "I saw them pull in, Audrey sitting like frozen in the car. Marmasette went in the office to get a key, a room, I guess. I came over here. Right away. I drove around awhile first."

LaLuna had his loafers on, both their backs folded under. He went out with them that way, no socks. He heard Chester yelling to his back, "Should I come? You want me?"

LaLuna thought he knew where the Ho-Hum was, but he had trouble shifting gears all the way, and the place wasn't there. He cursed and made a U-turn on 23A, hoped there wasn't a cop around to slow him down. He found the Ho-Hum on the way back, had driven right by it, looking on the wrong side of the road.

He pulled into the unlit parking lot, only a few cars there, maybe a Mercedes, maybe not, he wasn't sure, didn't check. He stopped in front of the office, place still had a light on, a red Vacancy sign in the window.

A kid reading *Sports Illustrated* was at the desk, looked up at him, put the magazine down quick.

"Police," LaLuna said.

"You don't look like it," the kid told him. LaLuna looked at him. Kid said, "All right. I just said you didn't happen to look like one. What do I know?"

"A fat blond guy, dyed-blond hair, he check in tonight?"

"Surfer Joe? Yeah, he got a key a couple hours ago."

"Anybody with him?"

"Well, you know, he made out like he was alone. Some kind of business-trip crap he gave me. But I could see a woman, sort of folded over, ducking over, down in the shotgun seat of his car. Like it's a big thing they're gonna spray the sheets for a few hours. I don't care."

"They still there?"

"Geez, I don't know. Are they? I didn't see them go in or out."

"Room number."

"They're probably still there. I don't think the guy was gonna take her out for dinner or anything. Maybe he was, I don't know. I'd give up my paycheck on this cheesy job if every screw job gave me five bucks. Yeah, right, a business trip."

"Room," LaLuna said louder.

"Fifteen. Odd numbers are that way, on the way out and down."

"What else?"

"What else what?"

"What else you see? In the car, anything."

"Nothing. You want the key? I'll have to see your badge, I think, you want the key."

The window to 15 was dark, plastic curtain pulled over. No sounds. LaLuna yelled and started to kick in the door. Took two kicks; the second did it, but it twisted LaLuna's knee up crazy. The pain made him yell louder.

Inside 15 was even darker. He could just make out the two heads and sets of shoulders, held stiff, coming up out of the sheets of the bed. LaLuna limped over quick; his knee wasn't working.

Two screams from the bed, his and hers. LaLuna dragged the fat slob out of the covers, down onto the floor. Part of a blanket stayed wrapped around his hips, legs. Incredible fat, felt like three hundred pounds, hard to move. LaLuna kicked in deep with his bad leg; both men screamed. LaLuna tried standing on the bad leg, kicking with the good. No force. Both his loafers had flown off, across the room somewhere.

In the dark corner, he could make her out, watching, but he kept his eyes on the fat, rolling over, groaning.

Guy tried to crawl away, lost the blanket, all naked. LaLuna dragged him back, like you would a bug you wanted to hurt, get rid of.

LaLuna used his fists and elbows, saved his bent knee. He was counting the solid hits he got on the porker. "One, two, three …"

Fat bastard tried crawling under the bed, too fat, the bed lifted up on one side with his bulk, most of him still hanging out there, easy to hit. Bed almost high enough to topple over the other way.

LaLuna lost count. Lot of hits, lot of hits. Ribs and ass and back and legs, getting red and swollen.

LaLuna waited, felt the blood, heard the air leaving the fat victim, just spitting blood, then a little whimpering, "Please, please." Familiar voice, but not like this.

Blood, wet and warm, all over the guy. In his hair. You couldn't see the blond of the hair in the dark, with all the blood.

LaLuna felt himself getting sick, getting too tired to hit. He kicked him once, wincing, and he stopped. His eyes started finding things, there in the dark of room 15. A little crummy table by the bed. A desk holding an ice bucket and a telephone. Upright lamp somehow knocked half over, leaning between the wall and the drapes.

The little whimpering "Please" coming from half under the bed.

She was still in the corner of the room, naked, screaming for him to stop, even though he already *had* stopped, was just looking around now.

She looked to be OK, except Audrey was screaming at him with a Spanish accent. And Audrey was a spic girl, nothing on but brown skin and a Mets cap crooked on her head.

And fat Felix Marmasette, whining and naked and hurting bad there on the rug, half under the bed, was really Captain Big Bob Bell.

TWENTY NINE

The only thing uglier than a white cop's ugly white legs, Hraska figured, was those ugly white legs with one knee swaddled up in Ace bandages to about the official size and weight of an NFL football. Worse, those legs poking out of madras Bermuda shorts left over from around 1963 maybe. All of this in Hraska's own living room.

Joe had moved into Hraska's place, sort of. If the poor guy was living anywhere, he was living here in Hraska's crummy little three-rooms-and-some. Joe had put his house on the market the week Duva died, got a quick sale to a Pittfield Petroleum yuppie who had been rotated in, wanted the place right away for him, his wife, his kid, and his ex-wife to share. Cozy. Price was right, not that Joe would give a shit about that these days. So Joe had vacated, dumped everything somewhere—maybe on secondhand consignment, Auction Louie's—and brought a trunk and a couple of suitcases and some brown paper Grand Union bags of stuff over to Hraska's. Naturally, Joe was also lugging his two cartons of papers on the cases, don't leave home without them.

What with the second mortgages, topped-out credit cards, bank loans, and all the doctor bills Lou Duva had stuck Joe with, he wasn't about to see any long-term pocket money from dumping the place, even if it did give him a little folding cash for just now. Another day older and deeper in debt. So who knows, Hraska might never get to see Joe move out of his place.

Joe's spindly white legs, the cartilage all ripped away in one knee from being used on Big Bob's motel door and then on Big Bob's ribs and crotch, were spread out like hairy vines across Hraska's little living room. Joe spent his day with his legs propped up on Hraska's collection of cheap crime paperbacks, whining.

Guilt, huh? And the things it can do. One thing about life—guilt is shit. Guilt is definitely shit.

"Big Bob ever wakes up," Hraska told Joe, "let's not tell him I'm putting you up here. Let's not tell nobody."

Joe, the cop turned felon, said he appreciated.

Joe had been arraigned on a variety of crap, the worst of it being only aggravated assault on a police officer, so he made bail easy, using just a little bit of the house money for that and to keep the lawyer awake. But Big Bob hadn't regained consciousness—how could anybody be sure of that anyway?—and if he died, Jesus, if he died, Joe was in for manslaughter, maybe even murder, didn't matter how many good years he had put in. This was the chief of detectives lying there with concussions, abrasions, contusions, mumbling like he always did but now officially mumbling on account of he was semicomatose.

"Semicomatose, business as usual," Hraska had said. "The doctors keep telling Big Bob breathe deep, breathe deep, Big Bob. Big Bob, he keeps forgetting what that is. Don't worry, Joe, he'll be all right."

Joe didn't answer.

The papers were playing it like a simple disgruntled-employee thing, wacko cop turned on bureaucrat, looked like. The whore was out of it so far, so Big Bob the Stud wasn't looking too bad with his ink. At the Ho-Hum on official. Bob had a little bit of clout with some locals, maybe even something going at *Newsday*. The *Daily News* ever got interested, he'd probably be screwed good, page two for a week.

"Just remember," Hraska had told Joe that night, down at lockup, Joe looking dazed, Hraska trying to cool things, "when it gets to the grand jury, don't take the rap for his stump. That was long before you got there. Years before." Wink had pocketed Big Bob's wedding ring—it had flown off during the beating; no knuckle to hold it on. Showed it to Joe, Joe gave it a zombie look.

Now Joe looked even worse than he had then, and not just because of the Ace bandage and the madras shorts that had replaced the just plain tan ones. Joe said, "I showed the kid at the Ho-Hum a picture of Marmasette. It was definitely him checked in, probably with the spic girl in the car. Maybe even carrying the milking thing, for effect."

"Sure," Hraska said, trying to read an old *National*. "Made himself known, snuck back out unseen, gave the spic chick the key, slipped her fifty bucks to get Big Bob's bare ass over there. You know Big Bob and his ass, it wouldn't have been difficult. Well, who knows, maybe this will cure him of his low-down, Rudolpho Valentino ways of the flesh."

"I just hadn't put Chester and Felix together. They got me good on this."

"Hell, your BAC was higher than Roger Craig's ERA, he was still playing, so it wasn't that tough to screw somebody like *you* up."

"I didn't see it coming at all. Just fogged out and mad."

"You were rousting Felix on the pressure he was giving Audrey, rousting them both, Chester especially, on the murders, one and two, it's no wonder they got together, came after you. They're two of a kind, those guys, wonking businessmen. Just a business deal for the two of them, that's all. They knew you were hurting, probably heard it from Audrey, but thought you were still carrying. How were they to know that you were already a washed-up nobody, added injury to insult. How's the knee? Draining pus? You want something to eat?"

Joe called him Madeline, said he didn't want anything, Hraska went in to cook anyway. He had this really good recipe, easy to do. Rice that came in little bags, you only had to microwave it, then this mixed-vegetable garbage, fry some chicken, mix it up, pour it over the rice after it's drained.

Hraska finished draining, called in, "C'mon, Joe, you gotta eat."

"Audrey's getting married."

Hraska went back into the living room, carrying the pan with the chicken and vegetables. Rice was ready, draining in the sink.

"Yeah," Joe told him. "I called her up, she told me. Asked me again to please get lost."

"So soon, with everything that's going on?"

"Yeah, well, they'll keep the plans quiet for a while. Maybe not do it, but it's all planned out anyway. All set. It's for real. I could tell."

"Chester, right?"

"Yeah, sure, who else? From the first, I been telling people he did Audrey's husband to get Audrey, and now he has her. He's got this business, doing very well now, I guess, getting bigger and bigger. I guess Audrey figures she'll be a CEO's woman again, I don't know. Plus I guess she's ready to take the money from Vor-Tech and split, give Felix the whole place, just be happy with the gelt. Maybe even invest it some in Chester's new deal, I don't know."

"They want you for best man? Nah, I'm kidding. That's too bad, really. You want to try this chicken?" He held out the pan to show Joe. "Vegetables and shit, very good. It's like moo goo gai pan, but it tastes different."

Joe said no, said he was going out.

"Where you going to? You limp too much, you go out. Rest up. The doctor said stay off it. Your lawyer said he's gonna call, lay things out for you, plus see if Police Aid will pay or not when one cop beats up his boss. Stick around for that, at least. Come on, we'll talk about what pressure we can bring to bear on this. Hell, between the two of us, we should be able to get the department, Big Bob, to ease up on it, don't you think? Lotta ways, I'm sure, as long as the big turd lives."

Hraska had to go back into the kitchen; his hand was getting hot. He heard limping steps, then the door slam. He finished off half the chicken with a beer, shoveled the rest of it into a microwave container and put it in the icebox.

He went out to the couch, the one Joe had been using for sleeping on. Moved some of his own mystery books out of the way. Joe's supermarket bags had underwear, black socks, some handkerchiefs and belts, and more neckties than Joe would use in a life.

The suitcases had shirts, pants, short pants that Hraska felt like getting rid of, a pair of flannel pajamas that would be too heavy for another three months, at least.

The trunk was locked. Hraska popped it with a screwdriver, one try. There were Joe's two summer suits folded on top. Under those a few framed pictures—Joe in his old blues, looking about sixteen; Joe with Duva in Eisenhower Park, it looked like; the kids, both dead—

and the *Aristocrat,* the same yearbook Hraska had on his own book-shelf in the bedroom. It fell naturally open to Audrey McKenna's picture. Hraska looked at it a minute, put it away.

More crap in the trunk under the picture stuff, nothing worth the look. Then, at the bottom, in a corner, a nice-looking wooden box, some kind of jet-black wood—ebony?—a nice grain and shine to it.

Hraska tried not to damage the wood finish as he worked with the screwdriver. Needed something sharper, went into the kitchen for a steak knife and an ice pick.

The top of the box popped off. Inside were some small and expensive-looking electronic things, bugs most likely, and, in its own leather sheath, a surgical syringe about the size of one of those Ginsu knives they advertise on TV, twenty-nine ninety-nine, plus handling and shipping.

Hraska picked up the needle. Big mother. The tube of it was marked by cc's, was holding about 50 cc's of a clear liquid. Hraska kept holding it, shaking it, kept thinking, couldn't put the damned thing down.

What the hell, Joe, what the hell. Jesus Christ, Joe, Jesus Christ. Have I said Jesus Christ, Joe, yet?

THIRTY

LaLuna said, "Whoever it is out there, Chester or whoever, he knows I'm closing in. I'm tightening the circle, Wink, I won't give up now. I can't give in. I'm closing in, and whoever it is knows it, see. There's nothing left for me to do except to not give up."

They were at a pizzeria, Larry's, across a busy 23A from the Waterchop Hotel. Waterchop was a flashy, four-story, lot-of-wings place—new, built for visiting executives, high-class hay tumbles. From their pizzeria table on the sidewalk, LaLuna could see a constant stream of well-dressed people going in and out of the place.

LaLuna kept trying to explain, about not giving up, going on. "I feel all right, closing now. I'm like Andy Robustelli going after the quarterback. I'm Sam Huff hanging on to Jim Brown's back until help arrives. Remember?"

"Until help arrives."

"Only trouble," LaLuna said, "only trouble, clock's running down."

"Yeah," Wink agreed with him, "two-minute warning."

Big Bob was still pretty bad off. Hadn't regained consciousness. LaLuna kept trying not to think about it. It was sad and scary, got him so pissed he wanted to kill somebody. Kill guys—maybe Chester, not so much Felix, he wasn't sure why. But he didn't want to be Big Bob's killer. Big, dumb, gentle Big Bob, chief of detectives, half under the floating bed, saying, "Please, now please," over and over.

The hotshot ex-DEA guy that Sheeney had gotten on loan was working on this Big Bob one too. Did that mean they figured it to turn into a homicide?

The IAD boys were swarming, locusts in heat. And Hickey the lawyer had told LaLuna that Campbell and Auffermann, two plaid ADA's from Philbrick's, were investigating it. The two plaids going around the Room with their eyebrows all crushed together in the center, not talking to anyone. Hickey had told LaLuna that too. Wink hadn't said much about it.

Just that there was a two-minute warning, and someone had said about "jail time."

"That was jail time even if Big Bob lives?"

"Yeah, looks like, that's what they're targeting for. Some time, even if he lives," Wink had told him.

Philbrick, using his boss Strickland's muscle because the boss was too stupid to even know it, could put anybody he wanted to in jail. Unlimited man-hours, money, manpower, paper, and memory, all right there on his desktop at his corner place in Town Hall. Plus more felonious targets than they could fit into Yankee Stadium on a Sunday morning. All Philbrick had to do was decide who he wanted carted off to jail, and sooner or later, that would happen. The poor shit didn't have to do much. Some, it was said, had never done anything. Some poor schmuck had cursed at Philbrick on his day off when he was buying his kid an ice cream at Jones Beach. Hard time for that poor stooge, it was said.

Nothing mattered; the DA wanted you gone, you're gone. Even if you didn't do anything.

LaLuna had usurped authority, been guilty of police brutality, broken and entered, illegally wiretapped, and beaten his naked chief into a two-week-minimum coma: working title—assault on a public official/police officer. Big Bob lives—please God, yes—LaLuna does time anyway, if that's what they decide on.

LaLuna could fight it off for a while. Hickey was pretty good. But he cost money, and he could only do so much. Sooner or later it would all cave in. It was the irresistible force meeting the very movable object. LaLuna was real movable.

Two-minute warning, Wink told him. Not much time. Busy day.

Wink had just finished saying something about indictments. LaLuna told him again about the tightening circle on the two kills. He wanted to hear that again, even if he had to say it himself.

Monte, who was really Larry, the place Larry's was named after, came out and over to their table, sat down. Monte owned three Larry's, still threw his own dough. He was known as a guy who liked cops.

"How's it going the battle, officers? More slice each?"

The cops both thanked him, said no.

"My boy at the counter said me to come over?"

"Yeah, true," LaLuna told Monte. "Thanks. Listen, Monte, I wanted to ask you. It's OK a van's parked out back, in the lot, couple hours, a couple days maybe, the weekend tops?"

"Sure. It's there now, huh?"

"Yeah, it is. It's rental, the dark gray, couple hours. Just don't have people bothering it, all right?"

"Yeah, sure," Monte told them. "What's up? Surveillance?"

"Well, something like that."

"Not *my* place, I hope, officers. This is all very clean here."

Wink broke in, said, "Across the street." He poked his head at the Waterchop.

"The Chop? Hey, that's a fairly classy place. What d'you make?"

Wink said, "Something, nothing."

Monte waved his palm. "Fine with me, fine. This isn't the first time I've been asked to help out on an ongoing."

LaLuna and Wink looked at each other. For a guy followed cops, he hadn't been reading the papers. Good.

"Officers, I'm a fairly suspicious guy, forgive me. That van, where it is now, you can't get a view of much of the Chop. You wouldn't be busting my chops here now, would you?"

LaLuna told him, "We don't gotta see. You understand, Monte?"

Monte asked, "Just wire?"

Wink said, "Christ, Monte, why don't we just we put you in charge of the whole wonking investigation. Might as well. You do all right here, we'll have you clean up the drug traffic on the whole damned East Coast, you know?"

"Hey, I could, probably," Monte told them. "Old Monte wouldn't do any pussyfooting about it, in and out, bang, bang, bang, just say screw to drugs. Course, I know you guys are hampered by the courts and our legal system. In this country, of course."

Wink told him he was right.

"So you guys know Johnson, something Johnson, he comes in here, he's a gambler or something? Kind of Chink eyes, big cheeks?"

Wink said they didn't know him. Wink said, "This is just a little snooping, listening operation Sergeant LaLuna here is running. I'm here strictly trying to talk some sense into the man. He's asking you to not do nothing, so that's easy."

LaLuna said, "So anyway, thanks, Monte. The van, it'll be there not long, so just leave it be, no problem."

Monte said he would, would tell his staff about it, to keep it quiet. He got up from the table.

"Don't tell *anybody* about it, for Christ sake," Wink told him. "Your staff, anybody. Now I don't know why the hell we told *you* about it at all. You gonna leave it alone, or you gonna leave it alone?"

"Yeah, OK, OK, just tell me what it is when it's all done, that's all."

"Yeah," Wink said, "we'll do that. You'll be the first to know. You'll get the wonking carbons, faxes. Maybe you can run it over to the DA for us, the entire case."

"Jesus," Monte said, walking away. "I told you guys I'd do it."

Wink just shook his head at LaLuna.

LaLuna asked, "You covering your ass, even with Monte?"

Wink said, "Sure. I'm stupid?"

When LaLuna had gotten back to Wink's place last night, late, Wink had been sitting in front of the TV, the needle lying there on the little tin folding tray in front of him. They both looked at it awhile; Wink leaned over, gave it a flick with his finger, like a used-up cigarette.

"It ain't the same, not the same one," LaLuna finally told Wink, sitting down across from him, so Wink would have to look right at him.

Wink punched off the TV with his clicker, said, "Joe, what I should do, I should arrest my partner. I been sitting here two, three hours, not even a beer, thinking how I do that. How's a guy cuff his partner, Joe, over ten years, the guy he's in the yearbook with from high school. How I do that, Joe? You tell me how I do that."

"I'm glad you said you should, Wink. So you won't. I swear to God, it's not the same one. There's ways to prove that, I'm sure. It's a knockoff, I swear."

"Who the fuck cares about *you* anymore? Who the *fuck* cares what you do. You bring *this*." Wink got out of the chair, on his pins— LaLuna had never seen him move anywhere near this fast—up and over him, his arm grabbing, whipping toward LaLuna. LaLuna covered up.

He felt the syringe hit him hard, where his shoulder and chest met, sting him; it fell to the ground. LaLuna looked at it hit the rug, couldn't help looking. Still intact, not leaking. Wink was over him, trying to lift him out of the chair. LaLuna just let himself hang. Wink struggled with his bulk awhile, cursed him, threw him back down in the chair.

"You bring *this* fucking thing"—Wink stepped over, kicked hard at the thing on the rug, missed it—"into *my* fucking house? You beat Big Bob half to dead, do all this other shit, you bring your death needles into my house? Whose eye *this* been in lately, Joe? Your *wife's*? Your wife's eye? Your fucking fuck broad's husband? *Whose*? Who gives a shit what *you* do anymore, Joe? Who cares about *you*? *You* don't, *I* don't. You don't care about me or *my* head or my reputation or my career or my fucking head on a platter. You never did, don't start now. You been in garbage, pal, since you got onto this thing, you been tripping over garbage, you kicked over garbage in the alleyway looking for this dream man been taking pictures, just like you been in garbage the whole time on this. Don't drag *me* down into it. This shit."

Wink leaned over, picked up the needle, held it two inches from LaLuna's face. The face didn't move. Wink whispered, *"This?* In *here?* You self-centered maggot-fuck."

Later, it had taken an hour, more, for LaLuna to explain the plan to Wink. He didn't want to hear. Just more shit on top of shit, Wink said. Finally, with LaLuna cashing in every last chip of friendship and memory and loyalty and feeling he could dig up, Wink had listened. Head turned away, eyes out the closed window, lips pressed together in fuck-you sarcasm, Wink had at last listened.

LaLuna told him, "The scam on me with Big Bob convinced me Marmasette is out of it. I figured, he's in for murder with Chester or even solo, he's not gonna be running these cheap side operations with the guy, just to get me off his ass from bothering Audrey. Seems to me to be just looking for the company, control, having some fun with Audrey on the side. He's too smart, too business wise, to be causing me shit if he's hiding a murder or two. What d'ya think? Wink?"

Wink just stared.

LaLuna said, "Chester's different. He's a mean bastard, probably runs his business ventures just to see who he can screw. He's killer emotion, wrapped up in Saran Wrap, that guy. You can see it. I wouldn't be surprised, I was beating Big Bob, Chester was outside with his photography equipment. Anyway, you know I don't think Audrey's part of anything, I still think that, but either way, Wink, here's where this comes in."

LaLuna reached over, picked up the syringe off the rug, put it back on the TV tray. "This. Chester and Audrey have a sort of pre-engagement celebration set up. At the Waterchop Hotel—you know that big new place across from Monte-Larry's first pizzeria, his first one he had? So don't ask me how I know, you don't want to hear any more about my skirting the law, I know that. I just know they got a date. Don't worry about it."

Wink told him, "Don't worry about it. Right now, pal, all I'm worried about's going to sleep, waking up with a fucking needle in my eye."

LaLuna was so glad to hear Wink talking like that, he said, "Wink, you're making my eyes tear."

Wink answered, "Yeah, just like a fucking needle would do."

LaLuna said, "What they're doing, Chester and Audie, they're eating somewhere nice, checking into the Waterchop for a wonk-all weekend. Room service and reserving the hot tub, private time, for some underwater wonking."

Wink got up, said, "I gotta go fix a bagel."

LaLuna said, "I got the room. Third floor they got. Jelly Craven's security. You remember Jelly Craven? I gotta maybe get somebody I know get the passkey from Jelly for a minute or two."

Wink, still standing, hadn't moved yet, said, "Yeah, somebody you know, one of your many, many loyal friends, those who cleave to you in your trials. I'm off to a bagel."

He left for the kitchen. LaLuna followed him in, leaned on a counter, told him, "First thing, a bug."

Wink asked, "How much that bug cost? Those ones you keep hidden from me, how much? They ain't no Whisper 2000, huh?"

LaLuna said, "No, they're good. Whole system, maybe three, four thousand. Hot."

Wink asked, "House money?"

LaLuna said, "Yeah, the house, always take real estate. So listen—I'm being square here. Audrey says, 'Honey, I just loved putting that needle in Milton, then into Joe's wife,' then we turn it over to Sheeney, to Philbrick, to his plaids, whoever you want, anonymous, immediate, that's it."

"Yeah, Philbrick'll have no idea, I'm sure, think maybe Boston Blackie delivered it to them."

"Don't matter," LaLuna told him. "It's not evidence, it's just motivation."

Wink asked, "What's the needle come in?"

LaLuna said, "Wait. I don't hear nothing on the bug, I wait, Chester's in the crapper, off getting more rubbers and booze or something, I give the room a call, I'm the desk."

Wink said, "Hey, yeah, you could put a handkerchief over the receiver, hold your nose, use your secret spy voice on them, nobody'll be wise. Neat." Good to have Wink back.

LaLuna said, "I say, 'Could you please check, ma'am, our Customer Satisfaction Survey Card, should be in the night table drawer, along with the Gideon and our complimentary, complimentary ...' I don't know, some kind of complimentary crap."

Wink said, "And so the needle's in there, right?"

LaLuna said, "Needle's in there, Chester comes back, I told you, the guy is nothing but Saran Wrap, we listen close, ready to bust in, him or Audrey or something tells us, their reactions, tells us what we want to know. He spills, he lies, she counters, whatever—something happens, we know."

Wink was creaming his bagel, inch-thick cream cheese.

"So?" LaLuna asked his partner. LaLuna said, "What I got, Geraldo, is an obsession with this thing, right?" LaLuna said to his partner, "Aren't you gonna tell me this is a crazy-crap thing I'm doing?"

Wink said, "Nah, every single thing you do is a crazy-crap thing. It's OK with me. You get your own room key for it, it's OK with me. I got my outside hobbies keep me busy."

LaLuna asked him, "Are you gonna tell me I'm not doing this all for the case, I'm doing this to screw up Audrey and Chester?"

Wink said, "Nah, everything you do screws up somebody. Usually yourself, mostly. I don't care. I don't care."

LaLuna said, "So tell me."

Wink said, "I'll tell you what." He finished creaming the bagel, both halves, pressed them together hard, gray cheese coming out all around, he turned and threw it hard at LaLuna, cream cheese spraying LaLuna's arm.

"That's what," Wink told him.

Now, at Larry's, Wink was finishing off the crust of his slice of pie.

LaLuna stood up, looked, said, "I'm going, you leaving?"

Wink said, "I'm leaving."

Wink had kept the needle at his place all night; LaLuna had gone back out. In the morning, Wink had let him take the needle back. LaLuna had spent the day busy, getting things lined up for what he was about to do.

LaLuna asked, "You couldn't do the van, just till I get back outside? Five, ten minutes?"

Wink shook his head.

LaLuna asked, "You couldn't cover, they come early, give me a call up there? 'Jo-Jo, better run, man.'"

Wink shook his head again.

LaLuna said, "That's OK. 'S OK. Look, pard, don't you worry about me, OK? I got me a plan. Oh, oh, oh, I *do* have a plan. Don't worry about me. Maybe worry about yourself, OK?"

LaLuna patted his pockets, turned to cross the street.

Wink called him back, said, "Look, Joe, don't feel too bad you went crazy, OK? Don't feel too bad about it. Everybody always said working with me all these years would drive anybody nuts. So really, you held on quite long."

The sun was in Wink's eyes. He was holding up his hand, for

shade, as he talked to LaLuna, looking up at him as he spoke.

LaLuna said, "Before it all ends up, man, answer me just one thing for me, please."

Wink jutted out his chin at LaLuna to ask him what one thing was that?

"Your father really invent Maypo?"

Wink looked down at the paper plates on the table, holding their crumbs and crusts. He waited awhile, LaLuna didn't move, Wink said, "Nah, was some guy up in Vermont."

He looked up again toward the sun, at LaLuna, and said, "But I'll tell you what. In my heart he did. In my heart."

THIRTY ONE

Hraska stayed sitting there, watched his partner cross the street to the Chop, still limping, still looking like he hurt pretty bad. Joe had on his gray suit, very quiet, gliding through traffic.

It would be a quick and easy trip across the lobby, no waves, elevator ride up to the third floor, then use a twist key Joe had muscled along with a guarantee from a quiff named Lombardo, into room 314, probably feeling just like Cary Grant.

Would take him, what, maybe a minute, two, to get up to the third floor, find the room, ease his way in. Hraska left the little pizzeria table, crossed over, looked around, snuck into the gray van.

He'd never worked a wire before; seen guys do it. He sat on a little yellow Naugahyde stool in front of the dials, put on this headset looked like a kid's Walkman, worked a couple squelch knobs, volume, figured the frequency was where it was supposed to be. Didn't mess with the recording crap. Hraska didn't know how much of this stuff Joe had ripped off from the department.

Hraska started hearing stuff. He knew Joe had brought in two bugs; Hraska didn't know how to switch back and forth between them. He heard bumps, moving around up there. If he had been helping his partner on this, had been in on it with him, they would've tested them now, had Joe say, "One, two, three, four," from all corners, flush the toilet, had Hraska call the room to report. These were thousand-buck bugs, though, didn't need a test.

Hraska heard more bumping around, static, a wind noise. More bumps, more racket. Christ, Joe, you're a worse cat burglar you are a cop.

No doubt about it, Hraska heard a door open, felt his skin prickle, brought his hands up and held the headset tight. Stared ahead, didn't want to fool with any knobs, just listened.

Voices. No words yet. Two voices. Just two of them. One was Joe. Joe and another. Female. Indecipherable.

First words Hraska made out weren't Joe's, they were Audrey's, they were, "Joe, what are you doing?" Clear as that.

Hoover High. Audrey McKenna standing there in Room 314 of the Waterchop Hotel, sounding as young as she did back at Hoover. Remember Audrey confronting Joe about the Popstooka affair, with the guys all watching, grinning, around the lockers, in the hall? "You really dating that Popstooka, Joe?"

"Joe, what the hell you doing?"

Hraska heard Joe's voice, starting to make out more words. "Audie. I'm sorry about everything. I didn't understand what was going on, neither of us did until, but—"

"What're you holding, Joe? What is that you got?"

Sounds of Joe fumbling with something. Nothing for a while. Then Audrey, trying to scream. Hraska should get his ass over there. Quick.

Joe, pleading: "It's OK, Audie, OK. Just water in it. I was gonna spring it on you, that was a plan I had, spring it on you and Chester, see what—"

Audrey: "I knew a long time, Joe."

Even through the wire, her voice was so tense now it hurt Hraska's neck just to listen to it. He kept holding the headset, could hear: "I knew, I didn't want to know it. That just for Chet, Joe? You gonna get me too? Both of us? You got enough shit in there to kill two, Joe, do you?"

Joe: "No, no, Audie, you don't understand this thing. Lot of shit going on, but this here is just water. This was just a kind of a frame. Not even. A setup. A setup is all. This isn't killing anybody."

Nothing for a couple of seconds. Hraska, get your fat ass over there. It's happening.

Joe: "Not me we have to look out for. It's everybody else. Everybody."

They both said something at the same time. Indecipherable. Then Joe again, indecipherable.

Then Audrey: "What for, Joe? To get me? You love me that much, Joe? Hate me?"

Joe: "I love you, Audie, yeah, guilty as always. Always have, never stopped. I don't kill people. I love you and I'm sorry, that's all."

Audrey said his name. She said it so sad, like it hurt so much, just to say it.

Joe: "Here, Audrey, watch. Look at me."

Had to be done, Hraska knew it.

Hraska knew his pal had got in wrong. It was the case he couldn't clear. Slabb was gone, Wright, Lou Duva, and he couldn't clear any of it. Too much lined up against him, people and things. For Big Bob, which he did, he'd do time. For Duva, which he didn't, he'd do time. Slabb was the only one he'd skate on. He'd gotten in wrong, and it had kept getting worse.

Was the case Joe couldn't clear.

Hraska heard Audrey say, "Joe."

Joe said, "I hate needles, huh?" With almost a little laugh at the end of it.

Hraska heard her say, "No."

Get over there, Hraska.

Hraska heard his partner say, "We were Joe and Audie back then, remember? Weren't we? Joe and Audie. Love. And water."

He heard her say, "Hey." Then louder, "Hey."

Man knows the difference between water hitting his system and something else, a little bit of poison.

"Joe. Hey."

Hraska didn't even take off the headphones. The jack ripped out of the console as he got off the stool and stumbled through the van door. The wire was still dragging from his head as he ran crazy across 23A, dodging traffic, heading into the Chop.

LaLuna thought about the dead.

The dead. Sharon Slabb, who had cut off her own face, was the worst in a way, somehow, she who never used anybody, never worked an angle, just tried to stay loyal to anybody she loved. She had a lab full of pieces of people and never tried to screw anybody up. Her partner, Dreeve, liked to wonk dead bodies, and Sharon never tried to hurt him with that knowledge. Maybe they even had Big Bob's missing finger in their lab, along with somebody's foot, the foot of somebody they couldn't find. And they'd have LaLuna there, too, soon.

What was that story in school: guy froze to death, saw himself doing it, saw the search party coming around the bend in the trail to find himself?

Dreeve would be the one to work LaLuna's body. On call. Audie would call 911 crying, here comes Buck Rodgers, crew chief who Mogie Hattes found out molested kids, then Dreeve and Crime Lab and rubberneckers and blues and Winky.

And LaLuna's wife was dead too.

LaLuna thought about his two dead kids every day of his life. Even lately, with so much he had to think about, he never missed a day thinking about them.

Audie, in the bleacher seats of Yankee Stadium, wearing a black beret and smiling up at the rain of food coming down on them.

Everybody he knew was either dead, didn't care, or was after his ass, so this was the best way out. Split the scene for good.

And Joey was four years old on a swing in some park he didn't recognize and Uncle Benny was pushing him. So high, higher than he'd ever been, and little Joe was just screaming and screaming, it was so great with Uncle Benny's big hands on his little kid back, and then him and the swing jolting out and up into the sky, he would almost get shoved off each time and he loved it. And he kept screaming and he loved it so much he knew he would have to cry soon with the love of it, but he knew he shouldn't because if he started crying he couldn't stop and then Uncle Benny would hear him and see and stop pushing. So he just kept screaming and screaming, trying not to cry, getting pushed higher up toward the blue sky above the park.

And in the next second he was going down and he was done, on the rug, still, needle dangling out, no thoughts, except that somewhere far off, somebody he had loved was screaming for him.

II

THE SURVIVORS

THIRTY THREE

Audrey didn't think all that much about Joe anymore.

Her ass hurt. She'd pumped the bike maybe twenty miles today, and they always made these seats feel like you were sitting cross-assed on a buzz saw. She got off, started limping around, feeling like her feet still weren't on real ground, feeling like she was still up, peddling the damned bike.

Chet was hoisting his bike up, putting it on the rack on the van's back door. He could go another twenty miles, probably another hundred, two hundred. But he was always good about it, never pushed her, always popped it into a low gear and stayed with her when she was slowing up.

She walked around the van, heard him stop fooling with the bike, now half on the rack, figured he had stopped to watch her.

She knew her hurting ass was still looking good in Spandex. She had on blue and black fluorescent biker shorts, down to just above the knee. Not so bad, for a woman her age.

How old could a woman be and still have an ass good enough for Spandex? Fifty? Fifty for Spandex sounded absurd, but it wasn't too far off. Fifty or forever, that's the only numbers she could figure for the answer. Fifty or forever.

How old, though, before it didn't matter? How old before you looked ridiculous, even if you *were* still tight there?

She got into the van and sat until Chet got in behind the wheel. She sat there ready to head back. He took the keys, turned to her, and said, "So what is it, Audrey?"

So he knew. Not bad. Pretty sharp.

"What's what?"

"Hey, you're acting like something's going on, happening, the whole trip."

He knew; still wanted to hear it, though, wanted her to say it.

She settled back into the bucket seat. All right, that's what you want.

"Chet, I'm a killer."

"What?"

"You're sitting next to a killer here. For instance, I killed Joe LaLuna. You want to marry a killer, do you?"

"No, you're not."

"I killed Joe. I stood there and let him die. That's a killing. One for me. One for the bad guys."

"Guy killed himself, Audrey, don't give yourself credit."

"Anyway, as I watched Joe LaLuna die, I knew him to be an innocent man."

Chet turned away, said Shit, like she was a stupid kid he had to listen to.

"I saw Joe LaLuna die, knew then he was an innocent man, Chet. I'd always in the back of my mind figured him to be the crazy in all this. I didn't tell you, I helped get the second autopsy done, the second on his wife. I thought sure Joe was a crazy killer. Flattered myself, figured he was killing for me. But when that needle went into himself there, I knew. Wasn't him. Wasn't him at all."

"Audrey, come on now."

"I don't maybe understand what he was doing. Maybe crazy, but not guilty."

"So what's that mean, Audrey? What d'you say?"

"Through all this, Chet, before that happened, if I wanted to be honest, I only knew one thing to hang on to."

"What?"

"That *I* wasn't murdering anybody. Honest, I didn't know about anybody else, anybody at all. I just knew *I'm* no murderer, that's all."

"So now what? I am?"

"I saw him kill himself, Chet, begging me to believe him. The needle, it met resistance, did I tell you that, Chet? Up around the eye, it going in, and then his thumb on the plunger, it didn't go in like butter, not at all. Tough muscle. And I dialed for help and I sat on the bed and I said, 'OK, now there's two innocent people to be dealt with here.' Well, no, innocent is wrong. I don't kill people, I just drive them there."

"Audrey, come on now, make some sense."

"Sense is, that reduced the field considerably. And, Chet, I hate Felix Marmasette more than anybody else alive, you know that, but I know he was doing all right with Vor-Tech with Milton still alive, better than he is now probably, and he sure as hell had no reason to kill Joe's wife. So."

"So I did? You're saying I did, right? LaLuna's a psycho, and so you blame this here guy. Audrey girl, you've gone as crazy as he did."

"All I'm saying, I'll never be sure, Chet. Never know. It'll always be there. I know what I am and what I do to people. I know what Joe was, just a poor cluck. So there's too much between you and me for anything good to grow. Hey, Chet, I talked to that Franklin."

"Franklin who?"

"Franklin Bugg."

"How you know him?"

"I didn't. I had a guy find him for me. I talked to him, Chet."

"Yeah, good, yeah, you talked to him, so what?"

"He told me more than he told to the cops. I don't know if he was scared, or he thinks it's cooled off, or if he just liked me. Talked to me. I gave him some money."

"Yeah, Audrey, that's probably it—he liked the cut of your jib. Like that, he told you stories. Audrey, the guy will say anything to anybody. You don't know him."

"So he'd alibi anybody?"

"I didn't mean that."

"He said something else too, Chet. He said he never saw you the night of the Chuck Berry, but he said something else then too, worse."

Chet leaned back into his seat, looked out the windshield. He sighed and said, "Yeah, that part is correct, Audrey. I admit. Stupid, but I got scared. All I did that night was talk on the phone to some people. No corroboration whatsoever. I got that moron Bugg to try to get the crazy cop off my ass. It ever came down to brass tacks, I knew Bugg'd renege. But that was all right. It was just for a convenience. What else he tell you?"

Audrey looked at him, waited a second until she was sure his eyes were on her, then she said, "Bugg said something about he used to get stuff for you. Needles."

She couldn't read him. Something was there, but she couldn't really get it.

He drove her home, got her bike off the rack for her, told her she had a crazy fried-egg brain from too much screwing and drugs and drinking and imagining, and he got back in the van to go. She gave back his diamond, through the van window. He put it in the ashtray, drove off.

Upstairs, she wondered again how long before her ass got big, and if Chet would come back and try to kill her. He ever came within a block of her, she'd be on the phone to the cops, tell everything. He knew that. She wasn't scared. Maybe Chet was right, what he had said there at the end. Maybe her brain was gone from too much happening, from doing and using up too much of herself. But at least she knew she had never killed anybody. She knew that about herself, and about her Joe.

She'd told him once that she was just a woman searching for a morality, any morality, really. She should have taken Joe's. It was a good one. It was good, but now it was too late.

She didn't like the feel of her finger without a ring, hadn't gotten used to it since she'd taken off Milton's simple gold band.

Her jewelry case. She saw an earring she had bought for Chet at LeGrande's right after the funeral, had never given to him.

Her old jewelry was in a separate box from the stuff she wore now. She found the old box, rifled through, couldn't believe some of the cheap stuff she had collected through the years. Some of it was pretty nice.

She found a washer from Milton's milking machine, Derek's Purple Heart.

She found what she was looking for, a big old blue onyx, ugly as shit. She slipped it on, lit a cigarette, sat by the window.

She sat there waiting for anything, expecting nothing.

Chet went home, took his eighteen-speed Peugeot off the back of the van, and went inside.

In his exercise den he had a five-hundred-dollar computerized stationary bike. He punched in a program and swung himself onto its seat. With a good kick, he managed to finish the run in PB time. He dismounted, looked at himself in the bedroom mirror, sweat and hair and muscle, then went in to take a shower.

Afterward, he cinched his ponytail, still wet, sat on top of the bed covers, and called up Bugg. Line was busy.

Chet went into his kitchen, got a quart bottle of green Gatorade, drank it all with the TV on, cruised the channels and flipped it off, tried Bugg again.

Bugg knew who it was first word, said, "Well, my Whitemeat, how you be, man?"

Chet told him, "Cut the jive crap, Bugg; remember, I knew you when you were Young Americans for Freedom."

Bugg told Chet, "You got me, you got me, Chet. OK, why you called. Let me tell you how things were. First off, let's face it, we both expected me to cave in sooner or later. Given. That's my makeup, man, it just is. We knew that going in, true? So snowing the black-haired cop was all right, your money was well spent there, although sometimes I get the feeling that people aren't buying what it is I'm selling, and that was such a time as that. With that cop there."

Chet told him, "Doesn't matter."

"Doesn't matter. So anyway, later, your gal comes to see me, I don't know what side of the street she's walking on. I mean, is she with you or not? Your squeeze or no? I should've called, I admit, I should've called you up."

"You should've eaten all your shoveling shit and choked to death on it."

"Well, maybe, probably, you're probably right there. But I told you I was going to paint the picture for you, so allow me. She come in—I don't know how it was she found me—she come in, I been sitting on the rug, just sort of screwing around with my dogger. Matter of fact, the dog's Carl, the one the very same cop gave me, LaLuna. Anyway, weeks my kids aren't here, Carl gets lonely, so I get down on the rug, shove his head around a little, let him bite me, anything, he likes it. So listen, Chet, I'm no fool. She comes in, sits down on my couch as I offered—I'm no fool—I sit back down on the rug, like I'm still half playing with the dogger there."

"Uh-huh."

"The view, Chet, with this gal, please don't be annoyed, is all the way to China, simply beautiful. Here she is, and to be honest, I don't really get a parade of lovelies passing through the apartment here. Here I have a lovely person, she keeps giving me twenty-dollar bills and long views of China from the couch, me down on the rug there."

"Bugg, what'd you tell her?"

"Chet, be honest, I would have told her anything in the world keep her sitting there. I mean, Chet, a man like me being treated to all of that *and* twenty-dollar bills too. It was a great time. Me cuffing the dog's head, sneaking beaver shots."

"You told her what?"

"More than I should have, I'm sure, I told. I never really said about what you told me to tell the cop, but I suppose I did intimate it. I figured she already knew most, I didn't know why she was here, even offered to deal her some light stuff, but she wasn't interested. I didn't have that much anyway, to begin with, but I offered to be polite."

"You tell her something about needles?"

"What? Needles? No. What? I guess I mentioned you as a past

and present good customer, that's all. You *have* been a market for quite a bit of paraphernalia in the past, right, Chet? Before the AIDS and all, right?"

Chet said, "When's the last time I bought anything from you, slime?"

Bugg said, "Long time, I admit, slime admits it, it's been a long time. Unless, of course, you're counting loyalty and testimony. Abstract things."

Chet told Bugg to keep his mouth shut, that shit works two ways, and Bugg said yeah, it did.

Chet said, "Listen to me, man. The only reason I'm not on my way over there right now to put your balls in a vise is I figure you probably did me a favor, getting rid of the bitch for me. But if you ever, *ever*, start singing a song with me in the lyrics, you're gone, you're a soprano for the boys' choir forever, you see?"

Bugg said, "Quite right, maestro, you're right there, my friend."

Chet hung up, with Bugg apologizing.

Chet spent the rest of the day doing paperwork, then watched a video on surfing. After dinner, he called up Felix Marmasette at home.

He told him, "Hey, Felix? I just got off the phone with the guy at the Ho-Hum. Yeah, the desk clerk. He's a kid, he's feeling randy. I don't know if he's been reading newspapers, trying to figure things and work some leverage, or what. Or if he just is tapped for money. Either way, he needs some money. I should have never let him know who we were."

"How much?"

"This is so much crap, isn't it? You think you've taken care of one little thing, it hemorrhages, bleeds into something else. I swear, it's never-ending, huh?"

"How much?"

"Didn't say. He's loose change, though; I would think two grand would buy him forever."

"Long time," Marmasette said.

"Yes, it is. But he comes back again, we make an arrangement, that's all. He's pocket money, this guy, Felix, that's all, no worry. Loose change."

"You want me to pay, of course."

"Well, Felix, starting up my business and all, I'm not flush. But it's not fair you do everything, so let me be the bag on it at least, OK? You buy, I fly. I'll come by tomorrow, pick it up, bring it over to the guy. What time would be good for you?"

After Marmasette had slammed the receiver down, Chet got back on the stationary bike, did an easy twenty-five miles, showered again.

Dripping shower water, hair all loose this time, he went into his closet and took out a leather case. He grabbed a rubber tube, used it to tie off his left arm, and shot some cooked drugs into his blood with a brand-new needle.

At least that dead bastard LaLuna would never find out about Chet's damned needles. He was getting close, talking to Bugg, when Chester got together with Marmasette to knock the cop out of the picture. The cop was a crazy man, was a dead crazy man now, but Chet knew somehow he'd always have a fear of the manic cop who got deflated into nothing and then blew away.

Getting groggy, Chet told himself he was ashamed at being what his mom would have called a dope fiend, ashamed of being what his mom would have called a blackmailer, ashamed at being what his mom would have called a libertine and a scoundrel.

Before he lost control of his mind for a while, he said to his mom, "At least I'm no murderer, Mommy. That's one thing."

THIRTY FIVE

After Felix had slammed down the receiver on Chet, hoping to crack the jerk's eardrum, he put his fist into the Sheetrock, trying to crack his own hand.

The girls were all up on Martha's Vineyard for the week, so Felix had the luxury of getting pissed in peace. After not even putting a dent in the Sheetrock—must have been a stud right behind it—he sat there on the couch and held his knuckles, and he stayed mad.

Why can't a man improve his own life? Why is he bashed back, right in the damned face, every time he tries to do things right for a change?

Vor-Tech was driving him nuts, firing up his BP to triple digits both upper and lower, and so were his wife and his three thigh-spreading daughters, so was the economy, so was all the crap with the cops and with Zumrad and Audrey Wright.

Felix, mortal, had decided to redo things, to undo things. He had managed to be a good boy with the diet; hadn't done him any good, but he figured he could do it with other things too. He had changed all the house's mattresses to Straight Arrow Posture-Aides, to help straighten out his backbone like he would straighten out his life.

He had decided to slowly liquidate Vor-Tech, take the money and run, worry about college tuitions later. They'd all be flunked out by another few semesters anyway.

He'd decided to quit smoking.

He'd decided to kibosh the trips to Audrey's boudoir every two months. That'd be the hardest to do, though, by far. Sweet legs, sweet ass. That part he wouldn't know if he could handle until the time came around. But handing over to her his copy of the contract, all ripped apart, would feel pretty good, maybe get her feeling good about him, get him feeling good about himself again. Maybe be worth one quick *au revoir* screwing and then off to the sunset. Even wish her brother Ronnie good luck, really mean it this one time.

Maybe send the kid a few bucks for the rehab clinic.

Maybe he should even call up the cops in the morning, make a full confession to them.

But damning things kept screwing it all up, all these fine plans of his. Maybe he was paying for his past transgressions. This ponytailed piece of street turd Zumrad calling him up, putting the screws to him. Wasn't no clerk at the Ho-Hum involved, they both of them knew that.

It was Zumrad cooked the whole thing up to begin with, sold him on it, spun it into play. Zumrad was bad news. Maybe, Felix sometimes figured, maybe even worse than a simple blackmailer, ballbreaker. The cop seemed to think so. Felix didn't think the cops really figured himself for a murderer, though. Was just a formality that got out of hand. Then the stuff with Audrey, pissed the cop off some. Felix admitted, in his time he'd been a lot of bad stuff, but never that bad. Never a rapist, technically, never a molester, never a murderer. What a track record—the Greg LeMond of morality.

And as far as this little drama at the Ho-Hum, it was just amateur summer stock. Felix was a bit player, in it for the fun, for the acting experience, for the thrill. Nothing really involved beyond that.

Felix took a drink with him to bed. He was going to do less of that stuff too, pretty soon. He stayed up most of the night, thinking. What did they have him for on this, really? No real fraud, no real swindle; no money had passed. A practical joke? Not much more. Certainly nothing felonious. Lying. Lying was all. There was no lying law he had broken. Hell, there wasn't even a commandment about lying. He was sweet-smelling on this one thing. Clear.

So who'd be after him if he did, did call up and tell? Well, first Zumrad. So what, he was already, and Felix could handle that little pile of waste just fine. Friends of the dead cop? Felix had heard the guy didn't have any. Besides, Felix didn't really cause the guy's death or anything like that. Wacko, killed himself over Audrey. Sad but true. The fat captain? Guy must realize he brought it all on himself, philandering on duty. A case of mistaken identity anyway. What's the problem? What's the charge?

Felix decided on it then, got to sleep finally, slept fine, made the phone call in the morning.

They jerked him around a bunch of different extensions, different voices, the desk to this department, to that one; he finally got to talk to a voice sounded a little bit black but polite, at some extension he didn't remember the name of.

The voice was pleasant, official, didn't seem dumb, just a little disoriented, not sure what it was all about. That was understandable, Felix figured; he felt that way a little bit too.

The voice was giving him the impression of writing everything down, asked him to repeat things a couple of times, spell them, but Felix got the idea it might just be for show. The voice told him they'd be in contact, thanks; they both hung up. Felix cursed, remembering that he should have gotten a name or department from the guy. He got the strong feeling that he'd never hear again. Anyway, worst scenario—a little scandal, too confusing for anybody to deal with or make anything out of it.

Felix felt good after the call. He got ready to go to work. He was a former lot of bad things, but hell, getting better, getting better, every day in every way. Saint Felix. Hey, Lord, which one is my cloud? Where do I park it for eternity?

He'd call the girls at the Vineyard tonight, tell them he missed them all, maybe even kiss the receiver.

P atrolman ElRay J. O'Keefe was working a desk and a phone, day shift, plain clothes.

It was just TDY, maybe a month or so, and just basic shitwork, phones and forms and doughnuts, but he looked upon it as an opportunity. The blues would come through, laugh at him, call him a titless secretary, he didn't mind. It was a step in the right direction. Up.

Pearley was gone for good, involuntarily retired. His daughter had used a cordless professional-model paint gun to spray her new boyfriend with fluorescent yellow, gone down to Bloomingdale's to do the same to the girl at the perfume counter, finally turned the spray on herself, then went home, killed herself with pills. Pearley said the undertaker had even charged him for the turp.

Pearley had wanted to come back active after that, did for a week, then got suspended for rabbit-punching a flower lady, and they had another hearing on the poor slob. Pearley was fighting retirement, had a lawyer assigned who didn't care much, Pearley just an old blue fighting to stay on the job too long. ElRay had testified against him at the hearing.

After, out in the hall, with blues all around, guys they knew, Pearley had called ElRay a bunghole, but later on had slapped him on the back and laughed and held his shoulders for a while.

The week after, Pearley had cuffed his ankle to a stolen moped, wheeled it off the Hell Gate bridge, called it, in his note, "Burial at sea, no frills."

So Pearley was loony leave, permanent, and ElRay started looking around for a new position. He felt bad for Pearley, but there were worse things to be than a climber, worse things to be than a comer. Pearley had always understood him, understood that. ElRay was no bad cop, didn't take graft or steal drug money or kill anybody. Just did things to get ahead, anything wrong with that? Since when was loyalty everything?

Pearley would've never taken this TDY assignment, but he would have told ElRay it was the thing to do, grab it, even if it was only for just a little while. Foot in the door, son.

So far, ElRay was doing all right at it, had worked three departments in five days, just bailing out detectives from underneath too much paperwork and time-waste stuff. Not too many decisions to make each day, fewer than on the street, but those calls he *had* made, he had done OK on. Learning ropes.

The conversation this morning with the strange guy had ElRay confused for a while. Working the phones at Fraud, ElRay had talked to a guy who rambled on a bit about working a scam on a cop. ElRay couldn't understand what the hell the guy was talking about, but he took down most of the information anyway. Then the guy had said a few magic names, ElRay's brain clicked in somewhat, and he started writing down everything.

After, he let phones ring as he copied his notes, got them straight on the pad, in his head.

"Get that, huh? Rook?" guys were yelling at him around the room, so he shuffled a bit, got the phones answered, got his notes straight. He stood up, told the detective he had to run something over, and he went out into the hall.

Pearley had told him, "Get yourself a rabbi, son. And once you got yourself one, you gotta kiss ass until your lips bleed."

ElRay got to Homicide, asked around, somebody said the guy was in Sheeney's office. Since Captain Bell was still on medical, indefinitely, Sheeney had been downstairs running the chief's operations, and nobody had really taken over for Sheeney. So the Homicides took turns using his office for a little privacy, a little quiet.

ElRay went to the door, knocked on the frosted glass.

"Yeah?"

ElRay looked around, leaned into the door, spoke quietly. He said, "It's O'Keefe. I got a call just now, a guy named Marmasette. You told me tell you if—"

"What? What the hell you saying?"

Why didn't he just open up the damned door? This was absurd.

A little louder. "O'Keefe, I said. I been at Frauds today. I got a strange call, a guy named Marmasette. Something to do with a scam or something he pulled."

"So what?"

"You told me, anything with LaLuna, you wanna hear. The guy mentioned, I think, about setting him up or something, I'm not sure. I got his name, number. It's confusing."

"You got notes?"

"Yeah, yeah, I do. They're brief. I think—"

"Put them under the door."

So ElRay slipped the notes to his rabbi, stood there awhile, then went back to work. He decided that the old cops, the good cops, like Pearley, like LaLuna, they were a dying-off breed, guys you could read and be sure all the time where they stood and what they stood for.

Hey, but did anybody ever tell him it would be easy, make any sense at all?

THIRTY SEVEN

Hraska took the notes that O'Keefe had slipped him under Sheeney's door. They were a neatly written half page of a yellow legal pad.

Hraska looked at them awhile, classified them quick as just so much crap and that's it. Looked like either Marmasette trying to work Hraska or maybe work the department for an angle, or else Marmasette actually feeling pangs of guilt for helping destroy a good man, a good cop. Either way, certainly nothing indictable, or even processable, or even interesting. Just one more thing to squirrel away somewhere, to be used someday to torque that fat blond pig with, or, more likely, never to be used again. Marmasette was nobody in the big scheme, just one more guy who had helped screw and screw up Hraska's only friend.

Joe had been his only friend, and Hraska was Joe's only friend. For Hraska himself to be friendless, he could easy figure out why. He was just a slimy, loudmouth, Polack muscle cop. Have to be crazy to have him over the house for supper or a beer. Why should you?

Joe, though, his friend Joe, that was a different ball game. Good guy, friendly as hell, funny, concerned, loyal, no loudmouth, heart like a diesel truck, a heart that could stop a train dead on the tracks.

Nobody had been at the funeral. Just about nobody. Well, it wasn't even called a funeral. Was a service, not even the urn with the ashes around in there. Hraska figured the Church still didn't let ashes in, just whole rotted bodies, but still. Just some priest, couple altar boys, some English that meant nothing to Hraska, nothing at all about Joe in it, and some Latin that meant nothing to nobody, not even to the priest trying hard to remember it all.

Where were those cocksuckers Joe would have called his colleagues? A couple them stuck their heads in quick, got out. Showing like that was worse than not at all. What, IAD was outside taking names? Taking down plate numbers like the FBI at a Mafia wedding? Shit.

That was the problem with being a cop and having nothing but cops for buddies. Stay blue and you got yourself a clot of good old boys punching your arm and buying you beers and telling you jokes about spics and niggers when they're not around, but start turning colors, suddenly nobody knows you. You die alone.

No real family of Joe's at the service either, couple faces Hraska didn't know. Just coming in to cool off in the church awhile? Even the undertaker guys, from the Ferrara Brothers, guys Joe knew, sprang them from a rape thing once. Just there paying respects, but looking like all they wanted to do was get out of there quick as they could, no questions asked.

Joe, I come to yours, but there'll be no one around come to mine—*my* funeral, my service. Joe, how y' doing, buddy? You wanna come to my funeral, my services, sometime? 'Cause nobody's gonna be there. Audrey? Yeah, forget that. Didn't see her at yours, even, did we, Joe? Appointment at the gym probably, getting her hair frosted, buns lifted.

Joe, I come to yours, you come to mine? What'd you say?
Gumbah?

Hraska looked back at the notes about Marmasette confessing to screwing up poor Joe. He took a manila folder out of his briefcase, took Sharon Slabb's suicide papers out of it.

He'd gone over them again just last night. Sharon "Sunshine" Slabb, what the hell was her story? He tried to study the papers awhile.

Then Hraska put the Marmasette notes in with the Slabb papers, tossed them all over onto an extra desk that Sheeney had in there, just to hold folders full of papers. The folder landed on top of photographs.

Hraska was surrounded by hundreds, maybe thousands, of photographs. Old Brownie snapshots, thirty-five-mils, Polaroids, three-by-fives, five-by-sevens, eight-by-tens, wallets, glossies, dull-finish, color, black-and-white, some ripped from newspapers and turning yellow. All over the desktop and tables, across the two windowsills, some spread out on the floor.

All together, they looked like a history of photography since the 1950s. A lot of changes, a lot of looks and sizes and tones. All the pictures had one thing in common. Audrey.

Every picture was Audrey. Audrey, thirty-five years old, wearing a black hat, Audrey walking into Bonwit Teller's, grainy shots of Audrey at the beach, Audrey graduating college, Audrey through her living room window, no nakeds, Audrey getting into a 1973 Mustang, Audrey's candids from the Hoover student paper and the Miss Hoover High contest, Audrey with Milton, Audrey coming out of the gym, Audrey long ago, Audrey last week. Hraska was nuts to have them spread out like this, right here in Sheeney's office.

There was one of her and her sailor-boy first husband, little curly-headed squirt, them walking away from the camera, in a mist, or a rain. After that guy had died in 'Nam, Hraska tried sending her some pictures, anonymous, then calling her up without a name, putting some moves on, but his words had twisted on him, turned ugly. He hung up.

Here were even the pictures from the roll Joe found on the ground.

You know the best one, though? Still the very best shot? Same one Joe would've picked, top right corner of page forty-eight, the blue and gold *Aristocrat*—Audrey's senior picture. Black gown off the shoulders, hair blonder than it is now, necklace with a single pearl hanging fairly low.

That was still the best of them, even after all these others.

Milton had caught Hraska in the street, shooting thirty-five-mils of his wife, just like Joe had almost caught him that time behind the gym in the little rental Omni. Milton had caught him from behind, after Audrey had left the house one day wearing a pink jumpsuit thing. Hraska had given him some crap about an ongoing, let Milton think about the drugs he was doing, let it go at that, no harm, no foul.

Then Milton had spotted a half-empty fifth of Walker Red that Hraska had been working on, lying on the front seat, along with the lens and the camera case. Milton mumbled something about taking it to the authorities, as if Hraska himself wasn't the authorities. Still, it got Hraska thinking.

Yeah, it sure started Hraska thinking. This shit punk was using Audrey, using her as a sex crate, using her as a mule. Hraska had through-the-window shots of the goddamned milking machine before they ever went into the house to finger it that night. This guy Milton was destroying her, day by day, year by year, so Hraska had showed up there the next night, flashing badge.

What was the plan? He didn't remember. Maybe muscle sweet Milton a little, get him away from his own wife, just have some fun with sweating him? Yeah, just tell the guy to lay off, be nice. Lay off Hraska, lay off Audrey. Yeah, but Hraska went in packing a hypo in his pocket, a big old hypo, pumping insulin. And a paperback in his back pocket, *Almost Perfect Crimes of the Century.*

The milking machine was Milton's capital crime. Hooking the spokes of that thing onto the tips of the woman, Audrey, was cause sufficient for a death sentence.

Hey, get Milton out of the way somehow, let Joe have Audrey. God damn it, best man wins.

Well, the plan was something like that. It was either that or stick your stupid, fat-ass, Polack tongue into an electric fan. Epiphany.

Milton had seen the badge, remembered the cop, coughed twice at the door, let him in. Down the hall, Milton so high he was talking like a whole throw pillow had been stuffed into his mouth. Milton blubbering mad. "You no goddamned good cop, you taking pictures of my wife? What for? I'll ruin you for this." Discussion or divorce seemed out of the question here as a solution, roll the punk down easy on the rug, stick him sharp. Once he was down and quiet, Hraska couldn't resist the temptation to look around, for something of Audrey's stuff. Came back, old Milton had flopped himself over on the rug. Drag him up, take him to bed like you would any drunk, make it look so natural. Tug the body of the guy who'd been quietly raping her for ten years, the guy been sending her out for his dope buys, back to his bed. Heart attack. OD. Tox. Whatever. If Hraska'd had a Sea Monkey enema with him, he would've administered it.

After, there was time for a little more nosing around—pictures of Audrey, her drawers. Her milking machine. Et cetera.

Hraska wanted Audrey. Little, slimy, five-foot-five Theodore John Hraska wanted her. Always did. If she'd laugh her balls off at the thought of that, well then, give her to Joe. Audrey and his friend Joe looked good together. Always had.

Slabb was one hell of a smart, wonking female, though. Why the ugly ones always have to be so smart for? Slabb was.

Still, though, Joe and Audrey it was for a while, looking pretty good. Joe deserved a sprout. Been loyal to everybody for ten years, twenty years, his whole life. Loyalty like that deserves something.

Lou Duva was different. Lou was just one plain, mean bitch. Hraska was sure she scratched her rashes raw, just so poor Joe would have to deal with the infections. Hraska went over there, Joe was busy wonking Audrey at the time, Hraska smiled, got let in, grabbed her.

He was either looking for an amiable separation for his friend, or looking for a way out for both of them, or looking to find out what it was to wonk your friend's wife while he was wonking the girl you had loved since grade school. Yeah, Hraska had seen Audrey first, seventh grade, St. Helen's.

Jealousy? You're damn right jealousy—who wouldn't be? Look at the picture, the graduation. Who the hell wouldn't be?

You never took chemistry, Joe? Hell, everybody did, I thought. Hell, even I did, me, who was held scoreless on the SATs. You don't learn anything in school, though. You teach yourself what you have to know, later on. You didn't know that much?

So Lou had fallen, unsullied but not any more ugly in death than she had been in life, and she had fallen because of either friendship or hate or lust or maybe just goddamn aesthetics, for Christ sake. But whatever, she had fallen, and Joe at that moment was gone too. Joe knew. Hraska didn't know it then, but he knew it now.

Hraska had killed him by calling him up in Audrey's bed and saying, "Joe? Listen, I don't know how to say this. Listen, they just found Lou Duva, dead."

With that, the coin had dropped. Had killed Joe right then, more than the Ermo crap in the third needle ever had. That last one was a mercy killing. Really. Joe was already gone by then. Easy to fool with a "you bring your death needles into *my* house?" routine. Hraska was busy loading up the needle for real, lying, calling up Audrey, sounding like the desk at the Waterchop with a message from Zum, have her show up early at the Chop, with Joe still in there holding the needle, doing all that stuff just to shake things down, just to give Joe a way to get out, just to give Joe some means over himself, just to see what would goddamn happen.

Hraska was just an angel of mercy by then. All his great, dangerous plans, to get his best friend the woman, to get himself the woman, had all gone completely, dead wrong. Joe was just a crazy shell by then, unemployed and homeless and loveless, hopeless, going around in short pants, beating up ghosts in motels he could hardly remember driving to.

Hraska, he was no murderer, no common shitbird drive-by murderer. 'Course, there had been his wife too, but that hadn't been murder, just a misunderstanding, even though it had required a certain amount of covering over at the time.

But the whole thing with Joe, mercy killing it was. Still, a bystander would look at it and say to him, Hey, Wink, it sprang Audrey for you, didn't it? Joe dies, Audrey is a free woman, huh? Or, Audrey calls him on it, they take it into the lab, Joe's still gone.

Who was shitting who here, anyways? A woman like Audrey McKenna would never let a slug like Hraska wonk her, no matter what he tried to convince himself when he was drunk. So he sat here at Sheeney's desk with just a picture in a yearbook, wishing for a drink.

Sometimes, honest, Hraska told himself this: He had loaded up the third needle for Audrey, the woman who had never, ever, acknowledged his existence. The voice on the tape in the van should've said, "Water, Audie, I'll punch it in you, prove it to you, you'll see." Joe was just destined for the scrap heap, Audrey for the graveyard.

Joe, you dumb wop, I was trying to help you. You wouldn't let the cases die. Should've just let them die, pal, cleared them, let them just float away, sink.

But hey, also, Joe's gone, then Major Crimes, when it came to be, Sheeney moving up, would have no head, right? Maybe. Doris Day, 1956 or 1957, sang "Que serà, serà, shit punk."

If Hraska wanted Major Crimes, he'd gotta work for it. Big Bob won't be back, Sheeney'll get chief of tecs permanent, Homicide would be open. Hraska would never get that one, but Major Crimes was a definite possibility, now with Joe gone. But he wouldn't make Major Crimes by locking himself in Sheeney's office, like a crazy man, beautiful pictures spread out all around him.

As he started to pick up the pictures, the sun came out, filled up the room. It seemed to ask, Who you trying to kid here, Polack?

And suddenly, maybe for the millionth time, Hraska was on the stand, and the DA of his mind, maybe Philbrick, was yelling at him, "Isn't it right, Sergeant Hraska, isn't it true that you killed Milton Wright because you couldn't stand what he was doing to his wife, your dream lover, with that defangled milking machine? And isn't it also true that you killed Madeline LaLuna just to break down her husband's obsessive behavior, to make him inoperable by drowning him in guilt and suspicion? You couldn't bring yourself to kill him, but you could bring yourself to kill his wife, isn't that true, Sergeant?"

Wasn't none of those guys could make Hraska cry by asking a question—not Philbrick, not Perry Mason, not Jack Barry on *a quiz show*. But still, to those questions, Hraska had to hang his head and then give one, almost imperceptible, nod.

"And isn't it true, also, that you filled the syringe with pure poison so that you could ride in at the last moment, like the Lone Ranger, and save the lady's life and leave your partner babbling and confused in the corner? While you won the lady?"

The future head of Major Crimes nodded again.

Hraska gently picked up all the pictures, put them in his fake-leather briefcase, locked it, put it down at one side.

He sat at Sheeney's desk, punched an intercom number.

Said, "O'Keefe? O'Keefe, listen, there's a file in Homicide about a foot. Go get it, bring it here. Yeah, just a foot. I don't know, look under *F*, for Christ sake. I gotta do everything?"

Good, hard, gutsy police work would be the thing got him Major Crimes.

It was tough for Hraska to get back to work. Tough, because he was all alone, and he was being crushed by a terrible, all-consuming loneliness.

He figured he'd get over it, though.

B y September the next year, Winky Dink Hraska was head of
Major Crimes.

It was what he thought he had wanted, but every day was filled
with little choking disappointments. His men, only three and a half
assigned, would mock him, barely keeping it low-key enough for him
to pretend he didn't notice.

The other heads ignored him, froze him out. Whenever he saw
Sheeney, it was like they'd never even worked together over at Homicide. Big Bob had never sent him a thank you for the flowers and
crap Hraska had given him when he got out of the hospital, never
told Hraska congrats for making head of MC. Hraska had even
returned Big Bob's gold ring from the Ho-Hum. Nothing from Big
Bob. 'Course, Big Bob probably couldn't come up with Hraska's business address to send to, or the right extension to call.

Maybe Big Bob was hating him, maybe he'd found out about how
Hraska told everybody the story of Big Bob, bare-assed, trying to
crawl under the Ho-Hum bed, looking like a rooting pig, as Joe was
beating his ass. Hraska had pieced that scene together from the few
things Joe told him, added the rest, told it around. Maybe it had gotten back to Big Bob. Careers, of course, had been ruined by less.

Plus there was that thing: Hraska had gone after some board
member's broad with a sharp pencil at the Fourth of July picnic at

Sunken Meadow. Hraska had said he was using the eraser end, but witnesses didn't bear him out.

Disappointing, all of it. Hraska hadn't even been able to solve the foot thing, which they had been kind enough to shovel on over to Major Crimes for him. Matter of fact, nobody could even find the damned foot anymore; it and a bunch of other body parts had disappeared from the ME's vaults. That freak Dreeve probably took them to the Catskills for the weekend, then home to meet the folks. Wouldn't've happened, Slabb was still around.

And Homicide wasn't even letting him get into the World Series Pool this year, told him he was Major Crimes now, couldn't do it. Disappointing. Big Bob had *given* him that pool, given him the folder, after Bob booted Joe off the job. Shit, Hraska had been one of the founders of that pool, for crying out loud, had always run the draft for it, chattering off the players' names, and now he wasn't even allowed in it to play.

There was another big disappointment—Hraska was still talking, talking always, talking too much. He had tried hard to stop—heads didn't blow off constantly like that—but trying to stop just made it worse. Hraska'd get around somebody and go crazy talking about anything, anything at all. Try as he might to change, he was still just the guy, would always be just the guy, the guy who would yell "Shake your booty" at the fat gal in the opera.

He'd gotten three laughs in his face, plus about ten hang-ups, from Audrey. Had kept on snapping pictures, scared about it all the time now, though. No joy to it anymore. Then about a couple months ago, Audrey had left, gone, like disappearing off the block or something. Word had said she was living in Bermuda or somewhere. People really live there, a place like that? They don't just visit? Who knew.

Anyway, for Wink, all this, it was like he had given up being a cop, to sit at a desk alone, just like his grandfather had given up the stage to become a mender of bad bowling shoes.

Even the mail he got thrown on his desk every morning was crap, disappointing, reminding him of what a nobody he was. Didn't look at all like the mail a head should be getting on his in-pile.

This morning, it was a little stack of cheesy interoffice Xerox memos, plus a gun catalogue, plus a postcard came in an envelope. That was it.

Hraska looked at the card, a color picture of a brown-skinned babe standing waist-deep in clear blue water; she was holding a pair of melons right below her own incredible set of knockers.

Card front said, "What Melons! Greetings From The Caribbean!"

Hraska thought about who he knew who was going to Mitchell Torok's territory for the fall.

Turned it over, the message was written small, almost too small to read without glasses, covered the whole back of the card.

Said, "Wink, My big fat mother always told me be careful, don't go poking yourself in the eye. Big dif between pure Ermo and a couple diluted cc's—dumped your cocktail for a small shot, mostly chaser. Splitting the scene doesn't always have to be so tough, so permanent. It's easy when you have info to help you squeeze some people who can cough up a dead body—911's and assistant MEs and undertakers. Some of the info supplied by a lady who lost her face. Me, I'm feeling great these days—Epiphany! Rested, trusting nobody. You knew what page Audie's pix was on, in the Aristocrap. You knew her first husband was a little curly-headed guy. You knew I tripped over garbage cans, in the alley, chasing the phantom photog. You knew too much. Madeline had out that pic of the '58 Giants to show *you* that night. Yeah, I feel great. Still feel like a cop sometimes, though. Hoping you don't spend too many Bobby Lewis nights worrying I'll come back to clear this case. J."